THE MOGUL AND THE MUSCLE

A BLUEWATER BILLIONAIRES ROMANTIC COMEDY

CLAIRE KINGSLEY

Always Have LLC

Published by Always Have, LLC

Edited by Elayne Morgan of Serenity Editing Services

Cover by Kari March Designs

ISBN: 9781697880847

www.clairekingsleybooks.com

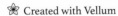 Created with Vellum

To my fellow lady bosses, Lucy, Kathryn, and Pippa. And to all women who lift each other up. Keep slaying, beautiful badasses.

ABOUT THIS BOOK

"I wanted this man's arms around me, cocooning me in safety. I wanted to feel like I didn't have to be brave for a few hours. I wanted to let him be my courage. My protection. My shield."

Cameron Whitbury—billionaire aerospace mogul—can engineer her way out of any problem. Sure, she's living with the threat of a potential sex scandal thanks to her lying ex. And that attempted mugging in her parking garage might not have been a random attack.

But she's totally got this. Sacrifice her privacy to an over-protective bodyguard? No thanks. She doesn't need a six-foot-five, motorcycle-riding, square-jawed, hazel-eyed man-beast shadowing her every move.

Jude Ellis—one-man security operation and professional problem solver—is ready to retire from the cloak and dagger stuff to live a normal life. He doesn't need another client. Not even one with coppery-red hair and mile-long legs who looks hot AF in a sexy pair of heels.

To appease her worried friends, Cameron hires Jude as her bodyguard. And despite their feisty banter and their rampant—and totally inappropriate—sex fantasies, they're both determined to keep it professional.

But as the danger to Cameron escalates, the heat simmering between them just might combust.

Author's note: Big wall-of-man hero with a fierce (and growly) protective streak. Confident and snarky heroine. All the banter. Sex in a closet. And a daring rescue with a big, heart squishing HEA.

1

JUDE

*T*he kid knew he was screwed.

He sat slumped in the chair, his eyes on the floor. Head tilted forward, shoulders drooping. I hadn't needed to lay a finger on him. Kind of a shame, in a way. Not that I wanted to beat the shit out of a twenty-two-year-old kid, but...

Actually, yes I did.

I stood in his father's study leaning against the huge mahogany desk. The walls were paneled with dark wood, and bookshelves housed leather-bound legal tomes. A credenza sat behind the desk with a crystal decanter and a set of bar glasses. There was even an oil-painted portrait of some stuffy old guy on the wall. This place couldn't have been more pretentious if it tried.

Hauling the kid in here hadn't been difficult. After a week of research and surveillance on behalf of my client, I'd nailed down his routine. Grabbed him outside the luxury Miami Beach condo his parents undoubtedly paid for.

Footsteps approached the half-open door and the kid flinched. Norman Cudello, Florida state senator, walked in dressed in a designer suit. His salt-and-pepper hair was neatly groomed, his jaw smooth. He saw me first and stopped just inside the study. Then his gaze traveled to his son—Owen Cudello—and I caught the flicker of annoyance.

"Who are you?" Senator Cudello asked, his voice betraying nothing but disinterest.

"Jude Ellis." I kept my posture casual. Relaxed. I could be physically intimidating if it was necessary. At six-foot-five and almost as wide as I was tall, it was harder to appear non-threatening than it was to scare people.

But it was always better when I didn't have to. If I threatened violence, I had to be willing to back that up. And I was really hoping to get out of here without getting any blood on my shirt. I had a date this afternoon.

"And why are you in my study?"

"We need to have a little chat."

"About?"

Your dipshit son, genius. I nodded toward the kid. "Him."

The senator walked around his desk and flipped over a whiskey glass. "I'm sure we can come to a suitable arrangement."

I narrowed my eyes but kept my posture relaxed. Of course the first thing he'd do is offer money. I hadn't expected anything less, but it still irritated me. "I'm not here to make that kind of arrangement."

"Then what are you here for?" he asked. "You're obviously not law enforcement."

"No, I'm not." I straightened to my full height. "It seems your son has a bit of a problem understanding English. Specifically the word *no*."

The kid didn't look up.

"Oh?" his father asked.

"About six months ago, the young lady he'd been dating, Mira Salinas, informed him that their brief relationship was over. Instead of handling it like a man, he chose to start stalking and harassing her."

The senator poured a finger of whiskey in the glass but didn't reply.

"Hundreds of texts, messages on her social media accounts, notes on her car. Hanging out at the restaurant where she works. Circling the block around her apartment building. You get the idea."

He took a drink of whiskey.

"That failed to charm her, though I can't imagine why— what girl wouldn't want to date a guy who stalks her?" I glared at the kid. "So now he's trying to use dear old dad's connections to get her kicked out of school. He even got someone in the university's administration to send her a warning of expulsion if she goes to the media."

"If this is all true, why hasn't she gone to the police?" he asked, his voice smooth.

"That's where it gets complicated, isn't it? Cops didn't take her seriously. I can't imagine it has anything to do with the fact that he's the son of a prominent senator."

The senator put his whiskey down. "So you're here to threaten me so I get my son under control, is that it?"

"No."

He met my eyes, his brow lifting.

"A threat's too much work," I said. "Maybe I tell you I'll beat the shit out of you both if your jackass offspring doesn't leave her alone. And maybe that works for a few days, or a week, or a month. And that whole time, I have to keep an eye on the little shit to see if I need to make good on my threat. Meanwhile, the fear wears off. You increase security so you know I can't get to either of you. He gets cocky. And then he escalates, and an innocent girl gets assaulted. So no, I'm not here to threaten you. I'm here to tell you what's going to happen."

The senator swallowed. His face was an almost expressionless mask, but I was good at reading people. I could see the fear he was trying to hide.

"Owen is going to cease all contact with her. He's going to stop following, threatening, and harassing her. Stop trying to get her fired or kicked out of school."

Owen's balls finally seemed to get the better of him, and he spoke up. "Or what?"

I ignored him, keeping my gaze fixed on the senator. "I'm sure your voters would be very interested to know that some of your campaign funds are being funneled into a privately-held LLC. Not to mention how much of those campaign contributions are coming from organized crime syndicates. I have to say, it's a bold move to take that much money from both the Russian mob *and* the Cuban mafia. They're practically at war with each other. I can't imagine they'd be happy to discover the senator they paid good money for is also in the enemy's pocket."

He paled. Good. He should be scared. If either side found out he was taking money from the other, they'd tear him apart.

"So like I said, Owen's going to leave the girl alone. Do we have an understanding?"

The senator's eyes flicked to his son. "If you so much as think about her again, you're cut off. Do you hear me? Not another cent."

"Are you serious?" Owen asked.

"Dead serious," he said, his voice hard. His eyes moved back to me. "I can assure you, Mr. Ellis, my son will no longer be an issue for your client. We have an under-standing."

I didn't offer to shake his hand. The dirty politician didn't deserve that kind of respect. I simply nodded once and walked out.

The heavy air hit me like a wall as soon as I got outside. It was humid as hell today, but it didn't bother me. I'd been all over the world and dealt with just about every weather extreme imaginable. Miami's tropical heat was nothing.

I put on my helmet and swung my leg over my restored 1940 Indian Chief motorcycle, glad the job was over. This was definitely the last one. I was supposed to be retired, for fuck's sake. I'd never set out to do this kind of work. But I had a certain set of skills—very Liam Neeson of me, but it was true—and it seemed like every time I finished one job, another one would pop up.

It was always the same thing. A sweet old lady with a nephew trying to get out of dealing drugs, and a dealer who wouldn't accept his resignation. A family man with a loan shark breathing down his neck. Owen Cudello wasn't the first stalker I'd dealt with. A lot of my clients had been young women with shitty exes who wouldn't leave them alone.

I'd never advertised my services. I didn't have a sign on my door that said *Jude Ellis: Personal Security and Professional Problem Solver*. It had started with Mrs. Dominguez. Nice lady, but her son had gotten in with some bad people. I'd handled the extraction and gone about my business.

Next thing I knew, someone else had gotten my name. A referral, apparently. The woman's ex-boyfriend had been on trial—an ex-boyfriend who'd also been involved with one of Miami's most notorious drug cartels—and she'd been a key witness. She hadn't trusted law enforcement to keep her safe, so she'd come to me.

And apparently I was a sucker, because I couldn't say no.

But this was the last job. Mira Salinas was safe from that little prick. And I was going to go back to being properly retired.

I stopped at the café near campus where I'd arranged to meet Mira. She was at a table near the front, wearing a floral dress, her dark hair in a loose ponytail. Her eyes widened with hope when I walked in.

"Oh my god, I've been so nervous." She was jittery, tapping her sandaled foot on the floor. "Is it over?"

I sat on the edge of the seat across from her. I wasn't going to stay. "It's over. He won't bother you again."

She let out a breath, her shoulders relaxing. "I'm so relieved. Thank you. I can't tell you how much this means to me."

"It's no problem." I stood.

"Wait." She set her purse on the table and drew out an envelope. "I know we didn't talk about price, but I have this."

There was no way I was taking money from a college student. "That's not necessary."

"Of course it is. I hired you to help me and you did. Take it."

I held up a hand. "I appreciate that, but keep it. And maybe don't date any more politician's sons."

"Don't worry. Never again."

"Take care, Mira." I slipped on my sunglasses.

"Thank you, Mr. Ellis," she said as I walked out the door.

∼

I GOT to the restaurant where I was meeting my date and parked on the street. Dating apps were hazardous at best, but I'd found one for the over-thirty crowd that seemed like it might work out better than all that swiping left and right bullshit. And at forty years old, my options for meeting women were narrowing. I didn't want to be *that guy* in the club—the guy who's too old. Last time I went out to a bar, people thought I was the bouncer.

Besides, I was convinced the type of woman I was looking for wasn't out at the clubs on a Saturday night anyway. I'd moved to Miami five years ago to start over and live an ordinary life. A quiet life.

I'd joined the Marines at eighteen and had been recruited to the CIA several years later. I'd seen—and done —a lot of shit. Now I just wanted to settle down. Stay in one place. Be a normal guy.

And dating a woman I didn't have to worry might kill me someday would be a plus.

The restaurant was only about half full, and Karen wasn't here yet. Our dating app profiles had photos, and we'd done the thing where we said what we'd be wearing so we could find each other. She'd said light blue shirt, and there wasn't a light blue shirt to be found.

I decided to get a table. It was a cute place—she'd suggested it—with bright blue tile and photos of Miami wildlife decorating the walls. I noted the exits, the location of the kitchen—which meant potential weapons in an emergency.

Damn it. I needed to stop thinking like that. This was a date, not a meeting with an informant.

The host led me to a spot next to a window and I chose the seat facing the front so I could see people coming in. My phone buzzed, so I checked, but it was Derek asking if we were boxing tomorrow. I told him I'd meet him at the gym at four.

After a quick glance at the menu Karen still wasn't here, so I swiped through the local news on my phone to kill time. There wasn't much going on that I didn't already know about. I kept scrolling until something about a foiled mugging caught my eye.

I skimmed the article. Someone had attempted to mug local billionaire Cameron Whitbury in the parking garage of her office building. She'd gotten away by stomping on the perpetrator's foot with her high heel. That made me chuckle. Nice move.

The article had a photo of Cameron with some rich pansy in a suit—the kind of guy who'd be no help in a crisis. It wasn't that he was tall and lean—almost skinny—that gave it away, nor that he was dressed in an expensive suit. I could see it in his eyes. In his posture. He was the kind of guy who'd crumble in the face of danger.

I didn't believe every woman needed a man in her life to protect her. But a woman like this—a billionaire CEO—could find herself a target of the wrong people for any number of reasons. Paid security was one thing, but a partner who could hold his own would be good for someone like her.

I put my phone down, realizing I was analyzing the story like she was an asset in a mission or a fellow operative. I needed to stop thinking like that.

The door opened and a woman in a light blue shirt came in. She had blond hair, cut in a short bob, a mid-length floral skirt, and sandals. She spotted me and lifted her hand in a hesitant wave.

I smiled, and she came over to my table. I stood and we exchanged a slightly awkward hug.

With a deep breath, I took my seat. I wasn't nervous, exactly. It was hard to get nervous anymore. But I'd been out with a bunch of different women over the last couple of years, and never seemed to connect with anyone.

It wasn't that I was wife-hunting, exactly. I wasn't sure how I felt about marriage, although I was open to it if it seemed right. But I was well past the *I just want to hook up* phase, and not really into *let's just be casual and fuck sometimes*. I was hoping for an actual relationship with someone interesting.

But normal. Ordinary. Not a woman who carried twenty concealed weapons underneath a black minidress and could use her stilettos as backup if necessary.

"Hey," Karen said, getting settled in her chair. "It's so nice to meet you."

"Nice to meet you too."

Seconds ticked by in silence. I rubbed my palms on my thighs beneath the table. I wasn't good at this part. I could face down a corrupt senator and threaten to out him to the rival mafia factions he was scamming, but I couldn't make small talk with a woman in a restaurant.

"So," she said, picking up the menu. "The fish tacos are good here."

"Oh, great. I like fish tacos."

"Me too."

I picked up my menu for something to do with my hands. And it made the ensuing silence less awkward. The server came to take our orders and I reluctantly handed over my menu. Kind of felt like I needed it for cover.

We managed a short stint of casual conversation— mostly about the weather—while we waited for our food. The server brought our meals and we both spread our napkins on our laps.

"So what do you do?" she asked.

"I guess you could say I'm a one-man security firm. I just finished up with a client before this, actually. Although I'm planning to retire."

"That sounds nice. What will you do with your time once you retire?

I opened my mouth to reply, but I didn't exactly have a solid answer to that question. What did I want to do with my time? More to the point, what did normal people do when they retired? "You know, play golf. Maybe start a small business."

"Like what?" She took a bite of her food.

"I'm not sure. Lately I've been thinking about a food truck. Something I can manage with just a few people. What about you? What do you do?"

"I'm a new accounts manager at a bank."

I nodded while I chewed a bite. She was right, the fish tacos were great. "Do you enjoy it?"

"Yeah, I do. I have really great coworkers."

"You know, bank robberies are more common than people think. Modern security technology has helped quite a bit, but the criminals keep getting smarter. You make a better lock, bad guys learn how to pick it."

She nodded slowly. "Oh. Yeah, I suppose so."

"And police response times can be abysmal, especially with the traffic."

"The traffic can be bad."

"Did you know only twenty percent of bank robbers are caught?" I took another bite.

She paused with her water halfway to her mouth. "No, I didn't know that."

"The best thing to do when faced with multiple armed assailants is stay calm and don't look them in the eyes. No matter how tightly organized they are, once a job gets going, tensions are high. They're probably nervous, even paranoid. The last thing you want to do is call attention to yourself."

"Oh."

"The exception to that is if it looks like it's turning into a hostage situation." I gestured idly. "In that case, tell them you have a health condition and you'll need your medication soon. The vast majority of the time, they won't want that kind of complication and they'll let you go. And you definitely want to get out as quickly as they'll let you. Once hostages get involved, the chance of there being casualties increases dramatically. That goes for any kind of armed perpetrator situation, not just bank robberies."

She stared at me, her face pale.

"I mean, that's what I've heard," I said, then cleared my throat.

Son of a bitch. I'd just scared the shit out of her with my rundown on how to handle an armed-robbery-turned-hostage situation.

It was no surprise that Karen picked at her meal for another few minutes, then thanked me and made an excuse about needing to feed her cat.

I finished my dinner alone, feeling like a dumbass. This was not the first time I'd made a date awkward. Like that time I'd explained how to dismantle a bomb on a second date. Or when my date had asked me about places I'd traveled, and I'd casually mentioned there were four or five countries where I was no longer welcome.

It was times like this that I thought maybe I was kidding myself about the whole *live an ordinary life* thing. I didn't know if a guy like me could ever learn to be ordinary.

But I had to. Getting back in wasn't an option. I knew where that life ended for most people. Or more importantly, *when* that life ended, and it was a lot sooner than I'd like. It was why I wanted to retire. I needed to put all the cloak and dagger shit behind me.

The truth was, I was tired of being alone. Tired of feeling like I couldn't trust anyone. My handful of friends and acquaintances were fine, but I felt adrift. I wanted connection. Purpose.

Otherwise I was always going to be the odd loner with the past he couldn't talk about.

2

CAMERON

*F*orm-fitting gold Versace gown. Check. Shimmering gold Louboutins. Check. My favorite sassy red lipstick. Check. Gin martini. Double check.

My dignity? That one was debatable.

Enormous crystal chandeliers hung from the high ceiling in the Biltmore Hotel ballroom. I glanced at the one above the silent auction tables, wondering how much it weighed and whether they'd had to retrofit reinforcements into the ceiling when it was installed. An odd line of thinking during a black-tie charity auction, perhaps, but that's how my mind worked.

It wasn't really the building's structure that had me gazing up at the ceiling with a drink perched in my manicured hand. It was a very satisfying fantasy of the giant chandelier breaking free from its supports and crashing to the ground. Right on top of Aldrich Leighton. He wasn't even here, and I was imagining his demise beneath a ton of crystal, glass, and metal.

"Cam?" Emily nudged me with her elbow. "Hello?"

Blinking, I tore my eyes away from the crystal monstros-
ity. Emily Stanton, one of my best friends and a biochem-
istry genius turned billionaire CEO, rocked her hot red dress
like nobody's business. Her blond hair was perfection and a
pair of very tasteful diamond earrings sparkled in her ears.

"Sorry, I was just... thinking."

She rubbed a hand up and down my arm. "Are you sure
you're okay?"

"Yeah, of course." I took a sip of my martini as if to
emphasize my okayness. "Why wouldn't I be?"

Emily opened her mouth to answer but Luna swept up,
her big brown eyes shining. "Have you tried the vegan
spanikopita? It's to die for."

"No, I'm sticking with gin." I lifted my glass. "Clear fluids
are good for you."

Luna tilted her head, her long brown hair brushing her
bare shoulders. Her white strapless dress practically glowed
in the low light. Luna da Rosa—known as Moon to her
closest friends—was a popular Instagram brand and the
founder of Wild Hearts, a cruelty-free cosmetics company.
Her big heart was my daily reminder to be a better person.
Tonight that big heart seemed intent on mothering me.

"Sweetie, you need to eat," Luna said. "I'll get you
something."

"I ate before we left," I said, but Luna ignored me in her
quest to find one of the appetizer-bearing waiters.

"Maybe we should have stayed in tonight," Emily said,
her voice laced with concern.

"It's good for me to be seen," I said. "If I disappear it'll
just blow the whole thing out of proportion."

Emily gave me the side-eye while she dug her phone out
of her clutch. A little smile crossed her lips as she typed.
She'd been dirty texting her boyfriend Derek all night. We'd

only been gone for a few hours, but the four of us—Daisy was around here somewhere—had come to the Florida Cancer Research Society's fund-raising auction as each other's dates. A slightly stuffy version of girls' night, but at least we were here for a good purpose.

"I'm not going to lie, Emily. I'm a little jealous of the hot sex you're going to have tonight," I said.

"What makes you think I'm having hot sex tonight?" Emily asked.

It was my turn to give her the side-eye.

Her lips turned up in a smile. "Okay, fine."

Luna came back and handed me a cocktail napkin with a pastry triangle.

"Thanks, Moon." I took a bite and the flaky pastry practically melted in my mouth. "Okay, you were right, these are to die for." I wasn't sure how Luna lived without bacon—or cheese—but I admired her dedication to her principles. And this spanikopita was amazing.

"Has anyone told you how fucking fantastic your ass looks in that dress, Cam?" Daisy appeared out of nowhere and grabbed my ass cheek. "I swear to god, whatever Inda makes you do is working."

"She loves to torture me," I said. Inda was my personal trainer and an Israeli goddess. My girl crush on her was no secret. I wasn't sexually attracted to women, generally, but if Inda had been single, I'd have given it serious consideration.

Daisy leaned back to check out my ass again. "Worth it. I'd totally do you."

"That would make for some fun gossip." I sipped my drink.

"If you want to go make out in a corner, let me know." Daisy winked at me. "Give them something else to talk about. I've got your back, babe."

"Careful, she's probably not kidding," Emily whispered.

I knew Daisy wasn't kidding. Her impulsiveness and flair for the dramatic meant you never knew what she was going to do next.

"Tempting," I said. "My hair does look great, so I'm camera ready. Although I think a public display of sexual experimentation might be the wrong PR move for me right now."

"Disagree, but suit yourself," Daisy said.

"Have you bid on any silent auction items?" Luna asked.

"I'm getting that." Daisy pointed to a large jewel-encrusted glass giraffe. "Isn't it fabulous?"

It was hideous, but that was probably why Daisy had to have it. "Why do I suspect they procured that specifically because Daisy Carter-Kincaid was on the guest list?"

Daisy was another member of our odd little foursome. On the surface, she looked like a socialite party-girl, with her constantly changing hair and intentionally scandalous wardrobe choices. What the gossip rags neglected to mention was how hard she worked managing—and expanding—her family's real estate empire.

A man in a black tux paused by the item and wrote on the bid sheet.

"Oh hell no. He is not getting my giraffe. I'm going to go outbid the shit out of him." Daisy paused, her lips curling in a smile. "I might do more than outbid him. He's cute."

"Girls' night, Daisy," Emily said. "No dates."

"Who said anything about a date?" Daisy asked. Her hips sashayed in her shimmery hot pink dress as she sauntered over to the silent auction tables. Poor guy didn't know what was about to hit him. Daisy was on the prowl.

The hairs on the back of my neck kept standing up, like someone was watching me. I glanced around the cavernous ballroom. Guests in designer gowns and custom-tailored tuxes milled around the auction items. Others were seated at their tables, finishing their desserts or sipping drinks. Clusters of people stood in knots around the room, chatting with cocktails in their hands.

And a fair number of them seemed to be casting judgmental glances in my direction.

"People are watching me, aren't they?" I asked.

"Yes," Emily said, and I appreciated her no-bullshit answer. "But can you blame them? It's been all over the news."

"What?" I hissed.

She looked at me like I'd suddenly gone insane. "You saw the articles. We were talking about them last night."

"Oh, the thing in the parking garage."

"Cam, someone basically attacked you. How can you be so flippant about it?"

"He didn't even get my purse."

I wished everyone would stop making such a big deal out of the so-called attempted mugging. Some random guy in a mask and hoodie had tried to grab my purse after work the other night. I'd stomped on his foot with my heel and rushed back into my building while he wailed in pain. It had barely been an incident worth mentioning, but the press was acting like it was big news.

"Do you really think that's why people are staring?" I asked.

"Why else would they be staring at you?" she asked.

"Because of the fucking sex tape," I said, lowering my voice.

I drained the last of my martini. Fucking Aldrich. A little over a year into our relationship, when I'd thought Aldrich might be *the one*, he'd talked me into letting him take a video of us having sex. I'd had a glass or two of wine and the allure of doing something a little bit kinky had overridden my good judgment.

Although I wasn't watched by the press like Daisy, being the CEO of a major aeronautics company and one of only a handful of female billionaires in the country meant I was susceptible to public scrutiny. It made me extremely careful to curate a professional public image. I acted the part. Dressed the part. And one little lapse in judgment—one night—was looming over my hard-fought reputation like a thundercloud.

I'd trusted Aldrich. That was what really stung. Aldrich's country club buddies weren't passing that video around because some jerk had hacked into Aldrich's computer and stolen it. He'd *sent* it to them. Sent a video that should have remained private. A video he'd assured me he had deleted long before we'd broken up.

Deleted, my ass.

"If it gets out, Derek and his team will help," Emily said. "And I don't think many people have seen it."

"God, I hope not."

Luna rubbed a few circles across my back. "It's going to be fine."

"Thanks. I should go bid on some things." I set my napkin and empty martini glass on a passing waiter's tray.

Daisy was busy flirting with the guy who'd bid on the ugly giraffe—which didn't say much about his taste, but to each his own. I wandered around the auction tables with Emily and Luna, absently bidding on things.

It had arguably been one of the worst weeks of my life— attacked in a parking garage and a potential sex scandal just days apart—so I was glad to be out with my girls. At thirty-six I still loved playing dress-up, and a black-tie event was a great excuse to dress to the nines. I'd hoped a killer gown and stilettos would take my mind off everything else.

So far I'd spent most of my evening fantasizing about bad things happening to my ex and having imaginary confrontations with him in my head. The good news was, if I did run into him, I had at least a dozen zingers ready.

Aldrich wasn't here, however, and I couldn't decide if that was a very good thing, or a massive disappointment.

We'd broken up six months ago, and until Monday, I'd been completely over it. Early in our relationship I'd imagined a future with him, but I'd eventually realized we were totally wrong for each other. Even in the immediate aftermath of our breakup, I hadn't been grieving *him* so much as the loss of nearly three years with the wrong man. I hadn't shed any tears. Mostly ranted to my friends while we drank wine in Daisy's hot tub.

After that it had been business as usual. I had an aerospace empire to run.

But Monday, a friend of his who was not a total douche had called to let me know Aldrich had shared the video with a handful of his buddies. His friend had thought it was a dick move and wanted me to know.

I'd thanked him and started plotting Aldrich's murder.

Except not literally.

Daisy sidled up next to me and slipped her arm around mine. "I think you need another drink."

"What happened to giraffe guy?"

"He was cute, but he's American, so, you know."

Daisy only dated European men. If you could call what she did dating. I admired her give-no-fucks spirit. Daisy Carter-Kincaid forged her own path and didn't care what other people thought.

Luna and Emily joined us, and we made our way to the

bar for another round of cocktails. We wandered back to our table—it seated eight, but we'd kept it to just the four of us by buying out the other seats—and sat down with our drinks.

"Cam, there's another reason we all came out tonight," Emily said.

"You mean other than the chance to bid on jewel-encrusted zoo animals? Do tell."

"Just hear me out." She glanced at Luna and Daisy. They both nodded.

Oh lovely. The vagillionaires—Daisy's term for the four of us—were about to gang up on me.

"You need personal security," Emily said.

"At least until we can be sure it was an isolated incident," Luna said.

"It probably was," I said. "And I have security."

"Not personal security," Emily said. "Derek knows someone who's very good."

"I appreciate what you're all trying to do, but I'm fine. I don't need some scary dude in dark glasses following me around everywhere."

"It's not nearly as bad as you think," Daisy said. She glanced around and waved to her bodyguard. "Alessandro's the man. You just need to find someone you like."

"I agree," Luna said. "It's comforting to know someone has your back."

I took a sip of my martini and set my glass down. This wasn't the first time they'd brought this up and I was bristling hard at the idea of a personal bodyguard. It felt so stifling. I already had a staff of people surrounding me. I didn't want to add someone whose job was essentially to follow me around all the time.

"We have building security at work," I said.

"That didn't stop some jackass from trying to snatch your handbag," Daisy said.

"I still maintain that was an isolated incident, and they're taking precautions so it doesn't happen again."

"You're not always at work," Luna said.

"We all know Bluewater's safe," I said. The Bluewater enclave—where the four of us lived—was our baby. We'd developed twenty-five hundred acres of swampland into a thriving micro-community. It was one of my proudest achievements, and there was nothing like being neighbors with your best friends. It made life a little less lonely.

Not entirely without loneliness, if I was being honest. But better.

"Well, I still maintain you need personal security," Emily said.

"I love you guys, but I don't need a bodyguard. I can handle things myself."

They gave each other undisguised *yeah right* glances. But I could tell by the way they shifted in their seats and picked up their cocktails that the discussion was tabled. For now, at least.

I did appreciate my friends' concern. But I already had enough on my plate without adding another complication, especially an unnecessary one.

And I ignored the little voice in my head that whispered tantalizing thoughts about having someone in my life I could rely on. About trusting someone else enough to let go —letting them shoulder some of the burden. I'd tried that and look where it had gotten me.

Yes, I was alone. But I was accustomed to it. It was what I knew.

And I wasn't sure if I could trust someone deeply enough to let them in.

I was a few minutes late to meet Derek at the boxing gym, thanks to Miami's shitty drivers. Sometimes I questioned my choice to drive a motorcycle. I was an experienced driver—hell, I was better on a bike than most stunt drivers—but that didn't account for other people being idiots.

Derek was already here, wrapping tape around his knuckles. An industrial-sized fan hummed in the background and a few guys were lifting over by the squat racks. I dropped my backpack next to the roped-off boxing ring.

"Afternoon," Derek said in his mild British accent.

My instincts prickled, which was weird. I glanced around the gym, but nothing seemed out of the ordinary. I didn't sense danger, exactly. Derek's face was impassive, his attention on taping his hands. If I didn't know better, I'd have thought he was up to something.

Then again, maybe he was.

"Afternoon," I said, keeping my voice neutral, like I didn't suspect anything. Not that I had reason to suspect Derek of anything, but my instincts were rarely wrong.

We gloved up and got in the ring without any conversation. That was normal enough. Bounced around and warmed up our shoulders. Life after forty meant both of us had to take better care of our joints.

I'd known Derek Price for a long time. We'd crossed paths when I was still an intelligence operative—he hadn't known that at the time—and I'd looked him up when I moved to Miami. Now he was a corporate fixer, specializing in public relations and image management, especially during and after scandals. I did some work for him once in a while, particularly when he needed someone on the ground.

With our joints and limbs sufficiently warmed up, we got to sparring. Jabs, right hooks, upper cuts. Boxing with Derek was mostly a way to work up a sweat. We knew each other's moves too well to surprise each other very often. And it wasn't like either of us was going for a knockout.

"Did you finish up with that last job?" he asked.

"The stalker? Yeah. He won't fuck with her again."

He swung and I ducked. "Good. What's next? You have something on deck?"

"No. I told you, that was the last one."

His grin irritated me, so I swung harder.

He blocked with his gloves in front of his face. "Sure it was."

"I'm serious, man. I'm retired."

"Keep telling yourself that, Ellis." He launched a solid right hook and I shifted my feet, twisting my torso so he'd miss.

"I'm not kidding. I'm done with all that shit. I just want to live a quiet, ordinary life."

Derek scoffed. "You've been saying that for five years and I still don't believe you."

"And I still don't care."

"What are you going to do? Play golf?"

"That's exactly what I'm going to do." I swung but he sidestepped.

"You don't even like golf."

"I'm getting better."

He rolled his eyes and threw a left hook. "That's not what I said, and no you're not."

I glowered at him from behind my gloves. He was right, I sucked at golf. And it was boring. But I was going to learn to like it, because golf was ordinary and I needed a fucking hobby.

"I don't know why you won't admit that you like the work you do," he said. "Come on man, you help people. What's wrong with that?"

"There's nothing wrong with helping people. That's not the point." I stopped and lowered my arms. "Do you know how hard it is to get out?"

Derek's smirk melted off his face. He knew I almost never talked about my time in the CIA.

"I was lucky to be able to tie up all my loose ends and walk away," I said. "Not a lot of guys like me get to do that. So yeah, I'm going to golf. And work out with your nosy ass. And then I'll figure out what I want to do with the rest of my life. Maybe I'll open a food truck."

He laughed. "It's a food truck now? What happened to starting a bakery?"

"The numbers don't really pencil," I said.

"So you're sure? No more security jobs."

"Positive." I put my hands up and gestured for him to come at me. "That was the last one."

"That's unfortunate."

I lowered my guard. "Why?"

Instead of taking advantage and landing a nice uppercut, he stepped back. "Because I have a friend who could use your help."

"No."

"Just hear me out—"

"No."

"Come on, man, listen first."

I raised my gloves and stepped closer. "No."

"Jude—"

I swung and missed on purpose. He wasn't even trying to defend himself. "Hands up, Price."

He lifted his gloves, his dark brow furrowing.

We kept trading blows without talking, but that determined expression never left his face. I bobbed and weaved around him, trading swing for swing.

Wordlessly, we finished up. Sweat dripped down my temples and soaked my shirt. We stepped out of the ring and Derek took off his gloves, dropping them in his open duffel bag.

"It's Emily's friend," he said, finally breaking the silence.

I pulled off my gloves and tossed them on top of my bag. Fuck. Emily was Derek's girlfriend, and she was... well, she was great. Wealthier than God, but she'd worked her ass off for every bit of her success. I wasn't exactly a have-a-big-group-of-friends kind of guy, but Derek and Emily were a great couple.

And if it was for her friend...

"I already said no, Price."

"Some guy tried to attack her in the parking garage of her building."

"That was Emily's friend? Wasn't that in the news?"

Derek nodded. "Cameron Whitbury, CEO of Spencer Aeronautics."

"Was it an isolated incident?" I asked before I could stop myself. Damn it. I wasn't getting involved. But something about the story was poking at me.

"Not sure. She's high profile enough for the usual— threats on social media, that sort of thing. But nothing up close and personal like this."

"Secured parking garage?"

"It is, although not too difficult for a pedestrian to gain access," he said. "An odd place for a purse snatching, however."

The location did make me curious. Purse grabbing tended to be a lot like pickpocketing. A crime of opportunity, usually out on the street.

"I'm sure the police are investigating," I said.

"You know they're not. They probably spent ten minutes searching the garage to make sure he wasn't still lurking in a dark corner, took a report, and called it a night."

I shrugged. "It was probably random."

"It could have been," he said. "But maybe it wasn't. Cameron's good at taking care of herself. But right now, she could really use personal security. Someone who can make sure she's safe, and figure out if there's more behind this than meets the eye."

I groaned. "No."

"It's not a long-term gig," Derek said. I could tell by the look in his eyes, he knew he had the advantage. "Consider it more seed money for your food truck."

"I have plenty of money."

"Look, I know there are other security companies out there who could handle this. You're massively overqualified. But she's Emily's friend. Hell, she's my friend too. I don't like trusting this to just anyone."

Goddammit. This was how it always happened. I'd say no, but they'd keep talking. And next thing I knew...

"Fine," I grumbled, crouching down to put my shit in my bag. "But only temporarily. If she needs long-term, she can find someone else. I don't do this kind of thing anymore."

"Absolutely," he said. "Consider it a personal favor to me, not a regular job."

"Mm-hmm."

"Thanks, man. This is going to make Emily feel so much better."

I glowered at him.

He smiled, ignoring my irritated glare. "I'll text you the details."

Derek left—he was a smart man who knew when to make an exit—and I gathered up my stuff to head home. His text came through before I'd even left the building. I rolled my eyes and walked out to my bike. Apparently I had to work tomorrow.

4

JUDE

*P*ausing on the sidewalk, I looked up at the glass office building. It reminded me of a safe house I'd used a few times in Prague. Unremarkable from the outside, just another high-rise with people in business attire coming and going.

I'd decided to stop beating myself up for taking yet another job when I kept saying each one was the last. This wasn't even a job, really. It was a favor. Totally different thing.

Granted, the last one had probably been more of a favor, too, considering I'd refused to let her pay me. But she was a college student, it wasn't like I could have taken her money.

In any case, I was only here to do Derek a solid. And maybe this would earn me some good karma. I could certainly use it.

Since I hadn't spoken with the client yet—and wasn't sure about attire—I'd opted for simple. Light gray button-down shirt. Slacks. I'd cuffed the sleeves, showing my tattooed forearms, because this was summer in Miami and it was hot as fuck.

I went inside, grateful to whoever had invented air conditioning. Checked my watch. Derek had said nine-thirty. I was early, but I'd wanted a chance to scope things out.

Uniformed security guards manned the front desk. I was pleased to see they looked alert.

"Can I help you?" one of them asked.

I swiped off my aviators. I'd already memorized the layout of the lobby and identified six things I could use as a weapon if necessary. "I'm here to see Cameron Whitbury."

"Your name?"

"Jude Ellis."

The second guard eyed me while the first turned his attention to his computer. A woman in a blouse and slacks walked by, flashing an ID badge. The guard nodded to her.

"Thirty-sixth floor," the first guard said. "Ask for Brandy."

I had an appointment, and I'd still have to go through a second layer to get to Cameron. That was good. "Thanks."

The elevator had stainless steel paneled walls that almost acted as mirrors. The dark carpet looked new. It took me up to the thirty-sixth floor and dinged, the doors opening.

The large Spencer Aeronautics logo was painted on the wall behind an imposing front desk. A receptionist with deep red lipstick and an earpiece watched me walk in.

"Can I help you?" Her voice was one shade shy of annoyed.

"I'm here to see Cameron Whitbury." I'd been instructed to ask for Brandy, but I wanted to see whether the receptionist would still make me go through another person.

"Do you have an appointment?"

I nodded once. "Jude Ellis."

"One moment." She tapped something into the phone on her desk. "I have a Jude Ellis here for Ms. Whitbury." She paused, then tapped a button on her phone. "Brandy will be out in a minute."

Brandy again. That was good, but so far, I didn't see any signs of further security on her floor.

A moment later, a woman came out. Mid-thirties. Blond, hair pulled back. Blouse and pencil skirt with black heels. Probably highly organized, but unlikely to be helpful in a crisis. Too smiley.

"Hi," she said. "Jude? I'm Brandy, Cameron's executive assistant."

I shook her hand. Small. Manicure, no callouses. Good grip, though. "Hi."

"I'll take you back."

I followed Brandy through a doorway next to the reception desk. Without meaning to, I picked out every hiding place and spot for an ambush. I couldn't help it; my brain just worked that way. I noted the exits, potential hazards, a conference room with a table that could be used for cover if turned over. People glanced at me as I walked by, faces showing expressions of mild curiosity.

Brandy stopped outside a closed door. The windows on either side were frosted glass, offering no view inside the office. She knocked, then opened it and stuck her head inside.

"Have a minute?" After a pause, she looked back and nodded for me to follow.

Cameron Whitbury stood behind her desk, her attention on a file. Thick coppery-red hair hung around her shoulders and her crisp white blouse had two buttons open at the collar. A thin gold chain draped across her throat.

A disconcerting sense of unease made the back of my

neck prickle. I shifted my shoulders and turned my head to rub my shirt collar against the back of my neck. What was bothering me in here?

There was a bathroom—door ajar, light off. Large windows showed a sweeping view of the city. Another wall had a framed blueprint of a vintage airplane. Neat desk with a laptop and a few files. Nothing unusual.

But something was off. I could feel it. The sensation intensified when my eyes went back to Cameron.

"This is Jude Ellis," Brandy said.

Cameron glanced up and smiled. "Oh?"

"Okay, so, let me know if you need anything." Brandy ducked out of the office and closed the door.

That was odd.

Cameron's eyes were on the door, her lips parted slightly. She had a dusting of freckles across her nose and cheeks that softened the angles of her face.

She was fucking gorgeous is what she was, but that wasn't why I was here.

Her gaze shifted to me and a little groove formed between her eyebrows. "I'm sorry, who are you?"

"Jude Ellis."

"Um..." Her eyes flicked up and down and she licked her lips. For a second, I could have sworn she was checking me out. But just as quickly, she was all business. She picked up her phone and swiped across the screen a few times. "Do we have an appointment? Because I don't have you on my calendar. Maybe Brandy forgot, although that's not like her."

"I was told nine-thirty, but if you're busy, you can just have someone show me around. Ideally, I'd like a schematic of the building and an org chart. Things seem fine in here for now, so if you could just point me in the right direction, I'll familiarize myself with the terrain."

She stared at me like she had no idea what I was talking about. Her green eyes were oddly mesmerizing. "You'll what?"

"I need to know the layout of the building."

"Who are you?"

Was she serious? "Jude Ellis."

"Right, but *who are you*?"

Wait, had Derek set me up? That asshole. "I take it Derek didn't tell you I was coming."

"Derek? As in Derek Price?"

"The very same."

The crease between her eyebrows deepened. "No, he didn't. Why would Derek ask you to come here?"

My neck prickled again. Maybe it wasn't danger I was sensing, but Derek's bullshit. Although this wasn't in character for him. He wasn't exactly a prankster. Why would he have done this?

"That's a great question. He said you needed security, but apparently he was screwing with me. Sorry to have wasted your time. I'm going to go rearrange his face now."

I turned to go, annoyed that I'd ironed a shirt for this.

"Wait," she said. "Derek told you I needed security?"

"Yeah. He said it was a favor for Emily."

Cameron rolled her eyes and shook her head. "That sneaky bitch. Don't move."

I raised an eyebrow. "Excuse me?"

She picked up her phone and tapped the screen a few times, then put it to her ear. "Don't pretend you don't know why I'm calling." Pause. "Yes, he's standing right here." Another pause. "I already told you I don't need a bodyguard."

She opened her mouth to say something else, but apparently whoever she was talking to—I assumed it was Emily—

wasn't letting her talk. Cameron's lips parted again several times, like she was about to speak, but instead, she kept listening. I couldn't hear the other side of the conversation.

Finally, Cameron pinched her lips closed and her nostrils flared. Those green eyes flashed. "We'll talk about this later."

She ended the call and set the phone back on her desk.

"Emily asked Derek to hire me behind your back," I said. It wasn't a question.

"Yes, she did."

There it was. My easy out. I didn't want another gig. She didn't want a bodyguard. I could tell her it had been nice to meet her, walk out that door, and never look back. Maybe go play golf.

Or go punch Derek in the teeth.

But something was wrong, and it was driving me absolutely crazy. The thought of leaving her here alone made my stomach twist into a knot. I wasn't sensing danger in her office, or even in this building. I sensed it in *her*. She was in danger.

"Look, it sounds like Emily's just concerned for your safety," I said. "Didn't someone attack you in the parking garage?"

She waved a hand. "It was random, and I was fine."

Her voice was flippant, but if I had to guess, she didn't fully believe that. Maybe she was trying to convince herself.

"Still, I could at least do a security evaluation for you." *Why are you still talking, Jude? You can leave.* "Find the weak points. Give you, and your friends, some peace of mind."

She lowered herself into her chair and motioned for me to sit. I took a seat across her desk from her.

"What are your qualifications?"

"Derek hired me."

"What does that mean?"

I crossed an ankle over my knee. "It means you can either trust his judgment or not. I don't exactly have a resume."

"So what is it that you do? Bodyguard-for-hire?"

"Sometimes. Depends on what the client needs. But this will be my last job. I keep trying to retire." I cleared my throat, not sure why I'd told her that last part.

"What was your most recent job?" She put up a hand. "I'm not asking for confidential client information. I'm just trying to get a better idea of what you do."

"Female college student. She was being harassed by an ex-boyfriend. His father was prominent politically. Made things complicated. She hired me, and now she no longer has a stalker."

She was hard to read, but the slight twitch of her eyebrows might have meant she was impressed.

"Did you use violence?"

I shook my head slightly. "Wasn't necessary."

"But you would have."

"Only if my client had been in danger of serious harm. What are you concerned about, Ms. Whitbury? That Derek hired a thug? I don't have a criminal record, nor have I ever broken anyone's kneecaps with a baseball bat."

Her eyes stayed locked on mine. They were such a bright shade of green. The intensity of her gaze, coupled with that danger instinct that wouldn't shut up, was making my adrenaline kick in. My heart beat harder, but I kept my posture casual. My face neutral.

"Okay," she said, finally. "I'll hire you—temporarily. We'll start with a security evaluation, and you can make your recommendations from there. I'll take them under advisement."

There was a challenge in her expression. In the set of her full lips and the way her eyes narrowed slightly. Like she was daring me to convince her she needed me.

All right, Cameron Whitbury. Challenge accepted.

5

CAMERON

*B*randy poked her head into my office, leaning around the partially open door. She'd put on her *you know you love me, don't fire me* smile. "Need something?"

I answered without looking away from the document I was reviewing on my computer screen. "A few minutes of your time, if you aren't too busy showing the Incredible Hulk around the office."

With a soft laugh, she came inside and shut the door behind her. "He's not green."

"We haven't seen him angry yet."

"Fair point." She lowered herself into a chair on the opposite side of my desk.

I clicked the mouse to save and close the document, then turned my attention to Brandy. "You knew about him?"

She winced. "Emily texted last night and told me to expect him."

"And you didn't give me a heads-up because..."

"She said not to."

I snorted out a laugh. "Of course she did. What do we know about him?"

"Not a lot. I looked him up after I got Emily's text, but I didn't find much. No social media. No mentions in news articles, at least not recent ones. He has a Florida driver's license with a motorcycle endorsement, but that's about it."

I tapped my fingernails on the desk. I shouldn't have been surprised that Emily had hired me a bodyguard. That woman was stubborn. But even if I'd been expecting a bodyguard to walk in my office this morning, nothing could have prepared me for Jude Ellis.

The man was enormous. I was five-nine with a love of high heels, so I was accustomed to looking men in the eye. But Jude? Even from across my office, he'd made me feel small. He had to be six-five, and I couldn't even guess his weight. He had the widest shoulders I'd ever seen. And those cuffed shirtsleeves and tattoos? Holy arm porn. He looked like he could flex his biceps too hard and burst the seams of his shirt.

But his size didn't tell the whole story. Sure, his thick tattooed arms and the way his thighs strained against his slacks made him look like most of his body's resources had gone into building muscle. But there was a sharp intelligence in those intriguing hazel eyes.

"He's friends with Derek Price," Brandy said. "And you know Emily wouldn't hire someone who wasn't trustworthy."

"I know." I trusted Emily. And Derek, at least as much as I knew him. But trust didn't come easily to me, and my ex's stunt with the sex tape hadn't done anything to foster my faith in humanity. "That's not really the point. I already told her I don't need a bodyguard. And if you say, *Cameron, you were attacked in our own parking garage*, I swear to god, you're fired."

"Cameron, you were attacked in our own parking garage."

I flicked my wrist, like I was shooing her out. "Pack your shit and go home."

"Fine, but if you don't hire me back by morning, I'll sell all your secrets to the competition."

"Traitor."

She shrugged. "You fired me."

"That's true. I have only myself to blame." My eyes flicked to my closed door. "What's he been doing?"

"Well, he asked for a tour, so I showed him around. He literally wanted to walk up and down every hallway. On every floor. It took forever. He looked in all the restrooms and supply closets, although I have no idea why. Then we went to the food court. I told him about the restaurants we have, but he didn't seem interested. Or hungry. I got a latte while he wandered around and chatted with people."

"Was he freaking everyone out?"

"You'd think, considering he looks like a pro wrestler crossed with an action hero. But he was very unobtrusive. If I didn't know better, I'd say he made himself smaller so people wouldn't notice him wandering around."

That was odd. And kind of fascinating. I didn't want to be intrigued by this man, but I couldn't help it.

"Where is he now?"

"He went down to the lobby to talk to the security staff. Am I still fired?"

I fake-sighed. "I guess not. I can't really live without you, so that's a consideration."

"As long as you realize it." She smiled. "Do you want me to send him in when he comes back?"

"Yeah, thanks."

Brandy stood. "Oh, don't forget—"

My office door swung open, interrupting her, and Bobby Spencer waltzed in like he owned the place.

Theoretically, he could have, if he hadn't turned out to be an entitled brat who knew nothing about the company his father had founded.

"Cami, babe, how are you?" He was apparently trying to resurrect the *Miami Vice* look with a turquoise shirt, its collar popped, and linen slacks. He'd even rolled up the sleeves of his white blazer.

I chose to ignore the fact that he'd called me Cami. No one called me Cami. My grandparents—the people who'd raised me—hadn't called me Cami. Bobby had used that nickname on and off since second grade. But whenever I called him out on it, he just used it more often.

"Knock before you come in, Bobby," I said. "What was that, Brandy?"

"I was going to say, don't forget I have to leave early today. Mateo has a dentist appointment."

"No problem." I kept my eyes on Brandy while Bobby sat on the edge of my desk. "If you want to leave now and grab lunch with Julio, feel free."

"Thanks. I'll see if he's available," she said with a smile. Her eyes flicked to Bobby, then back to me. "You also have that really important meeting in a few minutes. You wouldn't want to be late."

God bless her. "Right. Thanks, Brandy. I'll see you tomorrow."

"What meeting?" Bobby asked.

With a subtle roll of her eyes, Brandy slipped out.

"Just a meeting. Part of my job."

"I'm just wondering what's going on in your life, Cami," he said. "We don't talk enough. By the way, do you really just give your employees time off like that? You should dock her pay."

"Her three-year-old has a dentist appointment. I hardly think that's cause for disciplinary action."

"You give them an inch, they'll take a mile."

"Says the guy who's never held a real job."

He huffed. "I'm an artist-entrepreneur. An artistpreneur. Hey, I like the sound of that. I need to get that on my business card."

Bobby was neither an artist nor an entrepreneur. He lived off his father's wealth, and once in a while he pretended to start a new business. I knew better than to ask about his latest venture or why he was calling himself an artist now.

"Do you need something, Bobby? Because I need to get to a meeting."

"Did I tell you about the girl I've been hanging out with?"

I pretended to be absorbed in something on my computer screen. "Don't sit on my desk."

"She doesn't speak a lot of English, but we don't need words to communicate, if you know what I mean."

"Mm hmm."

"You know what we should do? Go clubbing. I'll bring Lola, and you can bring... Wait, are you dating anyone these days?"

"None of your business."

"Oh crap, I'm sorry," he said.

"Why?" I still didn't look at him. Hopefully if I didn't make eye contact, he'd get bored sooner and leave me alone.

"Me talking about another woman is making you jealous."

It was so hard not to laugh. "It's really not."

"You don't have a thing to worry about, Cami, you know my heart is yours. I'm just sowing my wild oats so I'll be ready to settle down with you when the time comes."

"That time will never come, but good luck to the girl who has to fill that position."

He stood, finally getting his skinny butt off my desk, and did a few hip thrusts. "She'll get all the positions, if you know what I mean."

"Gross, Bobby. Don't you have art or entrepreneuring to do?"

"Actually, I came up here to see if you want to come to my place tonight."

"Why would I do that?"

"To have dinner with me."

"I already told you to stop asking me out."

"Not a date," he said, holding his hands up. "I just figured you could use a little comforting after someone attacked you in the parking garage. We could talk."

"Someone *tried* to attack me and failed. And no thanks."

"Come on, Cami, you work too hard. You need to let your hair down. Take the edge off. I can help with that."

"Still no," I said. "Besides, I'm sure you have very important things to do tonight. Like jacking off to MILF porn and binge-watching *Miami Vice*."

"Already did both."

"Well haven't you had a nice productive day." I grabbed my purse, ready to get up and pretend to go to my nonexistent meeting. "Besides, why do you care if I work too hard?"

"Cami," he said, putting a hand to his chest. "I'm hurt. We're childhood best friends. Of course I care about you."

My grandmother, Dorothia Whitbury, had been one of the top engineers here at Spencer. She'd been with the company since the beginning, and she and my grandad had been good friends with Milton Spencer. When Milton had realized an eight-year-old me had an interest in aviation, he'd insisted on helping with my private school tuition. That meant I'd received an amazing education. But I'd also had to go to school with his dipshit son.

"We're not childhood best friends."

"I'll forgive you for saying that because you're traumatized by the attack. And you're probably on your period."

"Get out, Bobby."

"But first—"

I lifted my eyes. "Get. Out."

The corner of Bobby's mouth lifted in a smirk. He sucked in a breath, like he was about to say something, when a low voice came from behind him.

"You heard her."

Jude looked like he'd barely fit through the door. If he had some magical ability to appear unobtrusive, he was doing the opposite now. It looked like one of his tree trunk legs weighed more than Bobby's entire body.

Bobby turned at Jude's voice and I could see the smartass comment die on his lips. The color drained from his face and his barely-there Adam's apple bobbed in his throat.

Jude's eyes shifted to meet mine. "Problem?"

"No, he was just leaving."

Bobby glanced back at me. "Who's this guy?"

"Jude," I said, dropping my phone in my purse. "My bodyguard."

I probably shouldn't have said that—I hadn't agreed to hire him for more than a security assessment—but seeing Bobby's perpetually tanned face go pale made it worth it.

"Cool," Bobby said, his voice weak. "I guess you have that meeting, so I'll let you get to it."

Jude moved aside, but not quite enough for Bobby to get

past him. I tried to keep the amused smile off my face while Bobby shifted from one foot to the other, trying to figure out how to get through the door with Jude in his way. Finally, Jude side-stepped, giving Bobby just enough room to squeeze by.

"Who was that?"

I set my purse down, since I didn't really have a meeting. "Robert Spencer, aka Bobby the douchebag. He's the founder's son and a regularly occurring pain in my ass."

Jude's eyes narrowed slightly and he glanced back at the door. I thought maybe he'd comment on Bobby, but he didn't say anything.

"So, are you finished with the assessment?" I asked.

"No," he said, settling into a chair.

"I don't need you to make it formal. You can just email me your recommendations."

"I need to see your house first."

I leaned back in my chair. "I have adequate security at home."

"We'll see."

"I live in a gated community with twenty-four/seven security personnel, and my house is outfitted with a state-of-the-art alarm system. I don't need additional security."

"I don't think it was random," he said.

His square jaw with its careless bit of stubble was stupidly distracting. He was so hard and angular. Almost military. But there was a sophistication inherent in the way he moved that was a surprising contrast to his size. He wore a cuffed-sleeve button-down like a high-powered CEO but looked like he could lift the back end of a car without breaking a sweat. I had a feeling people often underestimated him.

I knew what that was like.

"What wasn't random?" I asked, mentally kicking myself for getting lost in that rugged face.

"The attempted mugging."

Points to him for calling it *attempted*. I wanted some damn credit for not getting robbed. "Of course it was random. It was dark and I was alone. Some guy tried to take my purse."

"Did he?"

"What do you mean?"

"I watched the security footage. The guy didn't try to grab your purse. He tried to grab *you*."

I crossed my arms. The entire incident had happened so fast. Had he been trying to grab me? I'd been holding my Chanel handbag tucked beneath my arm, so I'd assumed that was what he'd been after.

"What are you saying?"

"That it's possible you were targeted, and the objective wasn't your purse."

A sense of unease spread through my stomach, like a dribble of paint in clear water. "Well, if he was trying to kidnap me, he was terrible at it. All I had to do was stomp on his foot."

"That was a good move."

My lips turned up in a half-smile. "Thanks."

"Look, I can't give you a definitive answer as to what that guy was after. Maybe it was a random incident. But my instincts are telling me it wasn't. And it's rare that my instincts are wrong."

I believed him—about his instincts, at least. My brain was railing against the idea that I'd been targeted in a kidnapping attempt.

And I wondered what his instincts were telling him about me.

"Fine. You can come home with me. But don't expect me to put out unless you buy me dinner first."

His jaw hitched, an almost imperceptible tic. Nothing about his expression changed, and I wondered if I'd imagined it.

But the thought that I'd just ruffled this solid wall of man was oddly amusing. I kind of wanted to see if I could do it again.

I still didn't need a bodyguard, though. And once I had his security assessment, I'd smugly report back to Emily that she'd wasted her time. I'd hire a few more people here at headquarters if necessary. Maybe beef up security in the enclave. And let Jude get on with his retirement.

6

JUDE

I'd left the bike at home today, so I followed Cameron in my SUV. Interesting that she drove a Tesla. She could probably afford just about any vehicle she wanted. Of course, it had to have set her back at least a hundred grand, so it wasn't like the CEO of Spencer Aeronautics was tooling around in a practical sedan. I wondered if it was the engineer in her. She liked the tech.

We turned into the Bluewater enclave and stopped at the gate. I could see her speaking to the guard, then he waved me through after her. We drove down a street lined with palm trees, surrounded by lush landscaping.

I knew from my brief research on Cameron that she and three friends had developed Bluewater. They'd created a waterfront community with sprawling mansions, luxury condominiums, a private airfield, marina, and a village with high-end boutiques and restaurants. It was very exclusive—Cameron and her friends managed it personally—and it had a reputation for being home to the particularly quirky among Miami's elite.

A bridge took us over a canal toward several sprawling

waterfront estates. Cameron turned down the drive of the second one. She left her car in front of one of the four garage bays. I parked and met her at the steps of her enormous front porch.

Cameron's office had been sleek and functional with only a few feminine details. More elegant than pretty. But her house was like a tropical resort. The circular driveway was lined with palm trees and an explosion of flowering plants. Solar lights lit a wooden path that led to the covered front porch. The design was reminiscent of a beach hut, only sturdier—and much, much larger.

I noted the locations of the security cameras, including potential blind spots.

She punched in a code and opened one of the wide double doors. I stepped inside, although the palm trees growing right through the floor made it look like a tropical oasis. The glass ceiling let in light and a fountain trickled in the center of the room. Lush plants were everywhere. It was decadent without being garish. Tropical without being cliché.

"Well, this is it," she said.

"No butler to come take your coat?"

She glanced over her shoulder, giving me a wry grin. "It's Miami. I don't wear a coat often enough to need someone to help me take it off."

I took a few steps, my shoes clicking on the hardwood floor.

"Do you need blueprints, or will an old-fashioned tour do the trick?" she asked.

"A tour is fine. I'll get the blueprints later."

She raised an eyebrow.

From the moment I'd realized her friends had conspired to hire me behind her back, I'd felt like she and I were locked in a chess match. She didn't want to hire a body-guard. And although I'd started my day thinking I didn't want the job, my instincts were still tingling. Even here, there was a hint of danger lurking at the edges of Cameron Whitbury's life. I could feel it. And it was going to drive me crazy until I figured out why.

Which meant I had to convince her to hire me.

She set her purse on a side table and gestured toward a wide staircase. "Shall we?"

I nodded and followed Cameron up the curved staircase.

"We can start up here," she said as we walked. "There's not much to show you in the way of security in here. Blue-water is gated, of course. And the house is outfitted with an alarm system and outdoor security cameras."

The second floor had hardwoods and a subtle beach vibe. Blues and grays. Splashes of teal. Tasteful artwork, but no personal photos on display.

"Guest rooms," she said, pointing out several doors. "They have private bathrooms. They don't get used very much. Mostly by Daisy when she drinks too much."

"Daisy Carter-Kincaid. One of your Bluewater develop-ment partners."

She glanced over her shoulder. "You did your homework."

"It's my job."

"Naturally." She pointed to a set of double doors leading to a home gym. Floor-to-ceiling windows offered a view of Biscayne Bay. "That's where Inda, my personal trainer, tortures me. There's another bathroom through that door."

We moved on past more guest rooms. Then a set of closed double doors.

She opened one side. "My bedroom. There's a master bath and a closet through that other door."

Enormous windows offered an expansive view of sparkling blue water. A single chair with a throw blanket draped over the back sat next to a small table with a stack of books. A plush rug took up most of the center of the room. Her king-sized bed was slightly rumpled, one corner of her fluffy white comforter pulled back, like she'd gotten out of bed this morning and left it that way.

Something about that slightly unmade bed made my dick stir.

"Since no one but me is ever seeing the inside of my bedroom again, we can move on," she said, closing the door.

"That brings up another question." I cleared my throat. "Are you dating anyone?"

She tilted her head and the corner of her mouth lifted. "I don't date employees."

I held eye contact. "You haven't hired me. And I don't date clients."

"Touché," she said. "Although if this was all an elaborate ploy to get in my pants, I'd have to give you points for creativity."

"If this was an elaborate ploy to get in your pants, I'd already be in them."

"You're very confident in your abilities."

"When it's warranted."

Her lips twitched again, and she turned to walk back down the hallway. I followed.

"No, I'm not dating anyone," she said. "Not for about six months. And probably never again."

There was a hint of pain buried in her flippant tone. It made a coal of anger flare hot in the pit of my stomach. I didn't like the idea of someone hurting her.

"There's another bathroom through there." She gestured to a door, then to a large room on the other side of the hall.

"There's a TV and couches and that sort of thing in there. Nice for movie nights."

At the far end of the hall, I could see another stairway leading down.

"This leads to the kitchen, which brings me to Nicholas. He's my chef, and I'm warning you, whatever he's doing in there, don't interrupt. He makes magic in that kitchen and I don't like to bother him when he's working."

"Understood."

There was definitely something happening in the kitchen. A rhythmic thumping sound came from below. And was that someone breathing heavily? Maybe her chef was kneading bread dough.

"Nicholas is overqualified to be a personal chef, but he swears he likes the slower pace," Cameron said as we headed down the enclosed spiral staircase. "The restaurant industry is brutal. And he works a few days a week as a pastry chef at the Bluewater Bakery, so really, we all win. I—"

She stopped in her tracks, her words cutting off like she'd just had the air knocked out of her.

"Oh my god!"

"Shit!"

"Cam!"

I hurried down the last few steps and got an eyeful of her expansive gourmet kitchen. And an eyeful of a tall bearded man with his pants around his ankles. He had an athletic-looking woman bent over in front of him, bracing herself on the island. Also with pants around her ankles.

They both scrambled to pull their pants up, blubbering with embarrassment. I wasn't sure whether to laugh or grab them both and haul them outside. He better have been her chef.

Cameron put a hand over her eyes. "Oh god, Nicholas, I just saw your ass."

"I'm sorry," he said, still trying to pull up his pants.

"Damn it, Nick," the woman hissed, hauling a pair of tight workout leggings up her legs. She had a mild accent. Israeli if I wasn't mistaken.

"Are you decent?" Cameron asked, still covering her eyes.

Nicholas groaned. "Cameron, I'm so sorry."

"Okay, but am I going to see your junk if I open my eyes or can I look now?"

"You can look now," the woman said, shooting Nicholas a glare.

Cameron lowered her hand. "Were you guys just having sex in the kitchen?"

The woman bit her lip and looked at the floor.

Nicholas ran his hands through his hair. "Yeah, we... I didn't think you'd be home for a while, and Inda kept bending over, and she looks so good in those pants, I couldn't help myself. I'm so sorry."

"Don't blame me," Inda said, her voice indignant. "I was just helping you get stuff out of the cupboards."

Cameron blew out a breath. "Okay, we're all adults here. I'm all for a happy marriage where you can't wait to fuck the hell out of each other; it gives me hope for humanity. But you *cook* in here."

"I always wash my hands," Nicholas said.

"What?" The pitch of Cameron's voice went up a notch. "Is this like your pre-cooking ritual? Do you do this often? Is this why your food is so orgasmic?"

"No," Inda said.

"Because if it is, I'm tempted to let it happen," Cameron said.

"No," Nicholas said. "We don't... That's not... I was just being spontaneous. God, I'm so sorry."

Inda seemed to notice me for the first time. Her eyes widened and she put a hand to her forehead. "Oh my god, Nick, she's not alone."

I put up a hand. "Hi."

Cameron stepped down into the kitchen and I followed, standing beside her. "Right, you're here. This is Jude Ellis. He's—"

"I'm Cameron's new personal security consultant."

She whipped her head around to glare at me. "He's doing a one-time security assessment."

I just crossed my arms, my expression stony.

Cameron shook her head at me, then turned her attention back to her blushing chef and his wife. She flicked her hand toward a set of glass doors. "Go, finish."

Nicholas and Inda glanced at each other. "What?" Nicholas asked.

"Go finish what you started," Cameron said. "You don't need to suffer blue balls on my account. Go have sex with your hot wife. Just do it in your own kitchen."

"Cam, it's fine," Inda said.

Nicholas shot her a look of alarm.

"What?" Inda asked him, lowering her voice to a whisper. "You could keep going after this?"

"Are you kidding?" he asked, looking her up and down.

"Ugh, you're both disgusting," Cameron said. "Go have sex. I'm going to go bleach my eyeballs. You can make it up to me by baking one of those key lime things again. It's been a long day and I'd sell a kidney for one of your magical treats."

Inda opened her mouth as if to speak, but Cameron cut her off.

"Don't even start with me about my meal plan, Inda. I just caught you banging against my kitchen island. I deserve sugar."

Inda clicked her mouth closed and nodded.

"Get out of here, crazy kids."

"But, your dinner?" Nicholas asked.

Cameron started to answer, but I cut her off again. "I'll take care of it."

She looked at me, her eyebrows winging up her forehead.

I pushed my cuffed sleeves over my elbows and went to the sink to wash my hands. Nicholas and Inda glanced at each other again, then crept out to the terrace through the glass door.

"What are you doing?" Cameron asked.

"Cooking you dinner." I turned off the water and dried my hands on a towel.

The kitchen was spacious, with white marble counters, an ocean blue backsplash, and stained wood cabinets that matched her luxury beach hut vibe. Tropical potted plants added vibrant color, and it was no surprise that everything looked top of the line.

She watched me move around the kitchen without saying anything, her expression bewildered. I did a quick sweep, looking for ingredients. I was no gourmet chef, but I knew my way around a decent meal. And I liked keeping Cameron off-balance.

I found fresh chicken breasts in the large double-door refrigerator, along with a container of already-prepped vegetables. She had spices in a cupboard. I set everything on the counter, dug around for a cutting board and set of knives, and got to work.

"Is meal-prep in your usual lineup of services?" She

opened a cupboard and took out a wine glass, then raised her eyebrows, her hand hovering near a second one.

"None for me, and not usually," I said. "I just figured I could do Nicholas a solid."

"Getting in good with the chef is always a smart move. And I'm not helpless, by the way. I do know how to cook for myself."

"No one said you didn't." I started slicing the chicken.

She produced a bottle of red wine and went to work opening it, then poured herself a glass. I kept my attention on the food, but I could feel her watching me. That intense green-eyed gaze of hers was scrutinizing my every move. Sizing me up. It didn't bother me. I liked that she was being cautious, even though her close friend had hired me.

"Well, have you seen enough?" She took a sip of her wine. "Am I safe in my own home?"

"What's out there?" I gestured toward the doors.

She glanced outside. "Three guest houses. Nicholas and Inda live in one. The other two are empty. There's a terrace overlooking the bay and an outdoor pool. And lots of plants. My gardener likes to pretend we live in a jungle."

"How many people have unfettered access to your home?"

She raised an eyebrow. "Inda and Nicholas, obviously. Also my gardener, Bert. He doesn't really have a schedule, just comes and goes as he pleases."

My brow furrowed.

"I've known Bert since I was a kid. He used to work with my grandad. He loves gardening, and this gets him out of his wife's hair."

"Is that it?"

"I have a cleaning service. And Brandy has the entry

code. My friends do, too. Emily you know, plus Luna and Daisy."

From what I could see, she was reasonably safe here. But that danger instinct was still making the back of my neck itch. I found a skillet and some oil and got the chicken cooking on the large gas stove.

She slid onto a stool at the island and got out her phone. Her eyes darted up to me every so often as she scrolled through messages or texts and sipped her wine. I wondered what she was thinking. The woman had an excellent poker face. She could have been mulling over the potential details of our contract, already willing to hire me. Or planning to dig in her heels and refuse, maybe to stick it to her friend for going behind her back in the first place.

Of course, she could have been thinking about work. She had an aerospace empire to run.

I finished the impromptu stir fry and plated us each a portion. I slid hers in front of her and she set her phone aside.

"I will admit that smells amazing."

I took the stool next to her and handed her a fork. "Thank you."

"All right, Ellis. Do I have to wait for the PowerPoint presentation, or can you lay it on me over dinner?"

I met her eyes, my fork dangling from my hand. "You need me."

"Do I?"

"Yes. Your security staff at Spencer headquarters seem good. But they have an entire building to cover. And I assume you don't spend all your business hours in your office. You leave for lunches, meetings, that sort of thing?"

"I do. Quite frequently."

"So you don't have security coverage in those situations. It looks like your people do a decent job of keeping you out of the gossip rags, or maybe you don't do anything scandalous enough to draw attention." I might have imagined it, but I thought I saw her eye twitch. "But you still have a very high profile. There are hundreds of reasons you could be targeted."

She took a bite, her eyes never leaving me.

"In my opinion, your home security is adequate." I wanted to tell her it wasn't—that she needed someone here twenty-four/seven—but I didn't have anything to back that up. Just that persistent neck tingle, and I knew that wasn't enough. "Outside Bluewater, however, I do recommend full-time personal security."

"You actually think I need a bodyguard."

"Look, I don't have an ulterior motive. If you say no, I get to go home tonight and not set an alarm for tomorrow. I'm just being honest. You had an incident that warrants tightening security around you, at least for the time being. You can hire me, or hire someone else. But you won't find anyone better than me."

"And you can fill in for my horny chef in a pinch." She pointed to her plate with her fork.

I smiled. "Next time the meal costs extra."

"Naturally."

She went back to her dinner and we ate in silence for a few moments. It was odd. Cameron Whitbury was basically a stranger. Yet I was surprisingly comfortable sitting here in her enormous kitchen, sharing a meal with one of the wealthiest women in the country.

But I'd learned a long time ago that regardless of someone's title or the size of their bank account, they were still just a person.

Finally, she set her fork down. "Okay, I surrender. Emily wins. You're hired."

I raised an eyebrow.

"She and my other two girlfriends have been texting me all day. This is the only way to shut them up."

"So that's it? No negotiations? No conditions?"

"I want to make it perfectly clear why I'm doing this. It's not because I think I need personal security. It's to appease my friends and get them to stop riding my ass about it. So don't consider this a long-term gig."

"That works for me. I don't want a long-term gig."

"Good." She finished off her wine.

"Good."

"And if you think you can tell me what to do, what to wear, where to go, with whom, or when, you're mistaken."

"And if you think I won't stop you from doing things that put you in danger, you're mistaken."

Her eyes narrowed and her lips pressed together. Holy shit, this woman was sexy. The challenge in her eyes got my blood pumping in a way nothing had in a long time.

I just looked at her, keeping any expression off my features.

I could already tell Cameron Whitbury was going to be an enormous pain in my ass. But I'd always been a bit of a masochist.

7

CAMERON

*T*he breeze coming off the water was cool against my skin. I loved coming out here at night. The balcony outside my master bedroom had an incredible view of the water. The heat of the day had eased, and the blue serenity of the bay seemed to absorb every sound. Peaceful silence had settled over Bluewater.

"Suck it, asshole!"

Except for Frank, Bluewater's free-range parrot. He squawked from his perch in a tree somewhere to my left. I found it best to ignore him. He'd get louder if you gave him attention.

I stretched out my legs on the upholstered deck chair. I'd changed into a silky tank top and shorts pajama set—mint green with white lace along the edges. A glass of red wine sat on the table next to me, along with the remnants of one of Nicholas's key lime tarts. His *sorry for screwing my wife in your kitchen* gift.

Jude had left shortly after we'd finished dinner. His parting words had been *see you in the morning.* I picked up my glass and took a sip. How was this going to work? Was he going to stand in my doorway all day? Follow me to meetings and check the conference room before I entered? Run background checks on the wait staff at restaurants?

Daisy and Luna had bodyguards, but they trailed them at a distance, mostly at social functions. Emily had Jane, but she was more like a personal assistant who also happened to be a ninja.

Jude looked like a nightclub bouncer, only better dressed.

He smelled good, too.

I sighed. I'd told him that Emily, Luna, and Daisy hounding me with text messages was the reason I'd decided to hire him. That was partially true. They had been texting me relentlessly. And I did want to get them off my ass. But that wasn't the only reason. Maybe not even the main reason.

What he'd said in my office about that attack in the parking garage not being random had stuck in my brain, like a tiny splinter. A small irritation that wouldn't go away.

And when we'd come down the stairs to find Nicholas banging his wife in my kitchen, for a split second, fear had exploded in my belly. One thought had invaded my mind—someone was in my house.

The next second had brought another thought, just as fast and explosive as the first. Jude was behind me.

And all that fear had dissipated.

The entire experience had taken less than a heartbeat. But it had been so acute, I couldn't pretend it hadn't happened. I'd been terrified, and Jude's presence had made me feel safe.

I'd known right then that I was going to hire him. Of course, when he'd said he would make me dinner, he'd thrown me off. I hadn't been expecting that. So I'd dragged it out a little longer, too curious to see what he'd do next to tell him he was hired and I'd see him in the morning.

My phone buzzed against the glass tabletop. The girls were still waiting for me to tell them what had happened with Jude. So far, I'd mostly texted them with how mad I was that they'd done this behind my back. I didn't care that it had been primarily Emily. I was holding all three of them responsible. I knew them. They'd all been in on it.

Daisy: *I know you're awake. Answer us or I'm coming over there.*

Me: *No you're not.*

Daisy: *How do you know?*

Me: *Because you're already in bed.*

Daisy: *You can't see into my bedroom, you creeper.*

Emily: *Maybe she can. Cam, did you set up cameras in Daisy's house?*

Luna: *She would never do that.*

Me: *Um, no. Daisy's bedroom? Unsubscribe.*

Daisy: *Hey. A lot of good stuff goes on in my bedroom. You should be so lucky.*

Emily: *Can we focus?*

Luna: *How's your new bodyguard, Cam? I feel so much better knowing you have a professional watching out for you.*

Me: *I'm still mad at Emily for hiring him behind my back.*

Emily: *You didn't fire him already, did you?*

Me: *No.*

Daisy: *Where's he sleeping? Is he going to be in the room next to yours?*

Daisy: *Do you think he'll sneak in and peek at you while you sleep?*

Me: *Now who's being creepy? He's not sleeping here.*

Luna: *Why not?*

Me: *He declared my home security adequate.*

Emily: *So what does that mean?*

Me: *It means I have a bodyguard when I'm not in Bluewater.*

Luna: *What's he like?*

Me: *Enormous.*

Daisy: *OH SNAP. I bet he has major Big Dick Energy.*

I rolled my eyes, but mostly because she was right. Not that I was going to admit it to them.

Me: *He's tall and huge and looks like he could snap a guy in half. But he dresses nice.*

Me: *Also, he can cook. Don't ask me how I know.*

Me: *But it involves walking in on Nicholas and Inda fucking in my kitchen.*

Emily: *NO*

Luna: *That's not sanitary, but wow.*

Daisy: *Go big chef man!*

Me: *I can't even be mad. At least someone in this house is getting laid.*

Emily: *Aw, sweetie.*

Me: *I'm glad I've already decided I'm never dating again. Because I'm pretty sure Jude would be the world's biggest cock-blocker.*

Daisy: *I'm calling it right now. You're definitely boinking your bodyguard.*

Me: *I'm definitely not.*

Daisy: *I don't mean now, but eventually you will. When it happens, you have to tell me so I can gloat.*

Me: *How about no.*

Luna: *No you won't boink him, or no you won't tell Daisy?*

Me: *Both.*

Luna: *That doesn't make any sense.*

Me: *It doesn't need to. I'm closed for business. Only the battery-powered may enter my lady temple.*

Luna: *Approve of calling it your lady temple!*

Me: *I thought you'd like that.*

I paused and looked out over the water as it sparkled in the moonlight. I wasn't good at admitting when I was wrong. It felt like weakness. But maybe—just maybe—Emily had a teeny tiny point about needing personal security. At least until we were sure I wasn't being targeted.

Me: *Thanks for having my back, jerks. I love you guys.*

DESPITE MY INSISTENCE that it hadn't been a big deal, I'd been acutely aware of my surroundings in the parking garage ever since the attempted-mugging-or-possibly-worse. My designated spot was near the elevator, so I didn't have far to walk. But I'd started waiting to get out of my car until I was certain no one was lurking around a corner.

Brandy had suggested having my driver, Joe, start taking me to and from the office. She managed his schedule, making sure he was available to me during the day for my many offsite meetings and trips to our manufacturing or testing facilities. He wasn't exactly security, but it would mean I'd never be alone in the parking garage. But I'd deemed that unnecessary.

I turned off the engine and checked around me. There weren't many cars here yet. I was always among the first to arrive in the morning and last to leave at night.

It was possible I worked too much.

But I didn't have much else going on in my life, so putting in fourteen-hour workdays didn't feel like a hardship. I loved my job. I loved this company and the direction I was taking it. I loved that I was in a position to guide Spencer into a new era.

I was making a difference in people's lives. When Milton

Spencer had brought me in, this company had been on the verge of collapse. A dinosaur struggling to breathe in a world with a rapidly changing atmospheric chemistry. I'd pulled it into the next century, focusing on innovation, and poured resources into research and development.

It was paying off. Spencer Aeronautics was thriving. Instead of morale-killing rounds of layoffs, I'd saved jobs and hired hundreds of new employees. I insisted on paying well, providing good benefits, and making it easy for working parents to juggle their work and home lives.

If I was confident about one thing in my life, it was what I did here.

The mostly-empty parking garage was quiet, so I opened my door, clutching the pepper spray I hadn't admitted to my friends I now carried.

"Morning."

Whipping around, I pointed the pepper spray in the direction of the voice.

The corner of Jude's mouth twitched, like he was trying not to smile. "Nice reflexes."

"Don't scare me like that." I tucked the pepper spray into my purse. "I could have sprayed you."

He shrugged, like it wouldn't have mattered to him if I'd burned his eyes. He had a black backpack slung over one shoulder and was once again dressed in a crisp button-down shirt and slacks.

It was a good look on him.

"How long have you been here?"

"I arrived a few minutes before you."

"Is that a coincidence, or are you psychic? I didn't tell you when I'd be in."

"Emily texted me when you left home," he said. "And we can talk about schedules upstairs."

I wanted to argue with him. It was like an instinct I could barely control. But I had hired him, and it did make sense to coordinate our schedules in the comfort of my office, rather than standing here in the parking garage.

Still, I narrowed my eyes. I didn't want him thinking he'd scored points on me this early in the day. "I have a few things to take care of, then I can meet with you after my eight-thirty rundown with Brandy."

He acquiesced with a small nod.

I pretended to ignore him as he fell in step behind me and followed me into the elevator. My skin tingled at his presence, like he emitted biological radiation that warmed me from the inside. It was both comforting and disconcerting.

"What's in the backpack?" I asked. "Your secret bodyguard arsenal?"

"No. Laptop."

"That's very mundane," I said. "I suppose you keep a gun tucked in your belt or somewhere no one can see it."

"I don't carry a gun," he said. "Not unless it's absolutely necessary."

"How would you know if it's going to be necessary?"

He was quiet for a beat before answering. "I always know."

I wasn't sure how I felt about that answer.

Once in my office, I got to work, putting Jude out of my mind. Thankfully, he didn't linger in my doorway or try to stand guard behind my desk. I didn't know where he went, but somehow I could sense him nearby. Maybe he'd taken up a position at Brandy's desk or parked himself in the small conference room next door.

A report from my research and development team captured my attention. We were testing elements of a new guidance system that was going to be crucial to managing aircraft reentry into the atmosphere. Initial results were promising, although I could see from a quick sweep of the data that we had more work to do.

I blinked in surprise when Brandy poked her head into my office.

"Hey boss lady. Ready for me?"

"Sure." I minimized the report on my screen and took out my phone to open my calendar.

Jude came in behind Brandy and silently took the seat next to her, as if he'd been invited to our morning meeting.

My eyes flicked to him briefly, but I decided to allow it. I needed to figure out what to do with him while I was just sitting here working anyway.

Brandy went over my schedule and her list of reminders for me. She didn't seem bothered by Jude. In fact, when she noted I had a lunch meeting at a nearby restaurant, she glanced at him, as if acknowledging that he'd be joining me. Which was interesting, considering I hadn't had a conversation with her about his role yet.

"One more thing," Brandy said when she'd finished our usual rundown. "Do you need me to get paperwork for Jude from HR?"

"No, Mr. Ellis and I have a private contract," I said. "It's a personal expense."

"Sounds good. Also, Bobby was here about ten minutes ago, but he took one look at Colossus here and left."

Jude's brow furrowed and he glanced sideways at her.

"Colossus?" she asked. "He's a superhero. Big guy. Sorry, my husband's a comic book nerd."

"Wow, effortlessly saving me from a Bobby Spencer encounter," I said. "You've already earned your keep today."

"I aim to please," Jude said.

"Since we're on the subject, what am I supposed to do with you during the day when I'm working?" I asked. "Are you really going to hang around the office in case my would-be mugger gets through security in the lobby and rushes in here to try to grab my purse again?"

"Here's how this works," Jude said, clearly ignoring my snark. He shifted slightly in the chair, making his shirt-sleeves tighten around his bulging arms.

Not that I was looking at his bulging arms. Or his thighs straining against the fabric of his slacks. That would have been totally unprofessional.

"I am going to be here while you're working," he continued. "Ideally, you'll set me up at a desk outside your office or nearby so I have easy access to you, and you to me. I'll accompany you to meetings, both on and offsite. I'll be very unobtrusive. You'll hardly know I'm there."

I raised an eyebrow. It was difficult to imagine a man his size being unobtrusive, but I decided not to comment.

"I can take care of the desk situation," Brandy said.

I nodded to her. "Please do."

"I'll escort you from your car into the building in the morning and back again at night. If you leave the office, I go with you. That includes evenings and weekends. If you're going anywhere other than home, I'm going too. For the time being, at least."

Once again, the instinct to challenge him flared hot. But challenge him on what? I could insist he let me go to meetings without him. Did he really need to stand in the conference room while I listened to R&D's latest report or met with the accounting or finance departments? Probably not, but quibbling with him over small details would just make me look bratty. So I kept my lips pressed together.

"I also highly recommend filling your social calendar for

the next couple of weeks. Find reasons to be seen. If someone is targeting you, we want them to know you're not unprotected. It might be enough to get them to back off."

"Wait, Cameron's being targeted?" Brandy asked.

"No," I said at the same time Jude said, "Possibly."

We locked eyes but he gave me an almost imperceptible nod.

"There's a small chance the attempted-mugging wasn't random," I said. "But I'm positive there's no reason to worry."

"She's right, there's no reason to worry," Jude said. "She has me now."

I met his eyes again. There was no cockiness in his comment. Just a statement of fact. And for some reason, I believed him.

A layer of tension I'd been denying melted from my shoulders. I still had a million things on my to-do list and the future of this company—and its thousands of employees —in my hands. But for the first time since some jackass in a hoodie had tried to grab my purse—or me—in the parking garage, I felt safe.

8

JUDE

*B*randy set me up at a desk near hers, just outside Cameron's office. When Cameron's door was open, I could turn my head and see her. Although the threat level was on the low side, I was glad I had an easy view of her. Only because it made my job easier. Not because I liked looking at her.

I did. But I was a professional and my job had nothing to do with that thick red hair or those mile-long legs. The fact that she was gorgeous was a nice perk, nothing more.

This area of the building was spacious and open. Framed photos of aircraft in flight decorated the walls, some clearly decades old. Spencer's other executives had large, windowed offices. Their various support staff sat at desks arranged in a neat grid.

But what could have been a stark workplace was actually quite comfortable and relaxed. Brandy's desk had a string of chili pepper lights around the edge and a bulletin board with scribbled crayon drawings on the wall next to her. She had photos of her husband and son, and a mug with a rainbow handle held a supply of pens.

The other desks were similarly personalized. Family photos, kid art, and quirky décor seemed to be not only allowed, but encouraged. I'd noticed on my walk-through of the building yesterday that the other floors were similar.

There were the usual desks, office chairs, phones, and computer equipment. But I'd also seen an engineer in a bean bag chair, the accounting department had several vases of freshly cut flowers that looked like they'd come from someone's garden, and among the expected aerospace-themed artwork were framed prints featuring snarky quotes and sayings.

It combined to create an environment that was both professional and comfortable. Not typical for an old-school company filled with engineers. It made me wonder how much of it was due to Cameron's influence.

I'd done a brief search on the history of Spencer Aeronautics already, but today I needed to dig deeper, both into the company and Cameron. She'd hired me to handle her personal security and part of that was assessing potential threats to her safety. This was where I differed from some run-of-the-mill bodyguard for hire. My services included more than just muscle.

Cameron was back at her desk after I'd accompanied her to a short meeting in the large conference room on this floor. I had insisted on shadowing her during internal meetings, but not because I thought she was in danger here. I needed to learn her routine. See how she worked. Plus I needed to get her used to me being nearby.

My presence also sent a message. No doubt the office rumor mill had gone into full swing after the attack on her. It had happened here, in the parking garage most of them used. Tightening security around their boss showed that the threat was being taken seriously. It also implied that the potential danger was focused on her, not them, while simultaneously reassuring people that she was protected.

All things I'd been prepared to point out to Cameron last night. But she'd needed less persuading than I'd expected.

Brandy brought a white to-go container and set it on my desk.

I looked up from my laptop. "What's this?"

"Lunch. I ordered it for you."

A friendly gesture, but she eyed me with coolness in her expression.

"Thanks."

She pulled a chair up next to my desk and lowered herself down, crossing one leg over the other. "Who are you, really?"

Suspicion, probably a sign of loyalty and protectiveness toward her boss. I liked that. "Jude Ellis. We met before."

She arched an eyebrow. "Is that your real name?"

"Yes."

"It's the name on your birth certificate?"

"Would you like me to bring you a copy?"

She narrowed her eyes. "You offer security consulting."

"Among other things, yes."

"Then why can't I find your website?"

"Don't have one."

"What about social media?" she asked.

"Don't use it."

"Then how do you do business? How do you find clients?"

I flipped open the to-go container's lid. Sandwich on thick bread. Looked good. "All my business is referrals."

"You don't advertise?"

"No."

"And you stay in business?"

"Unfortunately."

"What does that mean?"

I shrugged one shoulder. "It interferes with playing golf."

"What qualifications do you have?"

Interviewing me when her boss had already hired me wasn't Brandy's job. But I didn't mind the interrogation. It was another sign that Cameron had people looking out for her. And making an ally out of Brandy would make my job considerably easier, especially if Cameron decided to stop being cooperative.

"I'm not qualified. I'm overqualified." I leaned back in my chair. Surprisingly, it didn't squeak under my weight. "Marine Corps. Then CIA. I retired and moved to Miami five years ago. Now I'm a security consultant and... problem solver. I don't have a website because I'm a one-man operation and I don't need more business. I don't do social media because I think it's a waste of time."

"Look, I know Emily didn't hire you for Cameron without doing her due diligence. I'm just worried about her."

"I know you are. That's why I'm here. How long have you worked for her?"

"I've been at Spencer for almost ten years. Four years working for Cameron directly. She's a really good boss."

"You like working for her. What about other people? What's her reputation like here?"

"Spencer employees are generally very loyal to her. They weren't at first—there was some grumbling when she took over—but she earned their respect. People don't always like change, but when they can see it's for the best, they usually come around. That's what happened here."

That matched what I'd learned yesterday in my lengthy

perusal of the building. I'd struck up casual conversations with people as I went, and had gotten the impression that Spencer employees were generally happy.

"Does she have any enemies on the inside? People who stand to gain if she steps down?"

Brandy's eyes flicked toward an office down the hall. "Most of the executives work really well with her. But Noelle Olson, our Chief Operating Officer, isn't exactly a fan."

"Was she here when Cameron took over?"

"Yeah, and she wanted the job. I wouldn't say she's openly hostile, but she pushes back a lot. If anyone's going to argue or try to stop Cameron from doing something, it's usually Noelle."

Interesting. An internal rivalry pointed to a potential suspect. "What about competitors?"

"There are quite a few companies in our space, especially because we have both military contracts and a large commercial division. But our biggest competitor in terms of where Cameron is taking the company is probably Reese Howard Aviation."

I made a note to look into Reese Howard. See if there were any personal connections to Cameron. "Have there been any issues with corporate espionage? Anything shady going on there?"

"Not that I'm aware of. And why would someone trying to steal trade secrets attack Cameron? Trying to get her phone or something?"

"It's possible. What about Cameron's ex? What's the story there?"

Her eyebrows drew together. "Aldrich Leighton? Why?"

"He's on my list."

She leaned closer and lowered her voice. "Wait, do you think Aldrich had something to do with it?"

"I just have to look at all possibilities."

Brandy glanced at Cameron's office. The door was open, but she seemed absorbed in whatever she was doing. "He's in finance—wealthy in his own right, but not at Cameron's level. They dated for almost three years, I think. It ended about six months ago. It's none of my business, but it was a long overdue breakup."

"Why?"

Brandy looked at Cameron's open door again.

"I'm not asking you to gossip about your boss," I said. "I need to know what's been going on in her life. Who might have motive to target her."

"She seemed happy with him at first. I actually thought they might get married. But as time went on, he started being kind of crappy to her. He expected her to change her schedule to fit his, or take impromptu vacations no matter what she had going on here. I don't think he respected the fact that she runs this company. Which was odd, because you'd think a peer would understand. He runs a company, too, so wouldn't he get that she can't just clear her calendar for two weeks on a Sunday night and jet off to the Bahamas with him?"

"Who ended it?" A personal, but not inappropriate, question. I needed to know. The dynamic of their breakup was important information.

But I also wanted to know if it had been her.

Hell, I *wanted* it to have been her.

"She did, but it was amicable."

I stifled a small grin of satisfaction. Good for her. "So you don't think Aldrich would have a reason to come after her."

"It seems far-fetched. But honestly, the idea of anyone coming after Cameron is. Most people like her."

I nodded. "What's the deal with the punk who came in here yesterday? Bobby."

She rolled her eyes. "Bobby Spencer. Milton Spencer is his father; he founded the company. Bobby's annoying but basically harmless. He's never worked here, and he doesn't have any actual power, but he likes to come in here and waste people's time and bother Cameron."

"He sounds like a pain in the ass."

"That's an understatement."

"What about his father? Retired?"

"Yep, he retired when Cameron took over. He's pretty old and now he spends most of his time on his yacht. I haven't actually seen him in about two years."

Something about Bobby Spencer bothered me, but I couldn't put my finger on it. Maybe it was Cameron's obvious dislike of him.

"Did Bobby have any objections to Cameron taking over?"

"Not that I've heard. He actually comes to the office a lot more now than he did when his father was in charge."

I wrote down a few more notes.

"Do you really think Cameron's in danger?" she asked.

"Maybe. Hiring me might turn out to be overkill and nothing else happens to her. Really, that's the hope. I don't mind being put out of a job; it's better for her. But if she is, I'll take care of it."

She smiled. "Good. Sorry if I was harsh with you."

"You weren't. Thanks for the sandwich. And the information. It helps me do my job."

"Sure. Did the calendar syncing work?"

I tapped my phone. "All set. And full disclosure, I put a tracking app on her phone. And yes, she knows it's there."

"Smart. Well, let me know if you need anything else."

"Will do. Glad to be on Team Cameron."

Her wide smile made a little ding go off in my head, like a signal on a game show that a player had scored a point. Ally acquired.

She went to her desk, and I started adding information to my growing file on Cameron Whitbury. I'd look into Reese Howard Aviation—corporate espionage was always a possibility—but my gut was telling me that wasn't it. This felt personal.

Which was why her ex-boyfriend was one of the people at the top of my list. As was Noelle Olson.

Now I needed to show Cameron—and Brandy—that their tentative trust in me wasn't misplaced, and track down who was fucking with the boss lady. Preferably before they did it again.

9

CAMERON

*H*aving Jude as a bodyguard was a lot like being followed around by a brick wall. If the brick wall smelled intensely masculine and seemed to possess the ability to melt into the background like a chameleon. How a man his size could move with so much grace and dexterity, and make people forget he was there, I had no idea.

I also had no idea how he smelled so good. It was very distracting. I'd almost asked Brandy if she'd noticed it too, but stopped myself. The last thing I needed was Brandy joining my girlfriends in predicting how long it would take before I slept with Jude.

Or more specifically, before I let him fuck me senseless on my desk, as Daisy had so eloquently put it.

I blamed her—and Luna and Emily—for putting the idea in my head. If they hadn't been teasing me about Jude, I wouldn't have found myself staring past my screen, imagining that very thing.

"Cameron?" Brandy leaned in through my partially open door.

Hoping she hadn't said my name more than once, I

clicked my mouse a few times, as if there were something other than a totally unprofessional sex fantasy occupying my attention. "Yes?"

"Do you need anything before I head home?"

I glanced at the time. It was almost six. Where had the day gone? "No, I don't think so. Have a great weekend."

"Thanks." She looked over her shoulder, then back at me. "So do you get to bring Mr. Incredible with you everywhere this weekend?"

"Apparently if I want to leave my house, I have to."

"It won't be that bad."

My eyes darted to Jude. He'd been here all week and true to his word, he'd been remarkably unobtrusive. I didn't even see him all the time when I was in the office. Often he was at his desk, but sometimes I'd glance up to find it empty. I assumed he stayed in the building, but at least he didn't stand guard over me every second of the day.

When I went offsite, he came with me. He insisted on walking ahead of me into restaurants, and he'd even checked underneath the table before my lunch meeting yesterday. I was pretty sure he did things like that to screw with me. His expression hardly changed, but there was a hint of fuckery in his eyes.

I kind of liked it.

But I was still chafing at the idea of needing a chaperone on my personal time.

"It adds a layer of complication," I said.

"Do you actually have plans this weekend?"

"What do you mean, *actually*? My schedule is always packed. You know this. You're usually the one packing it."

She shrugged. "I meant personal plans. Not for work."

I wanted to argue with her—particularly with what she was implying—but I couldn't. I was busy, even on weekends.

But that typically meant some combination of working at home, coming into the office, and attending events that were for networking, not personal enjoyment. Other than my monthly brunch and occasional wine nights in with my girlfriends, I rarely did anything that wasn't work-related. Not lately, at least.

"Still," I said, rolling my eyes at my own non-argument. "Now I have to coordinate my schedule with his."

"I'm sure that's very challenging when he has full access to your calendar."

"Do I need to fire you again?"

"Now would be a good time," she said, "since I'm on my way home anyway. You know, if I were you, I'd just move him in with me. You have plenty of space. Can you imagine coming downstairs in .the morning and finding him in nothing but pajama pants making coffee?"

"That's very specific. And you're very married."

"That's why I said *if I were you*. Besides, I'm married, not dead. I can still enjoy the view."

"I take it you've been enjoying the view all week."

"Job perks," she said, her voice cheerful. "Plus, I like him. He's funny."

"Funny?" That seemed like a stretch. He was quick with a comeback, but I wasn't sure I'd have called him *funny*. "I think you mean stoically unflappable. He's a brick wall."

Her smile seemed to say *you'll see*. "Well, have a good weekend with your brick wall."

"Give Mateo kisses from Auntie Cam," I said.

"I will."

Brandy left and I turned my attention back to my computer. My stomach rumbled—when had I last eaten?—but I needed to check a few more things off my list before I went home. Thankfully I had Nicholas's cooking to look forward to when I got there. Fridays were one of his days off, but he meal-prepped for me, so there was always something ready to go.

A message popped up on the corner of my screen.

Jude: *Check in. Departure time?*

Me: *Not much longer. Do you have plans tonight?*

Jude: *Just walking you to your car.*

Me: *I meant after that.*

Jude: *No.*

Funny, my ass. But now I was curious. What did Jude Ellis do on his own time?

Me: *What about this weekend?*

Jude: *I keep my schedule clear when I have a client.*

Me: *That sounds like a pain. No wonder you keep trying to retire.*

Jude: *The hours are terrible.*

Okay, maybe a little bit funny.

Me: *I won't be long.*

Jude: *Take your time.*

∾

EIGHT O'CLOCK SATURDAY morning and I'd already had two cups of coffee, been tortured by Inda in my home gym, reviewed data from R&D, and answered thirty-two emails. Sleeping in didn't exist in my world.

Except when the girls and I declared a Fuck-It Friday, cleared our schedules for twenty-four hours, shut ourselves in one of our houses, and gorged on terrible-for-you food and booze until we passed out. Although it had been a long time since we'd done that. Our lives seemed to keep getting busier and busier.

Feeling restless, I got up from my desk and wandered

over to the window. My home office overlooked part of Blue-water. Palm trees. Bright green vegetation and colorful flowers. Someone was driving a golf cart along a trail—it was the preferred method of transportation in Bluewater—and a small plane took off from the airfield in the distance.

I could see Emily's house and I wondered if she and Derek were enjoying a lazy Saturday morning together. They were probably dressed in matching bathrobes, feeding each other bites of breakfast out on the terrace.

It was possible I was a tiny bit jealous of my friend.

Not in a destructive, make-me-bitter-and-ruin-our-friendship way. I was beyond happy for her. But my no-longer-single friend reminded me of how single I was.

My phone buzzed, so I went back to my desk and checked. Another message from Noelle. She was upset about the financials. With a heavy sigh, I sat back down. That woman questioned everything I did. I wasted so much time typing diplomatic replies to her semi-aggressive emails. But I knew if I wasn't careful with every word, she'd find a way to use them against me.

Half an hour later, I hit send on what I hoped was a sufficiently mollifying email. Not ten seconds later, my phone vibrated again, buzzing against the surface of my desk. I was almost afraid to look, but thankfully it wasn't an instant angry reply from Noelle.

Brandy: *How many hours have you worked today?*

Me: *Why are you checking up on me?*

Brandy: *Because you need a day off.*

Me: *Since when is nagging me about my schedule on a Saturday in your job description?*

Brandy: *Stop replying with questions. There's nothing pressing on your calendar and it's been a while since that happened. Get out of your office and go do something.*

Me: *I have a lot of work to do.*

Brandy: *It can wait.*

Me: *Why am I arguing with you?*

Brandy: *Because you're stubborn. You know you need to get out of the house. Just call him. It's his job.*

I sighed. Brandy knew me too well. It made her amazing at her job, but she also had a knack for calling me out.

I did want to get out of the house—out of Bluewater. I was unsettled and I knew exactly what that feeling meant. I'd been working too much. For nearly three years, my relationship with Aldrich had provided a natural defense against burnout. Dating him had forced me to have a life outside the office.

Of course, he hadn't respected the fact that my job was just as important as his. But that was another issue. And one of the reasons we were no longer together.

Since our breakup, I'd focused the vast majority of my time and energy on work—even more than usual. Six months of that and I was starting to feel the effects. Add to that the usual aggravation of dealing with Noelle, plus the parking garage incident, and I was like a rubber band being pulled too tight.

But now I felt a bit like a kid who'd been grounded. I knew it was irrational. No one was keeping me from leaving my house. But it irritated me that I couldn't just go somewhere on a whim. Get in my car and go shopping by myself for a few hours.

Although, when was the last time I'd actually done that? I had a personal shopper because I was always too busy. And she was fabulous. But damn it, I wanted to go try on some shoes in a store.

Me: *Fine, you're probably right. But don't get cocky about it.*

Brandy sent a gif of a rooster strutting down a sidewalk.

I pulled up Jude's number and sent him a text.

Me: *I'm leaving the enclave and could use a big guy who doesn't talk much to follow me around. Know anyone?*

Jude: *I have a guy for that. He's good.*

Okay fine, he was funny.

Me: *Meet me at my house in an hour?*

Jude: *Destination?*

Me: *Shoe shopping. I'll drive.*

Jude: *No problem.*

10

CAMERON

*W*eekend Jude managed to surprise me.

He arrived at my house precisely fifty-five minutes after our last text. On a vintage Indian motorcycle.

Damn him.

I loved motorcycles. I loved men on motorcycles. I had a not-so-secret obsession with a TV series about a motorcycle gang and their very sexy and compellingly complicated leader. I read deliciously unrealistic motorcycle club romances.

And I just happened to have a view out to the front of my house when Jude Ellis pulled up on a bike, wearing black leather.

My heart skipped several beats when he pushed down the kickstand with his booted foot. Why was that so hot? He pulled off his helmet and set it on the back, then took off his leather jacket.

That left him in a white t-shirt that barely contained his thick chest and tattooed arms, and a pair of dark jeans. So simple. But god, he made that look good.

"Sorry, Cam, I can't let you go out with a boy on a motorcycle."

I gasped at the deep, slightly accented voice behind me and put my hand on my chest. "Oh my god, you scared me."

Bert, my gardener, stood just behind me, his smile deepening the wrinkles around his eyes. He wore his usual uniform of a loud Hawaiian shirt—this one yellow with pink flamingos—shorts, and an ancient pair of flip-flops. He had deep lines in his dark skin and his short hair was entirely gray. Crooked teeth gave him the most endearing smile.

"A bit early for a date," he said.

"He's not my date, he's security. Emily bullied me into hiring him after that thing at work."

"Good," he said, his voice serious.

Bert waited, facing the front door, his arms crossed. I raised my eyebrows at him, but he didn't say anything.

Jude knocked, then stepped inside when I opened the door.

"Cameron," he said.

Bert was still standing there, reminding me vaguely of my grandad when a boy had picked me up for my first school dance, junior year.

"Jude, this is Bert. He's responsible for all the glorious foliage around here."

The two men shook hands. Bert openly appraised him, his gaze moving from Jude's head to his feet in a slow sweep.

"What are your intentions with our lovely Cameron?" Bert asked.

Jude didn't show even the faintest hint of surprise. "I'm taking her shoe shopping."

"And?"

"And whatever else she wants."

Bert nodded slowly. "Do you plan to have her back by curfew?"

"Bert," I said. "He's not my prom date. He's security."

Bert's eyes flicked to me, then back to Jude.

"She's the boss, sir," Jude said. "I'm on her schedule."

"You aren't taking her on that death-cycle, are you?" Bert asked.

"I planned on letting her drive."

I felt a tiny dip in my stomach—disappointment that I wasn't getting on that bike. Not that it made any sense to ride Jude's motorcycle to go shopping. Not to mention how unprofessional it would be. I'd have to sit so close to him. Wrap my arms around him to hold on.

"All right, Cameron," Bert said. "You can go."

Shaking my head, I laughed. "Thanks, Bert. I'm glad I have your blessing to go shopping with my bodyguard."

"You treat her like a lady, son, or we're gonna have words," Bert said.

"Will do, sir," Jude said.

First my cook banging his wife in my kitchen, now my gardener interrogating Jude like he was my first date. At least Jude was getting a crash course in the weirdos in my life.

"See you later, Bert," I said, gesturing for Jude to follow me.

"Have fun, Cameron. Make good choices." He chuckled as he walked off in the other direction.

Jude followed me to the garage, and we got in my Tesla. Maybe it wasn't cruising the streets of Miami with the roar of a motorcycle engine between my legs, but it was a damn fine car. I was a sucker for innovation and new technology.

I drove us through the enclave, down a palm-tree-lined road. The guard on duty at the entrance nodded when I paused to wait for the gate to open. The sun blazed outside, but I was comfortable in an aqua sleeveless blouse and beige skirt. I was a Florida girl through and through—used to the heat and humidity. Every time I had to go somewhere with more moderate weather, I was freezing.

Jude pointed to one of several tubes of sunblock I had stashed in my car. "Always prepared?"

"I'm a redhead living in Miami," I said. "Sunscreen is life."

"Smart."

I glanced at him out of the corner of my eye. His skin was a healthy bronze, his short hair sun-kissed dark blond. Dressed in casual clothes, he looked rugged but still polished.

Traffic was light—which was a nice change. We raced down the highway to Bal Harbor, one of several luxury shopping destinations in south Florida—a tropical paradise with lush gardens, fountains, and koi ponds. It made for an enjoyable shopping experience, which was exactly what I wanted today. I needed to get out of my routine for a few hours. Wander, browse, and think about something other than work.

I pulled up to valet parking and Jude and I got out. He paused by my car while I shouldered my handbag and walked toward the shopping center entrance. I could sense him following behind me.

After strolling past a few stores, I stopped and turned around. "Do you have to do that?"

He took a few steps closer. "Do what?"

"Follow me."

"That's why I'm here."

"I mean follow me at a distance. Are you staying back there so you have a better view or something? Because I really don't think anyone is going to jump out and attack me."

His eyes darted around, like he was verifying my assessment. "Probably not. I'm just trying to stay out of your way."

"Can you just walk with me? It feels weird to have you back there."

"Sure."

I kept walking and he fell in step beside me. "See? Better. Now I can pretend we're friends out shopping."

He didn't reply.

I took my time, although I knew where I was going. My first stop was Jimmy Choo.

I still wasn't entirely comfortable with my level of wealth. I'd grown up an orphan, raised by grandparents who hadn't planned on returning to the parenting starting line. I'd worked my way through college. At one point in my early twenties I'd been so poor I'd lived on ramen noodles and cheap coffee.

Now I wore custom tailored suits and drove a six-figure Tesla.

I felt a strong sense of responsibility to use my resources well. I was working on creating a charitable foundation to organize my donations and charitable giving. My secret goal was to give away enough money that I dropped out of the billionaire category. Although with the way Spencer was thriving, that would be harder than it might appear, since much of my net worth came from ownership in the company.

But I also didn't feel guilty indulging sometimes. I'd worked my ass off to earn everything I had. Money didn't buy happiness, but it did buy security—something I appreciated deeply—and the most fabulous heels in existence. Shoes were my favorite indulgence.

Jude stood near the front of the store while I looked over the selection and chatted with the clerk. Wasn't he bored? He had to be bored. I glanced at him a few times, but his face betrayed nothing. He didn't look bothered or irritated that he had to stand in a shoe store while his client shopped. The man was a master at masking his thoughts. He didn't seem to be feeling anything at all.

Brick wall. Or maybe a statue.

The clerk came out with several pairs of shoes for me to try. I sat on a tufted stool and put on the first pair. They pinched in a way I didn't like. I could tell without even walking in them that they weren't going to work. I slipped my feet into the second pair—red suede pumps lined with crystals. They were bright and glittery and fabulous. I had no idea where I'd wear them, but I loved how brash they were.

Heels were my little rebellion. I'd spent most of my childhood being teased for my height. I hadn't even tried on a pair of high heels until I was out of college, assuming tall girls couldn't wear them. But now I wore them almost daily. I loved them. I loved the way they made my legs look. And I loved that they added inches to my already tall frame. They were my private *fuck you* to every asshole who'd made fun of me as a kid.

"Those look incredible on you," the clerk said.

I stood and took a few steps in front of one of the full-length mirrors. The shoes felt fabulous, and I loved the way they looked. I planted one toe on the floor and angled my foot to get a better look.

A hint of movement in the mirror caught my eye. I could see Jude's reflection behind me. He was staring, but not like a bored statue. He'd tilted his head ever so slightly and his eyes were on my legs. My long legs in a short skirt.

He was totally checking me out.

I felt a flush of heat and glanced at my face in the mirror, hoping I wasn't blushing. Thankfully there was only a hint of pink in my cheeks.

My eyes darted back to his reflection, but he'd looked away. Maybe I'd imagined him watching me with heat in his gaze. Had there been something other than professionalism in Jude's expression? Had I caught a glimpse of the man behind the wall?

I tried on a few more pairs but ultimately left with just the red ones. I thanked the clerk and Jude held the door, then fell in step with me.

I didn't have another store in mind, so we wandered past meticulously curated window displays and bubbling fountains. Mostly it felt good to be away from all things work. Brandy had been right, I'd needed this.

And I could grudgingly admit that it didn't ruin anything to have Jude along. He didn't talk much, but we strolled in comfortable silence. And any hint of anxiety I might have had about being in public since the incident in the parking garage was nonexistent. Jude was here. I was fine.

But I didn't need to spend an entire day shopping. My mind was already flitting back to my to-do list. I'd taken a break. I could finish out the day in my home office. Let Jude have the rest of his Saturday to himself.

Agent Provocateur, one of my favorite lingerie stores, caught my eye up ahead. I thought about Jude's statue impression in Jimmy Choo—and that glimpse I'd caught of him in the mirror. It had only been for a second, and maybe I'd imagined it. But I wondered if I could crack that stony façade again.

"One more stop," I said with a smile and veered toward the entrance.

We stepped into a world of soft pink paneling and gold accents. Venini chandeliers hung from the ceiling, their nineteen-seventies style just on the fashionable side of gaudy. Leopard print rugs with pink borders decorated the floor.

I pretended to be completely absorbed in the displays of lacy bras and panties, but I kept an eye on Jude, sneaking glances at him from my peripheral vision. He took up a position partway inside the store, probably where he had the best view.

Just doing his job.

A few other women wandered through the store. I took slow steps, pausing to brush my fingers over a sheer nightie. I found a gorgeous nude and black bra that would leave very little to the imagination.

I pulled it off the display and stepped in front of a mirror. Jude was behind me, arms crossed over his chest, that same stony expression on his face.

I held up the bra and tilted my head, like I was considering how it would fit. My eyes flicked to Jude.

No change.

He really was a brick wall.

I put the bra back and glanced at a few more things. My circuit brought me close to Jude. Pausing again, I ran my fingers over a very naughty rose gold cuff and choker set. The shiny metal cuffs were connected to a black braided rope. Luxury kink.

My eyes darted to Jude again. Nothing.

Except I caught sight of his Adam's apple bobbing in his throat with a hard swallow and a tiny bead of sweat glistened on his forehead. In the air-conditioned store.

There *was* a man under there. Interesting.

"We can go," I said, taking my hand off the cuff and choker set.

He cleared his throat and nodded.

Brandy had been right. Having a bodyguard wasn't all that bad. At least when I could have a little fun with him.

I sat at my desk outside Cameron's office. So far, there hadn't been any new threats. No suspicious activity. Business as usual for her. A lot of standing around and waiting for me. Which was fine. I was used to it.

Shopping with her had been... interesting. Not once in five years of doing this job had I been this intensely attracted to a client. But Cameron Whitbury was getting under my skin.

I couldn't let that happen.

But those fucking red heels.

Watching her try on shoes had been one thing. Her long legs were amazing. But when she'd put on those sexy red shoes, I'd seen the slightest change in her. Her hips had swayed, and she'd slid her hands down her thighs while she checked her reflection in the full-length mirror. Confident. Gorgeous.

Mine.

She wasn't, nor was she ever going to be. But the thought had hit me hard enough to knock the air out of my lungs. I'd recovered well. I was sure she hadn't noticed. But it had been difficult to keep my cool.

And then the vixen had taken me into a lingerie store.

That move had been to fuck with me, clearly. I'd seen the glint of mischief in her eyes when she'd said she had one more stop.

It made me want to spank that magnificent ass of hers.

Despite the way my dick was trying to take over the show, I wasn't going to let any of this get in the way of me doing my job.

I had Derek's people looking into Cameron's ex and Noelle Olson. I skimmed the first set of information they'd sent. On the surface, Aldrich Leighton was squeaky clean. No scandals. No affairs. No record of bad rich boy behavior in college. He'd never been married. He made appearances at elite social events regularly, most recently with a much younger Brazilian model on his arm. But there was something tickling the back of my neck, a sense that this perfect image was just that—too perfect.

Was he the kind of man to attempt revenge on an ex?

Noelle Olson had a similarly clean public image. She'd been with Spencer for fifteen years. Worked her way up from middle management. Married and divorced, with one child, now in college. Although she was free of scandals or any public record of bad behavior, Brandy had forwarded me copies of enough angry emails she'd sent to Cameron to wallpaper half the office.

This woman clearly had a grudge. She pitted herself against Cameron regularly, over issues big and small. But her habit of making Cameron's life difficult didn't mean she'd go so far as to hurt her.

I'd gathered a dossier on Bobby Spencer, too. According to both Cameron and Brandy, he didn't have a motive. But he'd sent up a flag when I'd met him, and despite the fact that it was looking more and more like Cameron didn't have anything to worry about, I wanted to be thorough.

His background was far more colorful. Bobby Spencer had been living the rich playboy life since high school. A regular in the gossip rags. There were stories about his obnoxious behavior and paparazzi photos of him partying in cities all over the world. He was the sort of guy who expected to be ushered to the front of the line, let in to every exclusive club and event based on his last name and the zeroes in his trust fund.

But why would a hard-partying rich boy want to hurt Cameron? The guy had it made. He'd never have to work a day in his life, and Cameron posed no threat to his decadent lifestyle.

No motive.

Corporate espionage was harder to trace, at least without a solid suspect. So far, I hadn't found any connections between any key staff members at Spencer and anyone at Reese Howard. I'd have to cast my net a little wider. See if I caught anything.

An alert popped up on my screen. Cameron had a breakfast meeting at a restaurant a couple of blocks away. I closed my laptop just as she came out of her office. We took the elevator down to the lobby and left out the front doors.

I walked down the sidewalk next to her, keeping her on my left, away from the street. She did something on her phone, then tucked it away in her purse. Her heels clicked on the pavement and she brushed her thick red hair behind her shoulders.

The restaurant was just close enough that we weren't sweating by the time we stepped into the comfortable lobby. I held the door for her, then went inside and did a quick visual sweep. The restaurant was elegant. Nothing of note. No sense of danger, other than the ever-present tingle I always felt when I looked at Cameron.

Everly Dalton, the woman she was interviewing, was already here. Pretty. Blond. Big smile. She and Cameron exchanged introductions and Cameron complimented her shoes.

"Are you ready to be seated, Ms. Whitbury?" the hostess asked.

"Yes, thank you."

I could only see part of the restaurant from here. Despite the fact that we still didn't have hard evidence that Cameron had been targeted—or was in real danger—I was still going to do my job. Thoroughly.

Plus, she'd messed with me the other day. I'd mess with her right back.

"I'll go first," I said.

Cameron only lost control of her expression for a second, but I saw it. A spark of annoyance made her green eyes flash. God, she was sexy when she was trying not to argue with me. Without a word, she gestured for me to go ahead of her.

I followed the hostess through the interior of the restaurant. The décor was subdued for Miami, sleek and modern with wood and chrome accents. About half the tables were taken. Couples, small groups, business meetings. Nothing unusual.

The hostess led us to a private terrace with a single table. I held up my hand and went out first. I didn't really need to inspect the entire area, but irritating Cameron was too tempting to resist. I could practically hear the snarky comments she was trying to hold back.

I checked the table, moved the chairs and inspected

beneath them. Did a quick walk around the terrace and looked over the balcony. An awning provided shade and planters held bright green plants. Nice ambiance. And obviously perfectly safe.

"Clear," I said and took up a position off to the side, my arms crossed.

Cameron and Everly came out onto the terrace and Cameron cleared her throat. "Sorry. Jude is... security."

I kept my lip from twitching in a smile, wondering what she'd stopped herself from saying with that little pause. Jude is overprotective? Jude is a pain in my ass?

Probably the second one.

"I suppose someone like you needs a bodyguard," Everly said.

"My friends seem to think so," Cameron said.

They both pulled out chairs and sat.

I stayed where I was while Cameron chatted with Everly. She'd flown her out from Seattle for a second interview. Cameron was creating a charitable foundation to organize her philanthropic efforts, and she was considering Everly for the executive director position.

I'd done a little digging on Ms. Dalton, just to see if there was any connection between her and anyone else in Cameron's life—specifically someone who could be a suspect. I hadn't found anything. Everly was an executive assistant to the elusive Shepherd Calloway, a businessman in Cameron's tax bracket. But her background checked out —nothing suspicious.

The waitress brought them mimosas and, a short time later, their breakfast orders. Cameron talked about her plans for the foundation. How it would be structured and what she'd need from an executive director. Everly's eyes were bright, a smile never far from her lips. She spoke with enthusiasm about her ideas. I could see why Cameron wanted her. She was smart and had a cheerfulness that even I found endearing.

Cameron folded her napkin and set it on the table. The interview seemed to be winding down.

Everly took a deep breath and her smile disappeared. "There's just one issue I wanted to talk to you about. I'm not sure how I feel about relocating. Miami is beautiful, and this sounds like such an amazing opportunity. But my entire life is in Seattle."

"I thought that might be an issue after we talked the other day," Cameron said. "If you don't want to relocate, I have no problem opening the foundation's headquarters in Seattle."

"Really?" Everly asked.

"Absolutely. I won't need to be there in person on a daily basis, and technology makes communication simple. If you want the job, we'll open the office in Seattle."

I liked Seattle. I wouldn't mind going with Cameron to Seattle when she needed to be there in person.

Not that she'd need me to travel with her. This job wasn't permanent. In fact, the more time that went by with no sign that Cameron was in real danger, the more likely it was this gig would be over sooner rather than later.

Which was exactly what I wanted. Wasn't it?

"Then I want the job," Everly said, her voice laced with excitement.

"I was hoping you would," Cameron said.

Everly put a hand on her chest. "I can't believe that just happened. Did you really just hire me?"

"I sure did." Cameron raised her glass. "Here's to doing some good in the world."

The back of my neck tingled as they clinked glasses. I glanced toward the terrace doors.

A second later, I heard the hostess inside. "Sir, you can't go out there."

A man was hurrying through the restaurant, heading straight for us.

Straight for Cameron.

Everything snapped into focus. I noted the exits. The number of tables and the reactions of the other patrons. People watched as the man strode quickly past them. No one responded with recognition. He was alone.

I stepped in front of the doors, blocking his access.

"Sir, that's a private dining area," the hostess said. "You don't have a reservation."

I knew who he was the second he stopped in front of me. Shepherd Calloway, Everly's boss. I'd seen photos of him when I'd looked into Everly, although he looked different from the slick business mogul with a reputation for being a hardass that I'd seen. He was oddly disheveled. Plain white t-shirt and jeans. Hair out of place. A beard more than a few days past neat stubble.

"Shepherd?" Everly asked behind me.

"Jude, let him by," Cameron said.

I could tell by the look in Shepherd Calloway's eyes that neither of the women in my care were in any danger from him. Not physical danger, at least. Everly's heart might be another matter. I was pretty sure he hadn't come all this way to interrupt her interview because she was a good employee.

The shocked yet hopeful look Everly gave him as I stepped out of his way confirmed my theory.

"Sorry to interrupt, Ms. Whitbury," Shepherd said. He moved closer to their table and held out a hand. "Shepherd Calloway."

"Cameron," she said, shaking his hand. The slight curl in her lips left her looking both curious and amused.

"I need to ask you not to offer Everly the job," he said. Cameron raised her eyebrows and Everly's mouth dropped open. "Not yet, at least. Don't get me wrong. You should absolutely hire her. You'll never meet someone who's as smart, kind, hard-working, diligent, and passionate about everything she does. As her boss—or former boss, I suppose —I give her my whole-hearted, unequivocal recommendation. But as a man, I'm asking you to do me an enormous favor and give me a few minutes to talk to her first."

"I'm sorry, Mr. Calloway, I've already offered her the position. And she accepted."

The moment of silence that followed made me feel terrible for the guy.

"Of course," Shepherd said. "As she should have."

Cameron picked up her purse. "I just remembered, I have another meeting to get to. Everly, thank you so much for coming. We'll connect later and work out the details. Mr. Calloway, it was nice meeting you. I hope you both enjoy your visit to Miami."

She met my eyes and I gestured for her to go ahead of me.

"Nice one," I whispered as she walked by, then followed her into the restaurant.

"Give them some privacy," she said quietly to the hostess. "They're my guests and if they need anything, I'll take care of it."

"Of course, Ms. Whitbury," the hostess said.

We left and turned up the sidewalk toward her building. I shifted so I was on the street side of the sidewalk.

"Was that what it looked like?" Cameron asked. "Because I think we just witnessed something in there."

"Everly and her boss? Oh yeah. That was something."

"I bet he chased her here because he's in love with her," she said, a hint of excitement in her voice.

"Definitely."

"Oh my god, it's like something out of a book. Do you think he deserves her?"

"I couldn't say."

"I wish I knew what was happening. I'm glad I trusted my instinct to offer her an office in Seattle. She's perfect for this job. I really want her."

"Looks like Shepherd Calloway does too."

She took a deep breath. "Exactly. Well, maybe she'll have her happy ending. A new job *and* the man she loves."

The hint of longing in Cameron's voice surprised me. No sarcasm. No snarky remark. That little glimpse of vulnerability did something weird to my insides.

"Aldrich would never have chased me like that," she said.

I wasn't sure what to say. "No?"

"After I ended things, I didn't want him to try to convince me to stay. And it still hurt when he didn't. What's that about?"

"You wanted to know you'd mattered."

From the corner of my eye, I could see her glance at me as we walked. "That's exactly it. And I don't think I ever did. Not really."

I squashed down the urge to reach over and clasp her hand. "At least you know you made the right choice."

"Yes, I did." She took a deep breath. "Sorry, I probably shouldn't have said all that. I guess now that you've witnessed sex in my kitchen, been interrogated by my gardener, and I've made things weird by oversharing, all we have left is for one of us to accidentally see the other one naked and we'll have our awkwardness bases covered."

I chuckled.

"Oh my god, did I make Jude Ellis laugh?" she asked. "I didn't know you did that."

"I can laugh."

"You should do it more often," she said.

"If it makes you feel any better, the last woman I dated long-term tried to kill me."

She raised her eyebrows. "You're serious, aren't you?"

I tried not to wince. Damn it, I shouldn't have said that. Normal people didn't have ex-girlfriends who'd held a knife to their throat. But I had said it, so... "Yeah. She did."

"Wow. How'd you stop her?"

"Talked her out of it."

"I'm impressed," she said.

"Thanks. It was a long time ago."

We'd arrived at her building, so I held the door open while she walked into the lobby. She didn't say anything else until we got into the elevator.

"Derek told me that you used to be in the CIA," she said as the elevator carried us up.

I wasn't surprised he'd told her, and my previous employment wasn't confidential. But I didn't like talking about it. People made assumptions, or asked too many questions.

"Yeah."

From the corner of my eye, I could see her looking at me. "I guess that's what makes you so mysterious."

"Mysterious was never my angle."

"No?"

I shook my head. "Because of my size, I played the

muscle. People would assume I was all brawn with no brains. My partner and I took advantage of that."

"Interesting. What does your partner do now? Is he semi-retired too?"

My back stiffened and I stared straight ahead. I didn't want to talk about him. "No."

The elevator dinged and the doors opened.

"Sorry," she said softly, then walked toward her office.

I let out a breath, feeling shitty. Some things in my past were classified. I literally couldn't talk about them. Those secrets weren't hard to keep. It was the ones I could talk about, but chose not to, that seemed to weigh the heaviest.

But that was simply something I had to bear.

12

CAMERON

I dropped my purse on my desk and grabbed the iced coffee Brandy had waiting for me. Not that I needed the caffeine. I'd spent the morning at one of our testing facilities and my body buzzed with the excitement of innovation. Our research and development team had made huge strides with our new heat-resistant exterior plating. It was light and thin but extremely durable, and preliminary tests were promising.

Since I'd taken over, I'd managed to secure a number of lucrative government contracts. Those were important because they were generally long-term and they represented stability for the company. But I had bigger plans for Spencer. We were one step closer to a prototype of a revolutionary long-distance passenger aircraft. Many of the new technologies we were working on had been ideas I'd sketched in notebooks a decade ago, before I had the resources to develop them.

It was one of the best parts of my job.

I'd also enjoyed showing off our research facilities to

Jude. Instead of hanging back like a disinterested layman, he'd struck up a lengthy conversation with one of the lead engineers on the project. From the snippets I'd caught, Jude was more educated in aeronautics than I'd realized.

I also got the impression that he might know how to fly a plane. And maybe a helicopter. I glanced at him through my open door, seated at the desk Brandy had set up for him. It made me wonder what else I didn't know about him.

Probably a lot. But I wasn't going to ask. He'd made it clear he didn't want me to, which left me feeling oddly lonely, and I couldn't understand why.

I settled in at my desk, took a sip of coffee, and went to work on my overflowing inbox. A few hours out of the office and I had at least fifty unread emails. Some I forwarded to Brandy; others I flagged for later follow-up. Then I got to one of the few names I always dreaded seeing. Noelle Olson.

Today she was edging out Bobby Spencer for the title of *biggest pain in my ass*.

She'd been with the company longer than I had, and when Milton had announced he was retiring, she'd assumed the CEO position was as good as hers. Milton had disagreed. Noelle blamed me. I'd hoped that she and I would have been able to develop at least a cordial working relationship. But she was just as hostile toward me now as she had been the day she'd stormed out of the high-level management meeting when my promotion had been announced.

I clicked on her email to find out what sort of trouble she was going to cause for me today. She wanted justification for the increased expenditures in the commercial R&D division. Noelle had long maintained that Spencer needed to focus entirely on government contracts and abandon our commercial projects.

With a sigh, I went to work drafting a diplomatic but very clear response. It was important that she remembered who was in charge.

Once I held a majority interest in Spencer, I was going to have to make some hard decisions about the leadership in this company. Noelle had good qualities that made her excellent at her job. But the way she constantly opposed me wasted a lot of my time.

Another email popped up just as I hit *send*, and I clicked on it.

DO THE RIGHT THING. *You'll know.*

MY BROW FURROWED. That was odd. And mildly threatening. What did that mean? There were no links. No signature. Nothing else in the email. Just those two sentences.

Do the right thing? I had no idea what it meant. It didn't have a subject line and the *From* field had my name, like I'd sent it to myself.

Brandy popped in to remind me it was time to go and my driver was waiting downstairs. I'd been asked to visit Miami Kid-Ovation, a summer and after-school program that provided art and STEM activities for kids, and an organization I personally funded. Jude was already standing, his laptop stowed in his backpack. Always one step ahead.

I forwarded the email to both Jude and IT so they could look into it, just in case it was relevant. Then I put it out of my mind.

Jude fell in step behind me and we took the elevator to the parking garage. Downstairs, Joe held the door for me as I slid into the back seat of the Mercedes SUV. Jude got in the passenger's side and moved the seat back as far as it could go.

The poor guy probably didn't fit in most cars. At least this was roomy.

He looked fantastic today in his cream button-down and slacks. I was going to miss the view when he didn't work for me anymore. Those arms were a work of art.

I felt an odd dip in my stomach at the thought of not seeing Jude anymore. And it wasn't just because of the arm porn. Or the shoulder porn, back porn, leg porn, or any other part of his gloriously muscular body.

So many of my private thoughts about him were exceedingly inappropriate. But there was something else simmering beneath the surface. Something I wasn't sure I wanted to admit.

I liked him.

A lot.

I found myself dreading the moment—which seemed inevitable at this point—when he'd tell me I didn't need him anymore. That I'd been right all along, and full-time personal security wasn't necessary.

What was I going to say when that happened? Thanks, it was nice to have met you, good luck with retirement? Wait, I was wrong, I'm terrified for my life and I need you to stay? Come home with me and lick key lime tart off my stomach?

This was a problem.

Trying to put my latest inappropriate Jude sex fantasy out of my mind—but god, what would it feel like to be pinned down by those huge hands?—I focused on the notes Brandy had sent me.

. . .

Give *short talk on why science and engineering are awesome.*
Bullet points below. Then the kids will show off their projects.
Indoors. No need for sunscreen.

I GRINNED at the sunscreen remark. She knew me too well.

We pulled out of the parking garage onto the street and
Jude adjusted the seat again. Thinking about his size, and
that stony brick wall impression he did so well, made me
wonder how this afternoon was going to go. He was so serious. I didn't want him searching the Kid-Ovation facility like
he expected to find assassins hidden around every corner, or
watching the kids with that suspicious glare that seemed to
come so naturally to him.

"Is there any way you can tone it down?" I asked.

He glanced over his shoulder. "Tone what down?"

"The scary bodyguard thing. We're about to be
surrounded by a bunch of elementary school kids."

"Do you think I've never been around kids before?"

"I wouldn't know," I said.

He chuckled softly, but didn't reply.

I'd just have to hope for the best.

I spent the rest of the drive reviewing the talking points
Brandy had outlined. We got to the campus—an old high
school I'd helped them purchase. Half of it was still under
construction. It was being remodeled in phases so they
could use parts of the facility, since their old location had
been too small for their growing program.

Joe parked out front and I thanked him when he opened
my door. I checked my email again while we walked in—
Jude in front of me to assess potential threats or whatever it
was he did—hoping Noelle hadn't sent another email to

argue with me further. I decided if she had, I'd ignore her until tomorrow. I had too much to do to get caught up in a debate with her.

Sheri Cruz, Kid-Ovation's executive director, met us just inside the double doors. Old lockers lined the hallway and the linoleum floor had seen better days.

"Cameron, it's so nice to see you," Sheri said.

"Thanks for having me. I'm excited to see what you've all been up to." We shook hands and I gestured to Jude. "This is Jude Ellis."

"Nice to meet you." Sheri shook hands with Jude. "We're ready for you, if you'll come with me."

"Sounds good."

We followed Sheri down the hallway, past banks of dented, slate-gray lockers. The faint sound of construction carried from the other side of campus, a series of loud bangs and the low hum of heavy equipment. She turned at a set of double doors leading into the old gymnasium.

Kids from the ages of six to fourteen sat on the bleachers, along with both paid and volunteer adults. Their voices filled the air, echoing off the concrete walls.

Much to my relief, Jude didn't insist on walking in first, nor did he do his customary sweep of the area. He followed just behind me, slightly to my right, keeping a comfortable distance.

Sheri and I stepped up to the microphone and she called for quiet. The kids shifted in their seats and a hush settled over the gym. Sheri introduced me and I waved to the kids while they applauded, then thanked them for inviting me to visit.

My talk was short and sweet, focusing on why art, science, and engineering projects are not only fun, but good for growing brains. I mentioned a few of the projects

Spencer was working on, particularly the flashy ones like advanced rocket technology, earning me excited oohs and ahs from the crowd.

When I finished, there was more applause. Then the teachers and volunteers led the kids to their respective workspaces. I chatted with Sheri about construction progress until it was time for me to make the rounds and see what the kids had been working on.

Jude was our silent companion as we walked to the first converted classroom. Instead of desks and chairs, it had long rectangular tables where the kids could build, paint, tinker, and craft. A dozen kids stood in front of their various creations, faces beaming with excitement and pride. A few wore safety goggles and one had donned a white lab coat.

I cast a glance at Jude. Brandy had said he seemed to have an ability to make himself appear less intimidating, and I could see what she meant. He was still enormous, but his posture was less rigid, his facial expression almost friendly.

"Okay, everyone, Ms. Whitbury is going to come around and take a look at your projects," Sheri said to the eager kids. "This is your chance to show off your hard work to someone new."

I visited Kid-Ovation every few months, and I always made sure Sheri and the teachers didn't make a big deal out of the fact that I was the primary benefactor and main source of funding for their program. I didn't want the kids to feel like they needed to perform for me. I simply enjoyed the chance to see what their creative minds came up with.

"Hi there," I said to the first child, a girl with big brown eyes and dark braids. Her nametag said Alicia. "What are you working on?"

"It's a catapult." She moved the contraption, made

primarily of large colored craft sticks and rubber bands. It had a plastic cup filled with mini marshmallows on the arm. "I made a different version, but it didn't shoot anything very far."

"Does this design work better?" I asked.

"Yeah," she said with a grin. "Wanna see?"

"Fire away."

She pressed the arm down and let go, sending three mini marshmallows flying.

"Nice trajectory," I said.

"Thanks."

"Have you tried shooting the marshmallows into someone's mouth?" Jude asked.

Alicia grinned. "Not yet."

"You know what, I volunteer," Jude said. He crouched down next to the table.

Oh my god, could he be any cuter?

"I think you just want marshmallows," I said.

"Hey, this is for science," he said. "Okay, kiddo, marshmallow me."

Alicia laughed and the rest of the kids quieted, watching. She loaded her catapult, pressed down the arm, and let loose.

All three marshmallows hit Jude in the face, none making it into his open mouth.

"Aw," the kids said in a disappointed chorus.

Jude picked up the discarded marshmallows and tossed them in the trash, then got back into position. "That's okay, let's do it again."

Alicia's tongue stuck out while she carefully loaded the catapult and repositioned it. When she was satisfied, she looked at Jude. He gave her a thumbs-up.

The room quieted with a collective intake of breath. Alicia pressed down on the arm, hesitated, then let go.

The marshmallows flew toward Jude. One bounced off his nose. Another ricocheted off his cheek. But the third sailed straight past his teeth into his open mouth.

Alicia's arms shot into the air and the other kids erupted with cheers. Jude stood, making a show of chewing the tiny marshmallow. He gave Alicia a high five—low enough for her to reach—then glanced at me and shrugged, his expression a little sheepish.

It was right about then that my ovaries exploded.

We spent the next hour getting mini demonstrations from the kids. Some had art projects—everything from paintings to clay sculptures. Others had built marble runs, rubber-band helicopters, and slingshot rockets. A fourteen-year-old in the middle school room had made a robot using mostly recycled materials.

They had fun showing off their creations. I couldn't decide what was more enjoyable—watching the kids demonstrate what they'd made, or watching Jude interact with them.

When the last straw roller coaster and paper kaleidoscope had been tried, Jude and I said goodbye to the kids. Sheri walked us out where Joe was waiting in front of the building.

We exchanged thank yous and goodbyes with Sheri, then got back in the car. I checked the time and was just about to ask Jude if he wanted to grab some dinner.

But I closed my mouth, the words unspoken. He'd been adorable with those kids, revealing a side I wouldn't have guessed existed. It made me want to dig deeper—get to know him better. And it was that very impulse that stilled me into silence.

That and the fact that I had an insane urge to offer to have his babies.

It was best if we kept things professional.

13

JUDE

*M*y new morning routine involved grabbing my phone off my nightstand and checking the tracking app I'd installed on Cameron's phone while I was still blinking sleep from my eyes. Like I couldn't even get out of bed without checking on her first.

I was always invested in my clients. Even when I'd been reluctant to take a job—which was most of the time—once I'd agreed, I was committed.

My level of commitment to Cameron, however, was something else.

I couldn't help myself. She was the first thing I thought about when I woke up in the morning and I had to know she was safe at home. It was a compulsion that had developed all too quickly, and one I couldn't seem to control.

It wasn't because she was smart and beautiful and a badass. It had nothing to do with those green eyes, sharp wit, or that ass.

God, that ass.

I was just jittery about her situation because my instincts were still whispering danger and I didn't have answers. I had one of Derek's people trying to trace the email she'd gotten, but whoever had done it had covered their tracks well. And it turned out, that wasn't the only one she'd received. There were several more that had been relegated to her spam folder, all with similarly cryptic and vaguely threatening messages.

Cameron seemed unconcerned, but I'd also learned that she hid her feelings well.

I was convinced someone was fucking with her and it was driving me crazy that I didn't know who it was. Or why.

I had most of my Saturday to myself. Cameron had an event to attend tonight, but until then, I was free. Luckily, she was being a reasonably cooperative client. I didn't need to worry that she'd go against my advice and leave home without protection.

But I still checked her location at least twice an hour.

What I needed was to get out of the house, and not be on high alert. So I went to the driving range to hit some balls. Took out a little aggression, although it was frustrating because my accuracy still sucked.

After grabbing a late lunch, I went home to shower and change. Tonight was an outdoor art show. In cooler weather, I'd have gone for a full suit and tie, but Miami evenings were warm in the summer. I opted for a button down and light-weight jacket. Still breathable. And maneuverable.

Cameron's driver would take us to the event tonight, so I drove my motorcycle to Bluewater. I parked in front of her house and glanced at my watch. I was early.

I hadn't meant to be. I was just being efficient. Early was better than late. It had nothing to do with her magnetic pull or an irresistible desire to see her.

Bert was out front, a set of keys in his hand. He put his hand up in a wave. "Mr. Ellis."

"Evening. Heading home?"

"Yes, the missus wants me home for dinner."

"The place looks beautiful, by the way," I said, gesturing toward the lush landscaping around Cameron's house. "You're very talented. Have you always been a gardener?"

He shook his head. "No. I was a construction foreman for a long time. Worked with Cameron's grandad years ago. After I retired, it drove the missus crazy to have me around the house all day."

"So you took up gardening?"

"Always had a passion for it. Never had the budget to indulge like I do here. Cameron lets me grow anything I like, as long as it won't poison anyone's pet."

"Sounds like a good way to spend your retirement."

"I can't complain. Here to see Cameron?"

I nodded. "I'm accompanying her to an art show this evening."

His face grew serious. "Have her back at a decent hour."

"Yes, sir."

He narrowed his eyes, then nodded slowly, like he'd decided he'd let me see Cameron. "Okay, then. Have a good evening."

"You too."

I let myself in and put my helmet by the door. The house was quiet, just the trickle of the fountain in the entryway. I glanced up the stairs, but I wasn't about to check up there. That was her personal space.

"Cameron?"

No answer.

Her office was empty, as was the kitchen. I glanced into her living room and noticed a huge pile of fur. Was that a dog? I hadn't realized she had a pet.

I left the dog softly snoring and went back to the

kitchen. She was probably getting ready, so I figured I'd check out her back terrace. I'd only seen it from the inside.

The large accordion door whispered open and I stepped out into the heat. Bert's handiwork was everywhere. Large planters overflowed with thick greenery, the wide leaves and bright red blooms shining in the sun. She had plush outdoor furniture shaded by large umbrellas and a sweeping view of Biscayne Bay. A path lined with plants led to the guest houses, smaller versions of her luxury beach hut mansion.

There was a splash in the pool and when I turned to look, I froze in my tracks, my hand still on the door.

Cameron emerged from the water. Topless.

Her red hair was plastered against her head and her eyes were squinted shut. I could see the rippling outline of gold bikini bottoms beneath the water line, but her top was nowhere to be seen.

"Inda, are you around?" she called. "My stupid top came off and I got sunscreen in my eyes and I can't see. Can you bring me my towel?"

Oh fucking hell. I was staring at her like I'd never seen a naked woman in my life. What was wrong with me? I was forty years old, it wasn't like I hadn't seen boobs before.

But I hadn't seen Cameron Whitbury's. And holy hell, hers were gorgeous. I hadn't been so turned on by a pair of tits at a distance since my first concert when I was sixteen.

"Inda?"

I glanced around the terrace. Cameron's towel was draped over a chair near the pool. No sign of Inda. Or Nicholas. Or anyone, for that matter.

This didn't have to be a big deal. We were both adults. If I went back inside and pretended I hadn't seen her, she'd be stuck out here with sunscreen stinging her eyes. She'd find her towel eventually, but it would be quicker if I just brought it to her.

Resolving not to stare at her tits, I got her towel off the chair.

The part about not staring at her tits was a lie. I couldn't take my eyes off them.

"Damn it," she said, feeling for the railing, her eyes still squeezed shut. She walked up the pool steps, water dripping down her body.

My heart thumped in my chest and my dick was so hard it ached. She was so beautiful and whatever bullshit I'd been telling myself about not being attracted to her was a big fat lie.

I was frustratingly, insanely, stupidly attracted to her.

Without a word, I held out the towel.

"Oh," she said when her hand brushed it. She took it from my hands. "Thanks."

I swallowed hard while she wiped her eyes, and before I could kickstart my brain into working again, she opened them.

"Jude! What the hell? I thought you were Inda."

It was right about then that I realized I really should have told her it was me. But my brain was still barely functional.

"Sorry."

Still blinking her bloodshot eyes, she huffed—and did not make any move to wrap the towel around herself. "I didn't know you were out here. Why didn't you say anything?"

"No one was here, so I got your towel."

"Well that's just great." She kept talking, gesturing with her hands, her towel flinging around. "You really had to dig into all my secrets, didn't you? Couldn't leave anything to the imagination. You just walk out here while I'm swimming and of course it's the one day my stupid bikini top falls off and the damn sunscreen gets in my eyes and now you've seen my boobs."

Fuck yes, I had. They looked round and soft with perfect pink nipples. Hard nipples. And they were bouncing a little as she ranted at me.

"You should really put those away. Then you can finish yelling at me."

"Who cares? You've already seen them."

I ground out the words through my teeth. "I care, Cameron. I'm the one who cares."

Her expression softened, her full lips parting. A light flush crept across her cheeks. The effect was only partly ruined by the way she still squinted one eye more than the other. Her gaze traveled down, stopping at my groin for a second before snapping back to my face.

I was a breath away from doing something very, very stupid when something big nudged my ass from behind.

"What the hell?" I spun around to find the dog I'd seen sleeping inside—an enormous Saint Bernard. "How did I not know you have a dog the size of a pony?"

"He's not mine. Brutus, what are you doing?"

"Then why is he in your house?"

She walked over to rub Brutus's huge head. She'd donned the towel while I'd been distracted by the dog. "He's free-range. Goes where he wants. His parents live over on Tequila Lane, but they've never had any luck keeping him contained. But he's a good boy. Aren't you a good boy?"

"Cameron, if a dog can just walk into your house, anyone can."

"Don't start. I'm safe here in Bluewater." She turned on her heel and headed inside. Brutus followed.

"Are you safe here, though? When I looked at your home security, I assumed you'd have the doors locked and the security system activated. But you're out there swimming topless while random animals, and who knows who else, wander around your property."

Brutus trotted away, maybe off to resume his nap.

"You were the one being a creeper," she said, pausing by the kitchen island. "And Bert probably let him in. He likes to nap in my living room."

"I wasn't being a creeper, I came to pick you up. I know I'm early, but it's not my fault you were flaunting your boobs."

"Oh my god, really? My top fell off and my eyes were stinging so bad I couldn't see. I'm in my own home, not standing on a balcony in New Orleans flashing my tits for beads."

I had a momentary—but very clear—vision of Cameron wearing nothing but cheap plastic beads draped between her tits.

"Look, I'm sorry."

She re-tucked the corner of the towel in the cleft of her cleavage. "There's only one way to solve this."

"What's that?"

"I need to see your dick."

Right as those words left her mouth, Nicholas opened the door from the terrace. Without missing a beat he said, "I'll come back," and left again.

I decided to pretend that hadn't happened. "I'm not showing you my dick."

"Come on, it's only fair." She crossed her arms. "Let's see your junk."

I raised one eyebrow, but made no move to do what she

said. I still had a raging erection. If I pulled it out now, she was going to get an eyeful.

The back of my neck prickled, like someone had moved just out of my line of sight, disturbing the still air. I looked toward the kitchen entrance, expecting to see Brutus. But it wasn't a dog. It was a woman with brown hair streaked with purple, a tight t-shirt with a large glittery D on the front, and a short pink skirt. She reached into a bag of popcorn and put a few kernels in her mouth.

"Don't mind me," she said. "I'm just here for the dick show."

"Daisy?" Cameron asked. "Why do you have popcorn?"

Daisy shrugged. "I made some before I came over. I had no idea how appropriate and mildly amusing it would be."

I put up my hands. "I'm not showing anyone my dick."

"You're no fun," Daisy said, popping another kernel in her mouth. "Why is he supposed to show you his baby-maker?"

"He saw my boobs."

"Then she's right, big guy. Whip it out and let the lady have a good look."

I ignored Cameron's popcorn-eating friend. "Cameron, you can't have a revolving door right now. You've got people and dogs and who knows what the fuck else wandering around your house."

"Don't keep trying to turn this around on me," she said. "I already told you my friends have the code."

"And I told you I'm sorry for looking at your boobs. I'm just trying to do my job."

The amusement disappeared from Cameron's eyes. "It's fine. What time is it? Are you insanely early, or am I late?"

"I was only about ten minutes early. Brandy told me six."

She grabbed her phone off the kitchen counter and swiped the screen a few times. "I'm late. Fantastic."

"Where are you off to?" Daisy asked.

"Art show at Wynwood Walls. I'm supposed to be seen with a bodyguard so the random thug from the parking garage knows I'm being protected now."

Daisy's gaze flicked to me, then back to Cameron again. "Or so whoever thought they could fuck with you knows they'd be stupid to try it again."

I gave Daisy a subtle nod and put her on my mental *allies* list.

Cameron had her boss face on. No hint of what she was thinking. "D, can you help me pick out a dress?"

"Sure, but it would be more fun if you picked something from my closet."

"You're like five inches shorter than me," Cameron said, heading out of the kitchen. "Most of your dresses won't cover my ass. Hell, most of your dresses barely cover your ass."

"That's what makes them fun," Daisy said and followed her out.

I slumped onto a stool and ran my hands up and down my face, trying to get the image of Cameron's fantastic rack out of my head.

14

CAMERON

*D*espite Daisy's protests that it was boring, I'd chosen a tasteful black sleeveless sheath dress. Maybe it lacked flash, but it was appropriate for the CEO of Spencer Aeronautics at tonight's event. And my sapphire blue heels spiced up my look quite nicely, if I said so myself.

The Wynwood Arts District was north of downtown in what had once been a rundown neighborhood filled with textile factories. Now it was one of Miami's artsy hotspots, with edgy street art, galleries, trendy bars, and studios featuring artists in action. Tonight was the premier of Carla Santiago's latest collection—a local sculpture artist who was known for her vibrant use of color.

Solar-powered lights lit the outdoor courtyard and the permanent installation of large wall murals made for an interesting backdrop. Carla's brightly colored abstract sculptures sat on concrete pedestals, each with a plaque displaying the piece's name. I stood in front of one entitled *Reflections on the Existential Meandering of Water and Time*.

Jude stood at a moderate distance, looking frustratingly

handsome in his light jacket and slacks—every bit the body-guard. Feet apart, arms at his sides, eyes taking in everything.

I didn't know if he was acting so serious because he wanted everyone in attendance to know exactly why he was here—in case the elusive mastermind behind the parking garage attack happened to see him—or if the distance between us was due to the boobs incident earlier.

Maybe it was a bit of both.

I took a sip of my martini and pretended to study the sculpture. Maybe I should have been more embarrassed about Jude seeing me almost naked. I wasn't an exhibition-ist, but I was comfortable with nudity. In private, anyway. Growing up in Miami, I was accustomed to seeing men and women in barely-there outfits. String bikinis and Speedos were standard attire for much of the year.

At work and in public I always dressed professionally. I was the CEO of an aerospace company, and I was exceed-ingly careful to maintain the right image. I wore business suits even on weekends if I left the house. But home was where I could let my hair down—or take my top off. Most of my home staff had probably seen me topless at some point. I only hired people I trusted implicitly, and a little nudity didn't bother me.

But I'd obviously made Jude uncomfortable. I'd thought we'd started to establish a relationship that was a little friendlier. More familiar. He'd started to feel more like a companion than a bodyguard.

Not tonight. He was all business, and I had a feeling that was my fault.

A man I recognized by sight and reputation wandered over to the piece I was pretending to admire. Nigel Houghton was a hotel mogul based in London, if I remembered correctly. He wore his button-down shirt and slate-gray slacks well. Neatly trimmed dark hair. Enough stubble to give him a masculine edge while still looking sleek and polished.

As far as I knew, he wasn't part of Aldrich's social circle, but I still felt a flash of worry that he'd seen the sex tape. My eyes darted to Jude, still standing off to the side. He was watching me, but didn't meet my gaze.

Nigel stopped next to me, holding a glass of whiskey on the rocks. "Is it just me, or do these make no sense?"

Definitely London. He had a nice British accent.

I studied the shiny mass of twisting metal in shades of aqua and green. "I was thinking the same thing. "I have no idea what this is supposed to be."

"That makes me feel better." He held out his hand. "Nigel Houghton."

I slipped mine in his firm grip and shook. "Cameron Whitbury."

"Nice to meet you," he said. "I think we've crossed paths once or twice, but never officially met."

Either he was good at hiding his thoughts, or he hadn't seen the sex tape. There was no hint of illicit recognition in his eyes. "It's nice to meet you, too. What brings you to Miami? Other than the vibrant art scene, of course."

His eyes flicked to the side, then back to me. "I'm looking at some investment properties."

"For a new hotel?"

"Yes. My people predict steady growth in Miami's tourism sector and we're looking to gain a foothold in the area."

"Then it sounds like now is a good time for new development."

"Absolutely." He seemed to look past me again. "But I

don't want to bore you with the details of real estate speculation. How terribly dull of me."

"Not at all." I doubted anything would sound dull in that
accent of his. But I felt a tickle of discomfort in my belly. I
wasn't sure I wanted to be having a conversation that was
even mildly flirtatious with another man.

Another man? What did that even mean? For there to be
another man, there had to be *a* man, and I didn't have a man
in my life. Jude was watching me like a hawk because it was
his job. Not because there was something between us. Just
because the man had seen my boobs—and for a second had
looked at me like he wanted to rip my bikini bottoms off
with his teeth—didn't mean I couldn't have a nice conversation with a good-looking man at an art show.

"So tell me about you," he said. There was that flick of
his eyes again, but he took a subtle step closer. "You work in
aerospace, do I recall that correctly?"

"Yes. Spencer Aeronautics. We started as a parts manufacturer and military contractor, but in the last several years
we've moved toward an emphasis on rocket technology,
particularly with passenger aircraft applications. And there
I go being dull."

"Not in the least." He looked past me again and cleared
his throat. "I suppose most people associate rockets with the
military or defense systems. I didn't realize there were
commercial uses."

"There definitely are; it's very exciting. What we're
working on will revolutionize air travel."

"Will it?"

I nodded. "Imagine a cross-Atlantic flight that only takes
an hour. The aircraft exits the earth's atmosphere, making it
possible to travel at much higher speeds. It reenters and
lands thousands of miles from the origin point in a fraction

of the time it takes a current commercial airliner to fly the same distance."

"That is truly fascinating," he said, but he was barely making eye contact. He kept watching behind me, like something else was attracting his attention.

I knew exactly what it was. Or *who* it was. Jude.

I glanced over my shoulder. Jude was doing his best brick wall impression—if a brick wall could look menacing. His eyes were locked on Nigel, his square jaw tight. He was ten feet away and completely unmoving, yet it looked like he could pounce on Nigel in an instant.

Yep, I'd been right. World's biggest cock blocker.

Nigel cleared his throat again. "Well, Cameron, it was lovely meeting you. There's a courtyard full of sculpture left to baffle me."

I smiled. "Have a nice evening."

Nigel walked away, casting a last nervous glance at my overbearing bodyguard.

I whipped around and marched over to him. "What are you doing?"

"My job."

"Your job doesn't include staring down attractive British men who strike up a conversation with me at a social event."

"I wasn't staring him down."

I arched an eyebrow. "No? Then why did he keep looking at you?"

"You'd have to ask him."

"Do you always have to be so intimidating?"

"Yes."

I pressed my lips together and took a deep breath, then took a long drink of my martini. "We were just chatting. You didn't have to scare him off."

A tiny twitch of his eyebrows betrayed a hint of smugness. "If me standing ten feet behind you scared him, I did you a favor."

"Why? Because he'd lose to you in a *who's the bigger caveman* contest?"

"Yes."

God, he was infuriating. Even more infuriating was that little voice in my head that said he was right.

"I hired you to keep me safe, not screen my potential dates."

"Would you actually date that guy?" There was an edge to his voice that stood out in contrast to the stoic brick wall thing he was doing tonight. "And didn't you say something about not dating again?"

"That's beside the point. Maybe he would have changed my mind."

"No, he wouldn't have."

I put a hand on my hip. "And how do you know that?"

"Money doesn't make him man enough for you."

I had no idea how to reply to that. Especially when Jude's hazel eyes smoldered with heat.

Was he picturing me naked?

I was picturing him naked.

This was ridiculous.

"I don't need your opinion on who I date, and I certainly don't—" I stopped mid-sentence, hoping the man I'd just seen from the corner of my eye was anyone but the man I thought he was.

No, it was him. Aldrich Leighton.

He was impeccably dressed, as always, in a lavender button-down and dark slacks—although the two buttons open at the top was new. The dark-haired beauty on his arm had to be fifteen years younger than him—at least.

I'd known this moment would happen eventually. We traveled in the same social circles. It was inevitable that we'd run into each other.

I glanced down at my dress, suddenly wishing I'd taken Daisy up on her offer to wear one of hers. This one *was* boring. One of her five-thousand-dollar sequined numbers that barely covered my ass might have been a better choice.

Aldrich's eyes met mine and a slow smile crossed his face.

"Oh, god," I mumbled.

Jude took a step closer. "Your ex."

I noticed he hadn't phrased it as a question. He already knew.

Keeping my expression smooth, I watched Aldrich and his date make their way across the courtyard. Frantically, my mind raced for the right words.

Now wasn't the time for a confrontation. Aldrich didn't know that I knew, and the sex tape hadn't been made public. As far as I knew, it had only been passed around to a handful of his buddies, and I wanted to make sure it stayed that way. One wrong word in a public place, with the wrong person within earshot, and the gossipmongers would be offering a hefty sum for a copy of that video.

But in the brief moment it took for Aldrich to cross the distance between us, I realized my fear of that tape making it into the media wasn't the only reason I couldn't say a word about it now.

Jude didn't know, and I did *not* want him to find out.

Jude accidentally seeing my boobs hadn't embarrassed me, but I was deeply ashamed of that video. Ashamed that I'd let Aldrich record it in the first place when I should have known better. Ashamed that other men had seen it—seen me in such an intimate act. I didn't know why the idea of Jude finding out about it hurt so much, but it did.

But I was Cameron fucking Whitbury. President of a multi-billion-dollar company. Badass aerospace mogul. And I wasn't going to let my ex hurt me.

"Cameron," Aldrich said with a smooth smile. He made a move to step in closer—probably to kiss my cheek—but he seemed to notice Jude. He hesitated, his smile faltering, then offered his hand.

I let him take my hand and shook his—hard. "Aldrich."

His only reaction was a slight eye twitch.

Jude no longer kept a respectful distance, the ever-watchful but unobtrusive bodyguard. He crowded my space, standing so close if I had leaned backward a fraction of an inch, I would have pressed against his chest. I could practically feel his body heat.

"I was wondering if I'd run into you," Aldrich said. "How have you been?"

"I've been well. You?"

"I can't complain. Busy, as usual. You know how it is."

The girl at his side didn't seem to care that he hadn't introduced her. She pulled her phone out of her purse and started typing.

"Yes, I do know how it is."

"What do you think of the installation?" he asked.

"It's interesting. Very colorful."

"You know what it reminds me of?" His eyes darted to Jude, then back to me. "That trip we took to Costa Rica. The place we stayed had that big painting above the bed. You said the colors were soothing."

Why was he bringing up a trip we'd taken more than two years ago? "Did I?"

"Don't you remember lying backwards on the bed so we could stare at it?"

I barely restrained myself from rolling my eyes. Was that comment for me, or Jude? Either way, it was clearly an attempt to show off the fact that he'd been with me.

"Vaguely," I said. Silently hoping Jude would understand my signal, I shifted my feet, just enough that my shoulder brushed against his chest.

I felt him lift his arm. Checking his watch? He put a hand on my arm and leaned closer to my ear. "It's time to go, Ms. Whitbury."

I kept the smile from my lips, but nothing could stop the rush of warm fuzzy feelings that poured through me. There were benefits to having a cock-blocking bodyguard.

"Thank you, Jude." I set my empty martini glass down on a ledge. "I have another engagement to get to."

"It was great seeing you, Cameron," Aldrich said, his lips curling in a smile that made me feel like vomiting all over his suede shoes.

I took a step closer to him and lowered my voice to almost a whisper. "I'd say it was nice to see you too, but that would be a lie."

Without another word, I walked away, allowing myself a little strut. A little hip sway. My dress might not have been club-worthy, but I did have a great ass. I'd worked hard for it.

I didn't have to look over my shoulder to know Jude was there. I needed to stop and text my driver to come pick us up, but I wanted to get out of Aldrich's line of sight first. I walked down the path, past the waist-high wrought iron fence, and continued up the sidewalk.

Cars were parallel parked along the street. I kept walking until there was an empty space, and fewer people nearby. Jude stopped behind me. I didn't turn around. I was flustered. Irritated at Aldrich. Wishing I could have chewed him out for lying when he'd promised he'd delete the video. For showing it to his friends. For acting so fucking smug.

And that little remark about our trip to Costa Rica? What an ass.

Trying to channel my inner Luna and breathe away my stress, I texted my driver.

"Where to next?" Jude asked.

Anywhere but here? Home so I could put on a pair of pajama pants and not share a bottle of my favorite cabernet?

But I didn't want Jude to think a two-minute conversation with my ex would rattle me enough to send me running home.

"I'm thinking Naoe. Sushi sounds good. I don't have a reservation, but I'll have Joe call ahead."

Jude didn't say anything, so I lifted my phone to text Joe again.

An arm cinched around my waist and spun me, knocking my phone out of my hand. Squealing tires and crunching metal filled the air, the noise shockingly loud. One second my feet lifted off the ground and the next I was curled up on the sidewalk, my legs tucked beneath me, my head down. Jude's large frame covered mine, his body shielding me from whatever chaos was erupting behind us.

Tires screeched again and someone yelled. Another voice hurled a stream of expletives.

My heart beat wildly and I held still, cocooned in Jude's protective embrace. I felt him turn his head, looking behind us.

"Oh my god, are you okay?"

"Did someone call the police?"

"Call 911!"

"Get the license plate."

"The car's gone."

"He drove off. What a dick!"

Jude slowly loosened his arms and inched back. He was crouched over me, his feet planted firmly beneath him. He put his big hands on my upper arms, as if to steady me while I uncurled myself from the pavement.

"Are you hurt?" His voice was low, concerned but calm.

"I don't think so." I'd lost a shoe and the other was barely clinging to my toes. Slipping my foot out of it, I took Jude's hands and let him help me to my feet. "What happened?"

"Black SUV swerved onto the sidewalk." He wrapped his arms around me and held me close, but his attention was on everything around us.

The back bumper hung off a maroon sedan that was parked along the street, and a handful of people stood around, most on their phones. A few were helping a guy in a tank top get to his feet not far from us. He had a bloody scrape on his leg. A man in a t-shirt and board shorts jogged over and stopped in front of the maroon car.

"What the fuck?" He raked his hands through his hair. "My car. Did anyone get the license plate?"

One guy said he'd tried to take pictures, but he'd been too slow to get a clear shot before the SUV had driven away. Another said the police were on their way.

"Let's go," Jude said quietly.

He let go of me and picked up my phone.

"Are you sure we can leave?" This wasn't just a matter of doing the right thing. There were already at least half a dozen people taking pictures with their phones. The last thing I needed right now was a scandal.

"Yeah, we weren't involved. There are plenty of witnesses. Are you sure you're not hurt?"

"I'm sure."

My hands shook as I grabbed my shoes. Joe pulled up to the curb a car length ahead of us and Jude ushered me inside. I scooted across the back seat while he scanned the scene. Blue and red lights flashed behind us.

Jude got in and shut the door. "Get her home."

15

JUDE

*C*ameron was quiet on the drive back to her house. Although she'd said she wasn't hurt, I'd be surprised if she didn't have some bruising. I'd tried to get her out of harm's way without letting her crash to the pavement, but a few bruises were preferable to being hit by a fucking car.

I'd been focused on her, not on the SUV, so I hadn't gotten the license plate. And I'd quickly determined that the other bystanders were useless. The cops would interview them, but I doubted they'd get anything. Half a dozen vague descriptions of a black SUV that swerved onto the sidewalk, hit a parked car, and drove off. Unless they got lucky and the SUV got pulled over somewhere else, they'd never track down who it had been.

The question on my mind was whether that had been a random hit and run, or another attempt on Cameron.

My gut was telling me it hadn't been random.

The guy in her parking garage. The untraceable emails. Now a hit and run. It all seemed so haphazard and strange. Were they trying to hurt her? Kill her? Was it a competitor vying for one of Spencer's contracts? Someone who wanted Cameron to step down as CEO?

Not knowing why someone was targeting her made it impossible to predict what they would do next. There was no pattern. No logic to it.

Her driver pulled to a stop in front of her house. She didn't wait for anyone to open her door. Carrying her shoes —one of them had a broken heel—she got out and went inside.

I followed her in, then shut and locked her door behind us. She headed straight for the kitchen at the back of the house. I checked the ground floor for any signs of an intruder or forced entry before joining her. Probably not necessary, but I wasn't taking any chances.

Not with her.

She sat on a stool at the island, a glass of bourbon in her hand. The only light came from the under-the-cabinet lighting, casting a soft glow over the shining surfaces. The bottle was still out, a second glass sitting next to it.

I took the stool next to her and poured myself a drink. We sat in silence for a few minutes, sipping our bourbon. The slow burn of liquor helped calm the aftereffects of all that adrenaline coursing through my system.

"Just when you thought this was the most boring security job ever," she said, lifting her glass.

I clinked mine against hers. "I'd prefer boring."

"I can't disagree with you there."

"Are you all right?"

She stared at her glass for a long moment, and I could tell she knew I wasn't asking her if she was injured. "I think so. This is going to sound ridiculous, but I don't know what has me more rattled. Seeing Aldrich or almost getting run over on a sidewalk."

Every bit of me wanted to gather her in my arms and hold her. The desire was almost overwhelming, but I held myself in place. "I don't think that's ridiculous."

"Did you get closure with your ex? The one who tried to kill you?"

"In a way. She thought I'd double-crossed her. Turns out I was set up by someone we both knew. So we... handled it. I wouldn't say we were friends after that, but at least we weren't enemies."

"That sounds like a good ending."

I took a sip of my drink. "It was. I don't like loose ends."

"I hear that." She took a drink and set her glass down. "This isn't because I miss him. I don't have unresolved feelings for my ex."

I nodded.

Aldrich had come across as egotistical, especially with his barely-in-context mention of a trip they'd taken together. He'd been like an animal marking his territory. I hadn't been able to tell if he'd been trying to get into her head with a look-what-you're-missing reminder of their relationship, or if that comment had been meant for me.

Either way, the brief encounter hadn't told me whether Aldrich was just a shitty ex, or something much worse.

He was still on the list.

Her phone buzzed on the counter, the screen lighting up with a call. She picked it up, winced, and set it back down.

"Do you need to take that?"

"No. It's just Bobby. The last thing I need right now is to listen to him tell me he's at the sickest party ever and I really need to get down there." She shook her head and took another drink. "You know, I used to defend Miami when people said the drivers here are the worst. But now I think they're right."

"That wasn't just a bad driver."

"He swerved onto the sidewalk, almost hit several pedestrians, smashed into a parked car, and took off. I think we can put whoever that was firmly in the *bad driver* category."

I didn't want to scare her, or make her feel worse than she already did, but I didn't feel right coddling her either. She needed to know.

"I think he was trying to hit you."

She closed her eyes for a second. "Fuck. I was afraid you were going to say that. The whole way here I was trying to come up with another explanation. Do you think..." She trailed off and swallowed hard before continuing. "Do you think whoever it is was trying to kill me?"

"That's one of three possibilities."

"What are the other two?"

I kept my hand on my glass but didn't move to drink more. "The objective could be to scare or intimidate you. Or to hurt you, but not necessarily kill you."

"But killing me is the third."

"Yes."

She rubbed her hands up and down her face. "Who would do that? Who would try to..."

"Noelle Olson and Aldrich are my main suspects. Someone attempting corporate espionage is another, although I haven't dug up any solid connections there. But I need you to be honest and tell me if there's anyone else who might hold a grudge against you. Any enemies you've made. I don't care how long ago or how minor it might seem now."

"No, there isn't anyone."

"Are you sure? A college boyfriend? A jealous coworker? Someone who might think they deserve credit for your work or a piece of your success?"

She shook her head slowly. "No. I dated off and on

before Aldrich, but nothing serious. And it's not like I clawed my way to the top, making enemies along the way. I didn't sleep my way to the top either." She side-eyed me.

"I wasn't implying that you did. Why don't you tell me how you ended up as CEO of Spencer Aeronautics."

"It's kind of a long story."

"I have time."

"Okay." She took a deep breath. "After college, I got a job with a company that made parts for commercial jets. It was stable, and a decent place to work, but I hated it. There was no creativity or innovation. Most of my job was trying to find ways to save money on materials without impacting safety. I can't imagine I made enemies there. I was just a young engineer, and I left on good terms."

"What did you do after that?" I wasn't just interested in hearing more for the sake of figuring out who might be after her. I wanted to know everything about her. How she'd become who she was. This woman fascinated me, but she kept her cards so close.

Her lips twitched in the hint of a smile. "I didn't have another job when I quit. What I had were some very big ideas and just enough money to get started. I downsized everything. Gave up my nice apartment for a cheap studio. Sold my car so I wouldn't have a payment or insurance. I rented some old warehouse space and got to work. Three years later I was broke, behind on my rent, and living off ramen noodles and cheap coffee."

I raised my eyebrows. "But?"

"But I'd filed four patents. Next thing I knew, I was juggling multiple job offers and had companies trying to outbid each other for the rights to my tech. In a slightly unexpected twist, I sold my first patent to the company I'd left a few years earlier. It made me a millionaire."

"Wow."

She smiled. "Yeah. My life changed quickly. And to answer your next question, no, there aren't any disgruntled engineers who think I steamrolled them and took all the credit. I worked mostly alone. When I needed help, especially with testing, one of my old college professors would hook me up with interns."

"Noted. How did you end up at Spencer?"

"Milton wanted my tech. His company was struggling, and he knew he needed to take it in a new direction if it was going to survive. I told him the girl came with the patents. I wanted a job. He brought me on to head his new emerging technologies division. I didn't know this when I started, but he was looking to retire. My initial position was basically a test run. He wanted someone with fresh ideas who'd be willing to take the company into uncharted territory, and he didn't see that in any of his existing executives."

"But he saw it in you."

"He did. And when he retired, he put me in charge."

"Did anyone other than Noelle oppose his decision?"

She shook her head. "No. I'd established good relationships with the rest of the executives. And they could all see what I'd done for the company. None of them would have still had jobs if it hadn't been for me."

"Then why does Noelle have a problem with you? She wanted the job?"

She ran her finger along the rim of her glass. "Probably. And she thinks I got the job because of favoritism, not because I earned it."

"Favoritism? Why?"

"Because I grew up knowing the Spencer family. My grandmother worked at Spencer. She was a brilliant engineer. Way ahead of her time, being a woman in a very male-dominated field. Milton didn't care about that kind of thing. He just wanted talent. She was one of the first engineers he hired when he started the company. Eventually she and my grandad became friends with the Spencers."

"But you didn't go to Spencer for a job after college," I said. "Trying to strike out on your own?"

"Exactly. I didn't want any favors."

I shifted on my stool. "What about Milton's son?"

"Bobby? What about him?"

"How did he feel about his father's decision to put you in charge?"

"It probably didn't make any difference to him."

"Are you sure?"

"Yeah. He's a trust fund kid. Even if Spencer went under, he'd never have to work a day in his life."

I tapped my fingers on the counter, mulling that over.

"Why?" She reached over and nudged my leg with her toe.

"He's on my list."

She raised her eyebrows. "Your list of suspects?"

"Yes."

"Bobby's not smart enough. He's just a spoiled douchebag."

I shrugged my shoulders. "Maybe you're right. But it's my job to be suspicious."

"Fair enough." She paused for a moment, licking her lips, then tucked her hair behind her ear and met my eyes. "Thank you. For what you did tonight."

I held her gaze and one corner of my mouth turned up in a grin. "Just doing my job."

"I'm glad you were there to do it."

"Me too."

She smiled, then looked down. "I should let you get home. It's getting late."

Part of me wanted to stay here all night to stand guard while she slept. But that wasn't exactly an option.

Unable to help myself, I stood and leaned in, cupping her cheek with my hand. I pressed my lips to her forehead. "Are you sure you'll be okay?" I asked softly.

"Yeah," she whispered.

With my hand still resting against soft skin of her cheek, I kissed her temple. "Call me if you need anything."

She nodded and I dropped my hand. The scent of her hair lingered, and it took a supreme act of will to make myself turn around and walk away.

I wanted to wrap my arms around her.

Hold her tight until she felt safe again.

I wanted to pick her up and lay her out on that island so I could devour every inch of her body.

If I'd thought she wanted me to, my self-control would have failed. But I wasn't even sure whether Cameron liked me very much, let alone shared any of my desires. I knew she was grateful that I'd saved her from that hit and run. But gratitude didn't mean she wanted me the way I wanted her.

And fuck, I wanted her.

Without another word, I left, hoping I was doing the right thing.

16

CAMERON

*T*he sun hadn't risen, but I was wide awake. I sat on a tall stool in my workshop, the parts of a dismantled blender spread out on the spacious worktable. The walls were lined with shelves, drawers, and bins, all my tools and materials neatly organized. I had everything from plastics and heat guns to a 3-D printer and a soldering iron.

Some women dealt with stress by going to the spa or with retail therapy. Others meditated, practiced yoga, or took long, hot baths with a glass of wine. I did those things, too. But my favorite way to de-stress was tinkering.

I'd been a tinkerer from the time I'd had enough hand-eye coordination to take apart my toys. As I got older, I started putting them back together again—only with modifications. I'd happily put motors on model airplanes to make them fly, built solar-powered robots that walked and had lights that flashed, and tried to enhance every household appliance I could get my hands on.

I didn't want to brag, but the modifications I'd made to my Lady Jam Personal Erotic Massager had become the stuff of legend. My friends had all bought the same model and made me trick out theirs too.

Pushing the safety glasses back up my nose, I inspected my handiwork. This blender had never worked as well as it should. I'd swiped it off the kitchen counter this morning while I'd waited for my coffee to brew, suddenly determined to make it better.

At the moment, it was still in pieces. But I wasn't finished.

Someone knocked on the partially open door.

"Yeah?" I asked, not looking up.

"What is that?" Inda asked. "Your blender?"

"Uh huh." I kept my eyes on the tiny screw I was reinserting.

"What's wrong?"

"Why do you think something would be wrong?"

"Because you're out here destroying your blender and it's not even six in the morning. Did you sleep?"

I tested the fit of the base that housed the motor. I was going to have to shave down some of the plastic to make it fit. Or maybe fabricate a new one. "Yes, I slept. I woke up early. And I'm not destroying my blender. It sucks. Or it did. It won't when I'm done with it."

"Okay," she said in a tone that made it clear she didn't believe me. "Are you going to finish up first, or…?"

"Why? Isn't it my day off?"

"From work? Yes, it's Sunday."

"No, from you."

She laughed. "Nope. Leg day."

I eyed her over the top of the glasses. Evil woman. "Fine. I'll be there in a few minutes."

"I already set your workout clothes on your bed."

"You think of everything, don't you?"

"Just doing my job," she said with a smile, then turned on her heel and left.

Of course she was just doing her job. Most of the people in my life were around because they worked for me. They had a job to do, and they did it.

I took off the glasses and set them on the table. I knew I was being sensitive because of what Jude had said last night. He was just doing his job. But what else did I expect? That in the aftermath of a tense and scary situation, we would have fallen into bed together? Had wild, adrenaline-fueled sex until we both collapsed from exhaustion?

The stupid part of me had thought that, yes.

The uncomfortable ache that still lingered between my legs was entirely my fault. I shouldn't have been fantasizing about him like that. Not when I'd almost been hit by a car.

And why did my thoughts keep returning to Jude and his annoyingly hot body? If he was right, and last night hadn't been an accident, I had an enormous problem on my hands. Someone was trying to intimidate, hurt, or possibly even kill me. This wasn't the time to be indulging in daydreams about getting naked with the man who was supposed to protect me.

But it wasn't just the sex fantasies that had me so distracted my brain was prioritizing the bulge in Jude's pants over the very real problems in my life. I liked him. There was more than physical attraction at work here, and it was scaring the hell out of me.

I wasn't ready for this.

My heart was still bruised by Aldrich's betrayal. I'd let him into my inner circle, and the number of people I allowed that close was very small. My three best friends. To a much lesser extent, the people who worked closely with me, both at Spencer and here at home. But even there, the natural boundaries of being the boss kept distance between us.

And Jude worked for me. I was his client, he was my contractor. That was the nature of our relationship, and I needed to remember that.

Leaving the still-dismantled blender, I went upstairs to change, then subjected myself to leg day with Inda. She coached me through heavy squats, walking lunges, stiff-leg deadlifts, squat jumps, and various other tortures.

I focused on her voice, giving me brisk words of encouragement. On the heat and burn in my muscles. On the sweat that dripped down my back and glistened on my forehead. On the steady stream of eighties music blasting in my home gym.

But even the musical stylings of Wham! and A-ha weren't enough to break me out of my funk.

When I finished, she sent me out to the kitchen for a breakfast protein shake. Nicholas was there, grumbling that the blender had gone missing. I patted him on the back, told him not to worry about it, and grabbed a premade protein drink from the pantry.

I showered off the effects of Inda's torture and dressed, feeling like I might be missing something. It was Sunday, so I didn't have any meetings. I'd worked out. Was there something else on my calendar?

With an unflattering squeak, I dove for my phone and swiped to my calendar. There it was, on my schedule for ten thirty. I couldn't believe it had slipped my mind, but at least I wasn't late. I never missed Drag Queen Brunch. And this time, I had a lot to talk about.

I paused with my phone still in my hand and stared out the window. DQB was at Mordecai's Bistro, over on Las

Palomas Boulevard. Not here in Bluewater. Certainly not in my house. Which meant I was supposed to bring Jude.

DQB was girl time. Sacred. It was when we shared the good, the bad, and the ugly of our lives. Asked for advice or gave it. Dished about dates and told each other the truths we kept from the outside world.

How could I do that if Jude was standing ten feet away? Especially when he was one of the things I was desperate to talk to my friends about?

Although the queens would have an absolute field day with him. That was tempting.

Before last night, I probably would have gone without him. Taken it off my calendar so he'd think it was canceled, then left my phone behind so if he checked up on me with his GPS tracker, he'd think I was home.

But last night had happened. And although we didn't have proof that I'd been the target of that black SUV, I wasn't stupid or childish enough to risk my safety by going alone.

With a heavy sigh, I texted Jude.

17

CAMERON

I'd been worried that seeing Jude today would be awkward, and sure enough, it was. For me. Not him. He showed no signs of discomfort. He was his usual slightly aloof, professional self.

He didn't arrive on his motorcycle—which I decided was good—and I took him up on his offer to drive. I sat next to him in his SUV, hands folded in my lap. I'd opted for a custom-tailored lilac blouse and high-waisted slacks. Over-size sunglasses and lavender stilettos were my nod to the fabulousness that was DQB. I dressed like a CEO whenever I went out in public, regardless of the day of the week. That was my image. Sleek. Smart. In control.

Not that I was feeling any of those things today. But I was hoping the clothes would help.

I walked into Mordecai's just behind Jude and spotted my friends at our regular horseshoe-shaped booth at the back. As usual, the place was busy, the noisy hum of dozens of conversations filling the air.

Crimson Delilah, a queen rocking an Ariel-red wig, zebra stripe pantsuit, and lace-up platform boots was at the front. Her heavily mascaraed eyes widened when they landed on Jude.

He gave her a short nod, then gave me his *I need to check the place out* look.

"Darling, who is this big tall hunk you brought with you?" Crimson Delilah asked, appraising Jude with open appreciation.

"He's security," I said.

"Is that what they're calling it these days?" she asked with an arch of her perfectly microbladed eyebrow.

"He just needs to take a quick look around. It's what he does."

"Be my guest," she said to Jude with a flourish, then turned back to me. "Have fun, my little ginger. The girls are already back there."

"Thanks."

Instead of waiting for Jude to decide Mordecai's was safe enough for me to take my seat, I beelined for the back and slid into the booth next to Luna. I swiped off my sunglasses and started talking fast.

"I really need to talk to you but I have to make this fast and I know how crazy this is going to sound but I was almost hit by a car last night and that isn't my biggest problem, so can we get that out of the way and just say it happened and I didn't get hurt and I realize it's insane that I'm more concerned about something else when I might have been the target of a hit and run attempt less than twenty-four hours ago but I can't help it."

I took a deep breath and smoothed my features, restoring my calm and collected façade while Jude got closer. My friends stared at me in silence. Luna's eyes were wide, and I could practically see her about to tell me to tune into my breath. Emily's eyebrows lifted and she slowly set her bloody Mary back on the table.

Daisy's face scrunched into an expression of uncon-cealed confusion. "What the hell is wrong with you?"

Tracking Jude's movement from the corner of my eye, I mentally calculated the distance between us multiplied by the approximate decibel level. My spine stayed stick straight, my hands folded, until I was reasonably sure he wouldn't hear me.

I leaned forward and splayed my hands on the table, my voice low as the words once again tumbled out in a rush. "I ran into Aldrich and Jude saved me from being hit by a car and before he left last night he kissed me on the forehead and I don't know what it means and I'm pretty sure I'm losing my mind."

So much for time spent tinkering and a good workout for calming me down. I felt like I was falling apart.

Jude came closer, finishing his sweep of the restaurant. I straightened my back and smoothed my hair.

My friends kept staring at me while Lady Raquel came over to our table. She was our favorite server here at Morde-cai's. Today's look included a bright pink wig and long pink dress trimmed with fluffy white feathers.

"Bloody Mary or mimosa for you, honey?" she asked. "And tell me about the blush you're wearing, because your face is all kinds of sexy pink."

Jude paused next to our booth and everyone's faces slowly turned toward him. He gave me his *everything looks good* nod. "Ladies."

"Mercy," Lady Raquel said, watching him walk to the front of the restaurant where he took up a position against the wall.

"He's security," I said lamely.

"Is he, now? How about I bring you one of each." Lady Raquel swept away, her feathery dress swishing.

I opened my mouth, another round of verbal vomit already racing its way up my throat, but Luna laid a gentle hand on my arm.

"Slow down," she said. "Maybe breathe first."

"Can we go back to the part about the hit and run?" Emily asked.

"I'm kind of fixated on the forehead kiss right now," Daisy said. "Although I really want to know if you punched Aldrich when you saw him. Or did you let Jude punch him?"

I took Luna's advice and breathed deeply before trying to speak again. "There was no punching. I didn't want to confront him about the you-know-what in public."

"And what about the hit and run?" Luna asked gently.

"We were outside Wynwood Walls and an SUV swerved onto the sidewalk. Jude got me out of the way. The SUV hit a parked car, then drove off. It was probably just a shitty driver."

"But maybe it wasn't," Emily said.

I nodded in acknowledgment. "Maybe it wasn't. And I know that represents a giant problem in my life and it's what I should be concentrating on."

"But the forehead kiss," Daisy said, her eyes flicking toward Jude. "Why forehead kiss? What's that about?"

Emily and Luna glanced in Jude's direction.

"Stop looking at him," I hissed, and their gazes snapped back to me. I took another breath. "He took me home afterward and we talked a little. Before he left, he asked if I was sure I was okay, and he kissed my forehead."

"That's so sweet," Luna said.

"It felt like a pity kiss," I said miserably.

Lady Raquel brought my two drinks and set them in front of me.

"And you wanted him to rip your clothes off and destroy your body in an adrenaline-fueled lust fest," Daisy said.

"Of course not." I was such a liar. "That would have been completely unprofessional."

Daisy rolled her eyes. "Do you want to know what your problem is?"

I actually did, and I knew my attempts to maintain my composed image in between letting my crazy out weren't doing me any favors. "What?"

"You're too worried about professionalism," Daisy said. "If you want the man to fuck your brains out, start by fucking his brains out and I'm sure he'll happily return the favor."

"That's terrible advice," I said.

"This isn't just about sex, is it?" Luna asked. "You like him."

I tucked my hair behind my ear, opted for the bloody Mary, and took a sip. Could I admit it out loud? Even to them?

And I was still mentally berating myself for letting this get to me in the midst of my other problems.

A female voice carried over from the booth next to us. "How are we feeling about butt stuff lately?"

I gasped. The one thing in the world that could distract me from my current emotional turmoil was the second reason my friends and I loved coming to Mordecai's. The first was, of course, the best drag queens in the business, coupled with a fabulous bloody Mary and great brunch menu.

The second was seated in the booth next to us. Our weird obsession. The romance novelists.

They were a group of four women who met here regularly to discuss their work. Sometimes they typed away on laptops while sipping coffee or cocktails. Other times they chatted about characters, plot points, tropes, and twists. From the time we'd realized who they were we'd started devouring their books and eavesdropping on their conversations, eager for a hint of what was to come for our favorite characters.

I'd been so caught up in my own internal drama, I hadn't even noticed they were next to us.

"I'm always down for butt stuff," one of the ladies said in an excited voice more than slightly too loud for the conversation topic.

"Just watch the hands," another one said. "If his fingers are involved, make sure they don't wind up on her face or in her mouth. Also, does anyone need more coffee? Because I do."

"Me, always," the enthusiastic one said. "And hard yes to watching the hands."

Daisy's face lit up with excitement and she mouthed, *One of them is writing anal.*

I stifled a laugh, but felt a little better. We were ridiculous. Four of the wealthiest women in the country—CEO, goal-getter, stiletto-wearing badasses—who also loved to hang on every word while four authors discussed their craft, and giggle at discussions of kinky sex in fiction.

"I'm just not sure if it fits," the first one said. "And as often as my kids make poop jokes, I don't know if I can make anything with butts sexy."

"If the story needs an edge, you can always take their sexytimes outdoors," the fourth woman said. "I wrote sex in a garden shed once. Readers loved it."

"Outside. That's not a bad idea."

"Oh my god you guys I think I just deleted my entire book. No, wait. False alarm. It's here. But has anyone seen my phone?"

"It's next to your drink."

"I should probably switch to water."

"Okay, ladies, are we ready to sprint? We have word counts to meet."

"Twenty-five minutes on the clock. Go."

"Damn, nothing about Salvio," Daisy said. "I was hoping they'd drop some hints about his next book."

"Sorry, Cam," Luna said. "You were saying?"

"It's okay," I said. "I'm just not sure what I'm feeling right now. Or what I'm supposed to be feeling. I kind of thought there might be a little something there, but he's my bodyguard. And I don't know if he feels anything, or if he's just doing his job. And I shouldn't be feeling anything anyway."

"Was there just a forehead kiss?" Daisy asked, her eyes narrowing. "Or was there touching?"

"There was touching." Unconsciously I brushed my cheek with my fingers. "He touched my face. And kissed my temple, too."

"Well, that changes everything," Emily said.

"It does? Why?"

Emily leaned closer. "A forehead kiss and a temple kiss are totally different."

"That's true," Luna said, nodding excitedly. "A forehead kiss is nurturing and protective. It can still be sexy, but if you're not sure about his intentions, it can be difficult to interpret."

"A temple kiss, though, that's a little more romantic," Emily said. "Especially if he was touching your face."

"I don't know," I said. "Maybe. I'm probably just having a delayed reaction to last night's trauma."

I risked a quick glance at him. He'd melted into the background, somehow inconspicuous despite being as tall as the queens in platform heels.

A romantic gesture? Had it been? I wasn't entirely sure if Jude even liked me all that much. We got along fine, but was there something else there?

Was that what I wanted?

I wasn't sure about that, either.

18

JUDE

*O*n the surface, things were business as usual with Cameron. Her schedule had been jam-packed with meetings, conference calls, and debriefings from her R&D staff. She went in early and stayed late. Went straight home after work and stayed there.

I could see what she was doing. Her guardedness couldn't hide the fact that the hit and run had rattled her. She felt out of control, and I had a very strong feeling that when Cameron Whitbury felt out of control, she dove into the things she *could* control.

Specifically work.

By Thursday, Brandy was giving me worried looks. Friday I heard Cameron tell Brandy to make sure her schedule was clear for the weekend. She had too much work to do.

Her demeanor was calm and collected. Her voice steady on phone calls and in her many meetings. The only outward sign that Cameron was struggling was her shoe choice. She'd been playing it safe, wearing simple black or nude heels every day.

If she'd been feeling confident, or letting her subtle rebellious streak out, she'd have been wearing something flashier on her feet. I'd already figured out that her shoes matched her mood.

I was also pretty sure I shouldn't have kissed her after the hit and run.

It hadn't been a real kiss. I hadn't gone anywhere near her mouth. But I felt like I'd crossed a line with her and now she was making it abundantly clear where we stood. Keeping me at a distance so I wouldn't get too close—wouldn't get too familiar.

It fucking sucked.

So while she spent the week buried in her job, I spent the week sticking to mine.

Friday I accompanied her home. She said she'd see me Monday.

That sucked too.

Two days without her. I wasn't sure how I'd let things get to this point, but the thought of having to wait until Monday to see her again made me feel like shit. Was this what I'd been reduced to? Pining for the company of my client—a woman who clearly had no interest in me beyond our professional relationship?

The air felt particularly heavy tonight and distant peals of thunder rumbled offshore. After seeing Cameron off, I stopped for takeout, then went home.

My food smelled good, but I set it aside while I did a quick Cameron check. Not that I needed to. I hadn't been gone very long, and she never left Bluewater without me. But I did it anyway. It looked like she was next door, at her friend Luna's house.

That was good. I liked that she wasn't alone.

I settled in with my food and turned on my secret guilty

pleasure, *The Great British Baking Show*. There was a simplicity to it that I liked. No drama or backstabbing. Just amateur bakers engaging in good-natured competition.

Maybe I liked it because the show had an air of normalcy to it. They were just ordinary people—talented people, certainly, but average citizens. They had regular jobs, regular homes, regular families. Even though it was a competition, there was a peacefulness to it that made it relaxing to watch.

Two episodes in—what an exciting life I led—my phone dinged with a text. I scrambled to check it in case it was Cameron, although I didn't know why she'd text me on a Friday evening when she didn't have anything on her schedule until Monday.

Derek: *Found something new on the ex. Check your email.*
Me: *Thanks.*

I opened Derek's email. My eyes narrowed at his brief explanation. He'd sent an attachment with more details. It would be easier to read on my laptop, but right when I got up to get it out, my phone rang in my hand.

This time it was Cameron. My danger instinct went crazy.

"Yeah?"

"Jude? Someone was in my house."

I was already grabbing my keys. "Where are you?"

"In my bedroom. They were in here, Jude. In my room."

The fear in her voice made everything come into sharp focus. Lightning flashed outside and thunder cracked.

"Stay calm. Do you think they're still in the house?"

"I don't think so. I had dinner at Luna's and when I came home, I felt weird. I can't explain it. So I looked around, checked all the rooms. I didn't see anyone. But then I came in here."

"Where are Nicholas and Inda?"

"Out somewhere. Date night."

"Did you call enclave security?"

"No, I called you first."

A swell of emotion hit me in the chest. She'd called me first. "Okay, good. Call them. I'm on my way."

"Okay. Hurry."

I shoved on a pair of boots, grabbed my helmet, and rushed outside into the pouring rain. My bike engine roared to life and the tires screeched on the wet pavement as I gunned it out of there.

My shirt was soaked before I'd gone the first mile—my SUV would have been a better choice in the rain—but I didn't give a shit. The bike was faster, and all that mattered was getting to Cameron.

I paused at the gate to the Bluewater enclave while security waved me through. Then I tore down the empty tree-lined road, crossed the bridge over the canal, and raced to her house.

I came as close to dumping my bike as I ever had when I skidded to a stop next to a Bluewater security vehicle. It was still pouring, the heavy rain making her entire driveway an enormous puddle. I pushed down the kickstand, pulled off my helmet, and Cameron's front door flew open.

She ran outside in a short white shirt and silky striped pajama pants. Dropping my helmet to the ground, I swung my leg over the seat of my bike and caught her right as she crashed into me.

Her arms flew around my neck, her bare toes barely staying on the ground. I wrapped my arms around her, one hand splayed across her back, the other holding the back of her head. Relief poured through me as her body pressed against me. Thank god she was okay.

Cameron made no move to let go, so I didn't either. The rain pelted us with fat drops, soaking her hair and her clothes. I was already wet through, but I didn't care. I'd stand here in the storm until I got struck by lightning if it meant I could keep holding her like this.

The wind was picking up, whipping the vegetation and making the palm trees bend. I smoothed down her hair and she gradually pulled back. Her hands trailed down my chest.

"Sorry, I..."

"Don't be." I gently touched her face.

She wasn't crying or hysterical. Her green eyes were clear, raindrops dancing across her freckled cheeks. Her wet shirt molded over her breasts, her lacy bra showing through the thin fabric. I'd seen her topless, but this tantalizing peek was so sexy.

"Thank you," she said, keeping her hands on my chest. "That really fucking scared me."

That reminded me why I was here. Without letting go of her, I did a quick visual sweep of the area. There wasn't much to see, especially with all the rain.

"God, we're soaking." She dropped her hands and stepped back. "The Bluewater security guys are here. They're checking everything."

"Good." I scanned the front of her house again and kept my eyes sharp as we jogged in out of the rain. Nothing looked amiss on her porch. No sign of forced entry here. I did a quick check of the electronic lock, but it seemed to be working fine.

We dripped water on the floor in the entryway. Cameron glanced down at herself and shook her hands, as if it would help. A big guy—although not as big as me—with a Bluewater Security logo on his shirt came down the stairs.

"I'll go get towels," Cameron said.

I shook hands with the security guard. He introduced himself as Dante.

"We've notified the police," Dante said. "My guys are checking for how the perp got access, but there's no obvious sign of a break-in."

"I'll check the security footage. Is the house clear?"

Dante nodded. "All clear. Whoever it was got in and got out."

"Did they take anything?"

"Not that we've found so far. But they left something. You just need to see it for yourself." He gestured toward the stairs.

Cameron came down with an armful of fluffy white towels. She'd slipped a silky pink robe over her wet shirt. I could see water spots starting to spread, but at least the Bluewater security guys weren't getting an eyeful of Cameron's amazing rack.

She handed me a towel and I toed off my boots, leaving them near the front door. I followed her upstairs, drying myself as best I could. She patted her long hair with her towel while we walked to her master suite.

Just outside her door, I noticed the faint odor of fish.

"It's there, on the bed," she said. "No one's touched it."

Her fluffy white comforter was slightly askew, the way it had been when I'd seen it on my first tour of her home. Right in the center of the bed was a red snapper, its reddish scales reflecting the light from the chandelier, its round black eye cold and dead.

She gestured toward the slimy fish. "I can't decide if the fish is fitting or a total cliché."

"What?"

She pointed to her hair. "It's a ginger fish."

I cracked a little grin. An intruder had been in her house and left a dead fish in her bed, and she could still make a joke about it. That was my girl.

I did a lap around the bed, checking it from every angle. On the far side was a typewritten note on a plain piece of paper, one corner tucked beneath the fish.

THE BOSS BUT STILL VULNERABLE. *You got lucky. Next time we won't miss.*

THERE WAS nothing funny about that note, nor the fact that whoever had done this had gotten in and out without tripping the alarm or forcing their way in. I checked the doors to her balcony, but they were secure. No sign someone had come in that way.

"You're sure you locked the door when you went to Luna's?" I asked.

"Positive," she said.

Damn it, I should have taken more precautions with her home security. Had her camera feeds sync to my phone. Set up alerts so I'd know when someone unlocked her door. But that kind of coverage hadn't seemed necessary.

It was now. Whoever did this was escalating.

This move reeked of ego. This wasn't in a parking garage or on a public street. This wasn't an email that could have come from anywhere. This was up close and personal. A message delivered not just inside her house, but in her bedroom. In one of her most personal, private spaces. I'd never even been inside this room before. Just looked in from the doorway on my first visit.

And it confirmed that none of this was random.

"Ms. Whitbury?" Dante's voice came from the hall. "The police are here."

I took pictures with my phone while Cameron talked to the police. Then she and I waited in the kitchen while they searched her house, including all the outside areas. The Bluewater security guards stayed to help, but none of them found any signs of entry, forced or otherwise.

The police cars in front of her house had drawn attention. Cameron's friends burst inside in a flurry of fuzzy robes, yoga clothes, and velour tracksuits. They were dry—apparently the rainstorm had passed—and they attacked her with hugs and offers of comfort food and alcoholic beverages.

Nicholas and Inda returned from their date, shocked and worried. Emily offered them one of her guest houses for the night so they wouldn't have to deal with the chaos.

"Derek and I are going to see what we can do about keeping this out of the media," Emily said. "Are you sure you're okay?"

Cameron's hair was bedraggled, curling haphazardly as it dried. Her clothes were still damp, her wet shirt having long since soaked through her robe. I was surprised she wasn't shivering. But she still gave her friend a calm smile.

"I'm sure."

Emily squeezed her arm. Her eyes darted to me, then back to Cameron. "Let us know if you need anything."

"I will. Thanks, Em."

Take care of her, Emily mouthed at me silently, then left with Nicholas and Inda.

A woman in her late sixties with a bob of sleek silver hair and dark-rimmed glasses wandered in. She was dressed in a peach tracksuit and what looked like a fortune in diamonds glittered on her ears, around her neck, and on most of her fingers.

"Oh no," Cameron muttered.

"What's the matter, sweetie?" Luna asked.

"It's Mrs. Vanderveld," Cameron said. "If she's poking around, the rest of the WWs won't be far behind."

"We're on it," Luna said. "Hey Daisy, we need to do some crowd control."

Luna and Daisy moved to intercept the woman, their arms out as if they were either going to hug her or attempt to corral her. I had a feeling it was both.

I leaned closer to Cameron. "What does WWs mean?"

"The WWs are the Wealthy Widows. It's a group of women who live in Bluewater's condo building. They're lovely, but very nosy. I just can't deal with them tonight."

Dante rushed past, grumbling about the growing number of golf carts showing up outside.

The police finished their search and asked Cameron a few more questions. I told them I'd get them a copy of the security footage. They said they'd be in touch if they found anything.

The Bluewater security guards successfully shooed away the residents who'd started congregating outside. Finally, all was quiet.

Cameron lowered herself onto the step at the bottom of her wide staircase. The entryway fountain trickled, the water meandering around the palm trees that grew through the specially-cut holes in the floor. I sat down next to her and she plucked my shirt.

"You're still damp."

"So are you."

She let out a long breath. "Did someone really leave a fish on my bed?"

"Yes."

"What the fuck." She rubbed her hands up and down her face. "Who does that?"

Questions and next steps ran through my mind. The police would investigate, but I wasn't going to leave this to them. I was going to find out who did this so I could make damn sure they never did anything to Cameron again.

"Jude?" she asked, her voice soft.

"Yeah?"

She hesitated for a few seconds. "Can I go home with you tonight?"

Putting my arm around her, I drew her in close. I didn't care if it wasn't professional. And when she melted against me, I stopped worrying about whether she wanted this from me.

"Of course." I kissed the top of her still-damp head. "Come stay at my place."

"Thank you."

I just squeezed her. *Anything for you, Cameron. Anything.*

19

CAMERON

*J*ude's muscular arm encircled me, and I rested my head against his thick chest. Closing my eyes, I breathed him in. His scent and the heat of his body were more relaxing than a glass of wine. I indulged in the comfort for a long moment before shifting away.

"Do you want to grab some of your things?" he asked.

I shook my head. My clothes were still damp from the rain, but I didn't care. I needed to get out of here. "No. Let's just go."

He smoothed my hair down and nodded. "Okay."

I kept several pairs of sandals in a closet off the entry, so I slipped my feet into a pair while Jude put on his boots. He did a quick check of the doors and windows, making sure everything was secure before we left.

Most of the runoff from the rainstorm had found its way into the canal, leaving the ground glistening wet but not flooded. The humidity would be intense when the sun came up and all the moisture left overnight evaporated. For now, the breeze coming off the water cooled the air and a bird called in the distance. Thankfully it wasn't Frank. That asshole parrot had a knack for ruining a quiet evening.

Jude insisted I wear his helmet, since he didn't have an extra one with him. I dutifully put it on and climbed on the bike behind him. I must have looked ridiculous, dressed in nothing but a thin pajama set and a hastily thrown-on robe.

The engine roared to life and I wrapped my arms around his waist. He drove us slowly down my driveway and through the enclave, pausing at the entrance gate.

As soon as we pulled out onto the main road, he opened it up. I felt the speed in my chest, in the way we sliced through the warm night air. The vibration of the engine hummed through my body as the scenery flew by. With a motorcycle between my legs and my arms around this gentle beast of a man, it was easy to forget the chaos I'd left behind. Lose myself in the freedom of speed.

We came to a stop in what looked like an industrial area, next to a building with tall garage doors on one end. A set of stairs on the adjacent wall led to a door on the second floor. It was hard to see much in the dim light of the single street-light. But as soon as we climbed off the bike, another light blazed to life.

"It's on a motion detector," Jude said.

I pulled off the helmet and handed it to him, feeling suddenly guilty. When I'd asked Jude to take me home, I hadn't thought about whether or not he'd want me to invade his private space like this.

"I'm sorry for springing this on you. Are you sure this is okay?"

"It's fine. I don't have company very often, but it shouldn't be too embarrassing."

He took my hand and led me up the metal staircase, his boots making surprisingly little noise. He glanced around—

it was like a reflex, I saw him do it everywhere—before unlocking the nondescript door.

And just like that, I stepped into Jude's world.

From the outside, the building didn't look like a residence. But inside was a sprawling loft. Exposed conduit and bare brick walls had been coupled with comfortable furnishings. A long section of wall had floor-to-ceiling bookshelves, stuffed with books. The kitchen was open with a bar-height island separating it from the rest of the space. Another area had a couch and two chairs facing a flat screen TV mounted on the wall. His bed—king size and neatly made—was in a shadowy corner at the far end.

"It's not much," he said, hanging his keys on a hook by the door. "But it's home."

"I like it," I said, taking slow steps and absorbing every detail. The deck of cards on a side table. The large desk with six monitors. The set of golf clubs in the corner.

"Thanks. I keep saying it's temporary until I find something else. I guess I've been saying that for five years, so maybe I should just accept that I live here. Anyway, you could probably use some dry clothes."

I glanced down at my bedraggled pajamas. Leaving without changing into something else—or grabbing a change of clothes—had been a stupid thing to do. I wasn't a wilting flower who could be scared out of her own home by some assface who thought he could fuck with me.

Except tonight, I was. And it was by choice. And maybe that was what made it okay to be standing in damp silk pajamas and sandals that, now that I looked down at my feet, probably weren't even mine. Inda's maybe? Or something Luna had left behind?

I was tired, an aching exhaustion that I felt deep in my bones. I'd been holding myself together—all by myself—

ever since the hit and run. No, ever since the parking garage. I'd been keeping my fear bottled up, hidden behind a wall of sarcasm and flippancy. I was fine. It hadn't been a big deal. I could handle things myself.

But I didn't want to handle things myself. Not tonight. I wanted to take off the mantle of high-powered CEO. Woman in a man's world. Badass engineer and literal rocket scientist who could do anything. Face anything. Be anything.

If I could be anything, tonight all I wanted was to be held. For someone else to do the heavy lifting.

I looked Jude up and down, doubting he owned a single item of clothing that wouldn't fit three of me. "Maybe just a robe while they dry?"

"I actually have something that might fit you," he said. "I'll be right back."

A doorway near his bed proved to be a small walk-in closet. He disappeared inside and I chewed my lip while I waited. Clothes that fit me? Did he mean women's clothes? I didn't like the idea of wearing something one of his exes had left behind.

He came out with a folded set of clothes and handed them to me. "Bathroom's through there."

"Thanks." I took the clothes—they were soft and smelled fresh—and went through the door.

The small bathroom was sparkling clean. One bath towel, folded precisely in half, hung from a towel rack next to a clawfoot tub encircled by a white shower curtain. A mirrored medicine cabinet hung over the vanity and the toilet lid was closed. A single toothbrush sat in a chrome holder designed for two, the second slot empty.

I set the dry clothes on the counter and peeled off my pajamas. The fabric stuck to my skin and a shiver ran down my spine. I shook everything out and hung it up on the shower curtain rod to finish drying. My bra and panties were damp, too, so I took those off and laid them on the edge of the tub.

Jude had brought me a pair of cotton boxer briefs and a faded green t-shirt. The underwear certainly hadn't belonged to a woman. They were loose on me, so I folded down the waistband once to make them a little more secure.

I picked up the neatly folded shirt and let it fall open. It said USMC in cracked lettering, like it had been worn and washed many times. I slipped it on and pulled it down, smoothing it over my bare skin. It was big on me, but I wasn't swimming in it. There was no way it would fit Jude.

US Marine Corps. Was this his? Who had he been when he'd worn this?

Catching a glimpse of myself in the mirror, I winced. My hair was flat and stringy. My mascara had held up—even in the rain—so that was something. But overall, I looked like hell.

Well, it wasn't like Jude hadn't seen me in all my hot-mess glory already.

I came out to find Jude in dry clothes—a plain white t-shirt and light gray sweats. He looked up from the sink where he was filling a tea kettle with water.

"Hey." His eyes traced from my head down to my toes, then back again. He cleared his throat. "More comfortable?"

"This is great." I smoothed the shirt down again. "Is this yours?"

"Yeah, it's mine."

"How did it ever fit you?"

One corner of his mouth lifted. "I wasn't always this big. Eighteen-year-old me sure wasn't."

"You've had this shirt since you were eighteen?" I asked, jerking my hands away, suddenly afraid I'd damage it.

"Eighteen or nineteen," he said, and set the tea kettle on the stove. "I don't really know what I'm doing, it just seemed like offering you tea was the right thing to do."

As sweet as it was, I didn't want tea. I wanted this man's arms around me, cocooning me in safety. I wanted to feel like I didn't have to be brave for a few hours. I wanted to let him be my courage. My protection. My shield.

I met his eyes, searching for a sign that he wanted me, too. For something that was more than a hint. More than a quickly smoothed-over glimmer of desire. Had we both been circling around the truth? Or was I alone in this infatuation?

As if he already knew me from the inside out—knew exactly what I needed—his expression turned hungry. No bodyguard mask hiding his feelings. His eyes swept over me, lingering on my chest where my nipples brushed against the thin cotton of his t-shirt. Down to the boxer briefs that were so loose they were in danger of falling off. Over my legs, bare from my upper thighs down to my toes.

With his eyes still on me, he let go of the tea kettle and crossed the distance between us. He slipped his hands around my waist, hauling me against him. He was so tall, I had to look up. Without a word, he tilted his face and brought his mouth to mine.

The sensation of his kiss exploded through me. Rising up on my toes and pressing myself against him, I threw my arms around his neck. He delved his tongue into my mouth, deep and demanding, and slid his hands up my back beneath the t-shirt, spreading heat across my skin.

His solid—and oh my god, so thick—erection pressed

against my belly. I rubbed myself against him and he groaned into my mouth.

God, it felt good to be kissed like this. With heat and passion. With strong arms surrounding me. With velvety tongues sliding against each other, urgency flowing through us both, making us frantic. Hot. Desperate.

This wasn't enough. I wanted to climb him like a tree. Feel his solid length between my legs. I jumped up, wrapping my legs around his waist. He caught me with his hands cupping my ass and groaned again.

"Bed?" he asked, our lips barely disconnecting.

"Yes."

"Are you sure?"

"Yes," I breathed again, then went back to attacking his mouth with mine.

I never did this. Not without careful consideration and planning. I hadn't exactly been free with my sexuality before I'd become the CEO of a multi-billion-dollar corporation. And now that I was, my body was on lockdown. No flings. Nothing casual. Ever. My ex was the only man I'd been with in the last several years, and we'd both signed a non-disclosure agreement before we'd slept together for the first time.

But I didn't want a contract with Jude. I wanted him like this—dangerous and raw. Unplanned and untamed.

And I wanted him now.

20

JUDE

*C*ameron's long limbs were wrapped around me, her magnificent ass in my hands. A torrent of sexual tension was unleashing between us. We weren't naked yet, but we were both stripped bare, casting off the masks of professionalism. Giving in to a healthy dose of pent-up lust.

With our mouths still crashing together, I carried her across the loft to my bed. I laid her down and climbed on top of her, reluctant to break contact. She kissed me hungrily, like she was as starved for this as I was.

Hell, maybe she was.

In the back of my mind, I knew this might be a huge mistake. Once we crossed this line, there was no going back. Not for me. Not with her. She'd already gotten deep under my skin, and if we crashed and burned, it was going to fucking hurt.

But nothing risked, nothing gained. And I was no stranger to a high-stakes gamble.

Pressing my erection between her legs, I felt her heat even through our clothes. My dick was hard as steel, ready to fire off like one of Cameron's rockets, especially with the way she rolled her hips to grind against me.

I lifted up, my groin still firmly pressed against hers. Her gorgeous copper-red hair fanned out across my bed and her green eyes were half-closed. She was killing me in my old Marine Corps t-shirt. It rode up her belly and draped tantalizingly over her tits, her nipples teasing me through the fabric.

"You are so fucking sexy," I growled.

She ran her hands up my chest and fisted my shirt. "Can I take this off?"

Something about the way she said that—asking for permission—made my blood run hot. How often did Cameron Whitbury ask for permission to do anything?

I thrust my erection against her, earning me a satisfying moan. "You can take it off."

Reaching behind me, I yanked on the back of my t-shirt to help her strip it off. She pulled it over my head and tossed it aside, then ran her hands through the dusting of hair on my chest.

The hem of the t-shirt was playing peek-a-boo with the bottoms of her tits. I splayed my hand across her rib cage and slid my hand beneath the fabric. Ran my thumb across her hard peak. She shuddered and bucked her hips against me.

"Slow down, eager girl." I traced her nipple.

Her eyes locked with mine and her hips relaxed. I lifted her shirt and tasted her pink nipple, circling it with my tongue. Her body moved in a gentle writhe beneath me, her eyes falling closed. Her tits were soft, but firm, and I lavished them with attention. With every kiss and suck, I felt her relax even as her breath quickened.

But my dick was starting to demand attention. I helped

her out of my t-shirt and rolled to the side so we could get rid of these annoying layers of clothing. I kicked off my sweats while she pulled off the boxer briefs I'd given her. They certainly hadn't lasted long.

But I wanted this more than I had let myself admit. Seeing her sprawled out on my bed was like a fucking dream come true.

"Condom?" I asked, although I was already reaching for the box I kept in the nightstand.

Shit, I hoped I still had some. It had been a while.

"Yeah, and I have an IUD, so we're covered."

Thankfully, I was prepared. She bit her lip, watching me openly while I rolled the condom down over my hard length.

"On your knees."

Her eyes fluttered, like the mere sound of my command did it for her. If she liked being told what to do, there was plenty more where that came from.

She rolled over, flipping her hair to the side, and got on her knees. I positioned myself behind her and ran my hands over the smooth skin of her insanely hot ass. She looked back at me over her shoulder, biting her lip again.

"Tell me what you want," I said.

"I want you to fuck me."

"Yeah?" I caressed her ass with one hand and held my dick with the other, rubbing the tip against her slick folds.

"Yes," she murmured. "Please, Jude."

Seeing her like this, on her knees and just this side of submissive, made me feel both powerful and protective. It was an exhilarating rush.

"Baby, I'll give you everything you need," I said, my voice low.

I kept rubbing my cock against her, focusing on her clit.

She arched backward, moaning, letting her head drop to the mattress. I desperately wanted to be inside her, but couldn't help taking my time. Drawing out the agony. She was firmly in my control and I loved it.

Finally, I lined up the head of my cock with her opening, grabbed her hips, and thrust inside.

I'd started slow, savoring my first tastes of her body. Now I hit the gas, driving into her hard and deep. My glutes flexed as I thrust my hips, the ecstasy of her pussy surrounding me.

Her enthusiastic stream of breathy yeses spurred me on. I knew exactly what she needed. I could feel it without her having to say a word. She needed to get fucked. To feel me deep inside her. To release her inhibitions and let someone else be in charge for a while.

I was more than happy to give that to her.

This view was incredible—her ass lifted, her red hair falling across her back. I watched my cock slide in and out of her, glistening and wet, and grunted with every thrust.

Her uninhibited cries made my head swim with lust. She gripped the sheets, her head turned to the side, eyes closed.

So fucking beautiful.

"Turn over," I said and slid out.

She obeyed immediately, rolling onto her back. I climbed on top of her and she hooked her legs around the backs of my thighs while I slid back inside her hot pussy.

"Fuck, you feel good." I kissed her mouth, licking across her tongue. "Tell me what you need."

"More."

I thrust into her.

"Harder."

I thrust again.

"Harder," she breathed. "Fuck me like you can't break me."

Unleashing a frenzy of heat and passion, I drove into her, over and over. My muscles flexed, my hips thrust, and a sheen of sweat covered my chest. She bucked her hips against me, her fingernails digging into my back.

It was raw and intense and so fucking real.

The pressure in my groin built fast. I growled into her neck while she clung to me, drawing her legs up so I could sink in deeper.

"Yes," she moaned in my ear. "Don't stop that."

Her pussy was hot, tightening around me. I kept my steady rhythm, drawing us both closer to the brink.

"Come for me, beautiful," I growled in her ear. "Let me feel that pussy clench."

Her desperate whimper was the sexiest thing I'd ever heard.

I thrust again, tilting my hips enough to grind against her clit before sliding out again.

"Holy shit," she breathed.

That was what she needed. I did it again, grinding against her with my cock deep inside. She shuddered, breathlessly moaning, and her pussy clenched hard.

One more and I felt her come apart.

Her silky inner muscles pulsed around me, squeezing my cock. I groaned as she came, the pressure in my groin skyrocketing. I thrust again, burying myself deep, and unleashed inside her.

My back stiffened, muscles tense, and my cock throbbed. I slammed into her with every pulse, coming so hard my eyes rolled back and a growl rumbled in my throat.

The intensity abated and I stopped, my cock buried

deep. She clung to me with her long limbs while we caught our breath.

Thoroughly sex-drunk, I propped myself up and blinked my heavy eyelids. Her cheeks were flushed the sexiest shade of pink and her mouth twitched in a smile.

"I'm not even going to pretend that wasn't the best sex I've ever had," I said. Because holy shit, it was. I'd never felt that kind of power and connection with someone.

"Oh good, I thought it was just me," she said, still a little breathless.

I laughed softly and climbed off her so I could deal with the condom. When I got back, we pulled down the covers and slid into bed.

Gathering her into my arms, I held her close. Kissed her forehead. There was something terrifyingly right about this moment. Cameron in my bed, our bodies sated. I could get used to this, and I'd never felt that way about anyone before. Not like this.

I knew Cameron had needed this tonight. What I didn't know was whether it was merely a way for her to cope with the fear and stress in her life, or if she was feeling something more.

A question for later. There were so many of those, I'd just add it to the list. For now, I wanted to hold her, feel her soft body snuggled against me. I couldn't imagine anything better.

21

JUDE

I woke to Cameron's face smashed against a pillow. It was the cutest thing I'd ever seen. Her cheek squished, her lips puckered in a bow. The sheet draped across her chest and her hands were tucked beneath the pillow.

It was tempting to haul her against me so I could feel her warm skin, but I didn't want to wake her. So I got up and quietly slipped on a pair of boxer briefs. Used the bathroom, then wandered into the kitchen to start coffee and breakfast. I needed to get started reviewing her security footage, but it seemed like I ought to be a good host and feed her first.

Doing my best to be quiet, I got coffee brewing and found some eggs and an unopened package of gruyere cheese in the fridge.

I heard the sheets rustling while I cracked an egg into a bowl.

"Nice ass," she said, her voice sleepy.

I glanced at her. She was on her side, the sheet pulled up over her chest, her head propped on her arm.

"Thanks. That's high praise, coming from you. Didn't

you rank in *Indulgence Magazine*'s Best Butts in Business poll last year?"

She rolled her eyes. "God, that article. You know, they didn't even mention my company. Although the unauthorized photo they used did make my ass look fantastic."

"Bright side?"

"Exactly," she said with a smile.

I gave her a little grin, relieved things weren't awkward this morning.

"Do you always cook breakfast in your underwear? Because a girl could get used to that."

God, Cameron, I could get used to this too. I cracked another egg. "Only on special occasions."

"And what's special about today?"

"I have a beautiful naked woman in my bed. What isn't special about today?"

She laughed and rolled onto her back, reaching her arms overhead in a lazy stretch. "I suppose I should get up. Do you mind if I wear your clothes again?"

"If you can find them." I tapped another egg to crack the shell.

From the corner of my eye, I saw her toss the sheet aside. She stood up, completely fucking naked, and walked to the bathroom. I didn't mean to stare, but I couldn't take my eyes off her.

Cold egg dribbled through my fingers. "Shit."

I made sure there weren't any bits of shell in the bowl—a naked Cameron walking brazenly through my loft was distracting—washed my hands, and went to work scrambling the eggs. She came out while I was stirring the eggs in a pan. Still naked.

"If you want breakfast, you might want to put some

clothes on. If you keep walking around like that, there's no telling what I'll do."

She glanced at me over her shoulder, the boxer briefs from last night in her hand. "Is that a threat?"

"No, it's a promise."

Everything about this was pointing to last night having been more than just a one-time comfort fuck for her. Which was good news because once was never going to be enough for me. Not when it was her.

It was hard to imagine ever getting enough of Cameron.

She came into the kitchen, and even covered up in my old Marine Corps t-shirt and loose-fitting boxer briefs, she was the sexiest woman I'd ever seen. She paused and leaned against the counter.

I put down the spatula, leaving the eggs to cook on low heat, and slipped my arms around her waist.

"Thank you," she said quietly.

"For what?"

She wrapped her arms around my neck. "Everything."

I leaned in and kissed her, enjoying the softness of her lips and the way her body pressed against me.

"Careful not to burn the eggs," she said.

I kissed her again. "I can make more."

She giggled as I kissed down her neck and squeezed her firm ass cheeks. I gave her ear a quick nibble, then went back to the eggs.

"Mugs are up there," I said, nodding toward the cupboard next to her.

"Thanks." She got out a mug and poured herself coffee. "I know we should probably talk about everything."

"But?"

"I didn't say but."

"I could hear the but."

She sighed, cradling the mug in her hands. "But I like pretending none of it exists."

"Are you referring to the fish in your bed, or the sex last night? Because I have to be honest, I'm hoping you mean the fish."

"I don't mean the sex, although maybe we should talk about that too."

I loved seeing the hint of a smile on her lips when she looked at me. "It's a better topic."

"I don't usually do that," she said. "And I'm not one of those women who says *I never do this on a first date* but really I do it all the time. I mean it."

The cheese was nicely melted, so I took the pan off the heat. "I know."

"I actually wasn't sure if you liked me. That way, at least."

I raised my eyebrows. "Are you kidding?"

"No. I didn't think you *disliked* me. But last week after the hit and run you kissed my forehead, and I had myself convinced it was a pity kiss and you didn't have any sexual feelings for me."

"Was that what had you so upset at Mordecai's?"

She bit her bottom lip. "You noticed that?"

I pulled out two plates and dished up portions of the eggs. "Most of the time you have an excellent game face, but yes, I could tell something was wrong. And it wasn't a pity kiss. It was my attempt to keep from ravaging you on your kitchen island."

Her mouth twitched. "What stopped you?"

"I wasn't sure if you liked me."

She laughed. "What are we, thirteen? I guess I should have dropped a *do you like me, check yes or no* note on your desk. Where are the forks?"

"It might have helped." I pointed to a drawer. "Forks are in there."

I set the plates on the island while Cameron poured me a cup of coffee. Then we sat down on the tall stools.

She took a bite and moaned before the fork even left her mouth. "Mm, this is so good."

"Thanks. The trick to good scrambled eggs is the low heat. You cook them slow and don't add anything until the end, not even salt and pepper. If you add anything too soon, it breaks down the proteins and they get rubbery."

"Wow. I'm guessing you didn't learn that in the Marines."

I shook my head. "Food Network."

"Well, now that we have food, serious topic: What do I do about the fact that someone broke into my house without a trace last night?"

"Two things. First, I'm staying at your place for the time being."

She picked up her coffee. "Wow, you get in my pants once and you think we're shacking up? Bold move, Ellis."

"Don't you have eight guest rooms?"

"Six. But I hear the master suite is getting a brand-new mattress. It might be more comfortable for you."

I was trying to stick to business, but she was making it difficult. And making me hard. "Is that an invitation?"

"It might be. You're a good cook, but your coffee's mediocre. I'm still deciding."

"I ride a motorcycle. Does that tip the scales in my favor?"

"God yes," she said, her eyes rolling back. "I should have known I'd end up sleeping with you the first time I saw you on that thing."

"So sleeping arrangements to be determined, but I'm not

leaving you alone there. Second, I'm going to figure out how someone got in. I need to talk to everyone who has a code."

"You think it was an inside job?"

"I know you don't want to think someone you trust enough to have access to your home would do this to you, but the fact is, whoever it was didn't break in. That means they were either let in, or they had the code to unlock your door and disable the alarm."

"No one was there to let someone in. Nicholas and Inda left before I went to Luna's. Bert wasn't there yesterday, and I can't even fathom him doing something like this. You're welcome to interrogate my friends, but if you do, I have to be there, because I want to see them chew you up and spit you out."

"I have no doubt they will, but I'm still going to ask them some questions. What about your cleaning service?"

"They're very reputable."

"All it takes is a little money. Someone could have slipped some cash to one of the cleaning people."

"It's possible, I suppose." She took a sip of coffee. "I wish I knew why they were doing this. None of it makes sense."

She was right about that. The only pattern was that there wasn't one.

"I still think the most likely suspects are Noelle and Aldrich."

"The note referred to me as the boss," she said. "Doesn't that imply something about Spencer? Aldrich doesn't have any connections to my company."

"Derek sent me an email last night right before you called. It turns out Aldrich bought a large share of Reese Howard Aviation not long ago. And guess who was just elected to their board of directors?"

"What?" she asked, her eyes widening. "Aldrich got

himself elected to the board of directors of our biggest competitor?"

I nodded.

Cameron got off the stool and put her hands in her hair. "That asshole. Why would he do that? He never cared about my business, only whined that I worked too much."

"Maybe that has something to do with it. If he blames your career for your breakup, he could be trying to hit you where it hurts. Take away the thing that took you from him."

"Why didn't I see it?" She started pacing around the loft. "I should have known he was evil. He waxes his chest, Jude. He's neither a model nor a swimmer. Why would he wax his chest?"

"I'm not sure what that has to do with anything, but it is weird."

"I just mean it should have tipped me off that something wasn't right."

"The question is, does Aldrich have your door code?"

"No. I changed it after we broke up."

"Regardless, I'll know more when I review your security footage."

"Why haven't you reviewed the footage?"

"I was a little busy fucking you last night."

She put her hands on her hips. "Well, you should have reviewed the footage instead. No, I take that back, I'm just upset and talking crazy. Fucking me was the right choice."

"I'm glad you think so."

"How could I not? It was amazing. But we need to focus. You still think it could be Noelle? Her hatred of me is fierce, but putting a fish in my bed seems odd for her."

"Can you see Aldrich leaving a fish in your bed?"

"Not really. But I'm starting to doubt my ability to judge people's character. Oh my god, I'm going to turn into one of those eccentric paranoid billionaires. How long before I start trying to build an impossible-to-engineer airplane in a massive hanger out in the middle of nowhere?"

"I'm sure you have a few good years left. And yes, I still think Noelle is a possibility. The fish could be for shock value, or to throw you off her trail. Regardless, I think you should get Derek involved. His firm can help manage the media if things start going sideways."

"I was thinking the same thing." She grabbed her phone and groaned.

"Another email?"

"No, a text from Bobby Spencer. He's throwing an *intimate soiree*"—she made air quotes—"on his stripper plane tonight."

"What's a stripper plane?"

She rolled her eyes while she typed a reply. "A few years ago, he bought a private jet from some Saudi prince. I think it's literally from the early nineties, and it's hideous. I'm talking red velvet and leopard print with gold-plated everything. I've only had the misfortune of seeing pictures, but it's outfitted with a rotating bed, a full bar, and a stripper pole. It's another one of his brilliant business ideas that's done nothing but waste a bunch of his trust fund."

"Classy."

"Oh dear, I was about to RSVP with a plus one, but he texted again to say I don't need to bring my bodyguard."

"The fuck you don't," I said.

Her lip curled in a smile. "Mm, territorial. I like that. I honestly don't know why he keeps inviting me to things. I've never gone to one of his parties."

"So he's clueless, delusional, and wealthy. That's a charming combination."

"At least I won't have to tolerate him much longer." She

sat back down on the stool. "I can exercise my option to buy more shares next month. Then I'll own a majority interest in Spencer, and I can tell him to fuck off."

My brow furrowed. "Does Bobby know you're buying out his family?"

She shrugged. "I'm not sure what Milton's told him. I've always kept my distance from their private family matters."

"Bobby might not be happy about the fact that someone else is on their way to owning his family's company."

"I don't know why he'd care. He lives off a bottomless trust fund. He's an only child of an elderly multi-billionaire with no other heirs. Spencer could go bankrupt and he'd still never run out of money."

"What about Bobby's mother? What's her story?"

"Ruby Spencer-Kensington-Alviar. She and Milton split up years ago. Last I heard, she was living in Spain after leaving her third husband and taking half his fortune. Some women marry well, Ruby divorces well."

"That helps explain Bobby."

She sipped her coffee. "Yeah. Milton is actually a decent guy, but he was almost fifty when Bobby was born, and I don't think he was a very involved father. Ruby was much younger, but I doubt she ever wanted children. Bobby was raised by a string of nannies who never stayed on very long because he was such a spoiled shit. I'd feel sorry for him, but he's thirty-six years old. At some point, everyone has to stop blaming their problems on their crappy childhood and either be a good person or not."

"True. And you said Milton was friends with your grand-parents?"

"Yeah." She slid off the stool and picked up her plate. "I'll clean up."

I eyed her for a second. Was that an intentional evasion

of my question? Or was she just ready to move on from breakfast conversation and get home?

"I can take care of it."

She took my empty plate and set it on top of hers. "You cooked, I can do the dishes. It's not like I forgot how. Plus, don't you have some packing to do?"

"That's right, I talked you into shacking up with me."

"To be fair, you're shacking up with me."

"What's Bluewater going to think of that?"

She smiled. "You'll get to find out tonight. It's Eighties Night at the Bluewater Disco. Everyone will be there."

"Eighties night? Why is this the first I'm hearing about it?"

"It's in Bluewater, so I didn't think I'd need to make you work on a Saturday just to watch me dance with a bunch of our weirdo residents wearing bad interpretations of eighties outfits."

"People are going in costume?"

"We dress to the theme. It's my favorite event of the year."

A community event tonight was perfect. It would give me a chance to casually find out if there was anyone else who might be responsible for the break-in. "Then I guess we should get moving. I have a lot of work to do before tonight."

Her smile faded. "Oh crap, I can't forget it's my day to feed Steve."

"Steve? Do I even want to know?"

"He's our three-legged alligator."

I blinked at her. "You have a three-legged alligator? Where?"

"He lives in the canal. He lost a leg and even with the prosthetic leg one of our tech-genius residents made him, he can't survive in the wild, so we let him stay. But don't worry, he's harmless as long as we keep him fed."

"What do you feed him?"

"Rotisserie chickens," she said, her voice matter-of-fact, as if feeding cooked chickens to a three-legged alligator was the most normal thing in the world.

"Let me get this straight. Bluewater has a free-range Saint Bernard, and a three-legged alligator?"

She smiled again. "Mm hmm. And Frank."

"I'm afraid to ask."

"Frank's a parrot with a talent for mimicking human speech. And his previous owner was kind of a dick, so he mostly spews profanity."

I had a feeling I was about to get a crash course in the quirkiness that was the Bluewater enclave.

)

22

CAMERON

I sat in a chair in my spacious master bathroom, turned away from the mirror, while Valentina attacked my face. She was dressed in a fabulous floral romper, her dark hair in a braided updo, her fingernails painted a deep red that matched her lipstick. One of Miami's best stylists, hairdressers, and makeup artists, Valentina—she went by her first name only—had just inked a deal to star in her own makeover show.

"Not many girls can pull off peach, green, and gold the way you can," she said in her light Puerto Rican accent. "Look down."

I lowered my eyes while she smoothed on eyeliner. "Are we sure that's eighties enough? I was thinking hot pink and bright blue."

"Too cliché," she said. "And with your skin, you'd look like a cheap whore."

I smiled. Valentina's blunt honesty was one of the reasons I loved her. That, and the fact that she could style me for a black-tie gala or a silly themed party with equal perfection.

Last I'd seen, Jude was downstairs, going over the security footage for the fifth or sixth time. One thing we knew now with absolute certainty, whoever had broken into my house had used the door code. The video showed a person walking right up to the door, like he or she belonged here, and typing in the code with a gloved hand. The problem was, we couldn't tell who it was.

They'd worn nondescript dark clothing. No logos or labels. We couldn't even tell for sure if it had been a man or a woman. The person's face had been buried deep in a hood and they'd kept their head down.

I didn't have cameras inside—although Jude was gradually talking me into letting him install one in the entry. Indoor surveillance had always felt like an unnecessary infringement on my privacy. But after this, I had to admit, the idea had merit.

It still sent a tingle down my spine—and not the good kind—that someone had waltzed right into my home. How had they gotten access? The police were investigating the cleaning service. Jude had talked to Nicholas and Inda earlier, as well as Bert, and he agreed that it was highly unlikely any of them were involved. He'd also ruled out Brandy, which didn't surprise me, but was also a relief. I was worried I'd sorely misjudged someone close to me. But I trusted Jude, and he'd said he was as sure as he could be that my closest employees weren't the culprits.

If it was Aldrich, I was going to have his ass. It made me want to sue him for breach of contract over the sex tape— we'd both signed that non-disclosure—even though that was a guarantee it would be made public. But it might be worth it to bury him in the legal system for a while.

A twinge of guilt fluttered in my stomach. I still hadn't told Jude about the sex tape. With Aldrich a potential suspect, I knew I needed to just come out and tell him. But I couldn't seem to get the words out.

I didn't want him to think less of me. I thought less of myself, and that was bad enough. I couldn't deal with the thought of disappointment in Jude's eyes.

My phone buzzed against the gray marble counter. When I'd built my house, I'd let my architectural and design team go nuts with their luxury beach hut concept. What they'd given me was a gorgeous home that was stylish and unique. My master bathroom was a soothing mix of grays, ocean blue glass tile, and a sprawling teak-style vanity that was actually constructed from more sustainable bamboo.

While Valentina consulted her sizable collection of eye shadows, I checked my phone, stifling a groan.

Bobby the Douchebag: *Are you sure about tonight? You can still come over.*

Me: *Positive.*

Bobby the Douchebag: *I'll get your favorite dinner.*

Me: *What's my favorite?*

Bobby the Douchebag: *I'll know when you tell me...*

Me: *No thanks.*

Bobby the Douchebag: *Come on. I told you, not a date. I don't even want to date you.*

Bobby the Douchebag: *That was a lie. We'd be the hottest couple in Miami.*

Me: *Nope.*

Bobby the Douchebag: *Think about it, Cami. We're the ultimate power couple.*

Me: *We're not a couple.*

Bobby the Douchebag: *Only because you're being stubborn.*

Me: *Still no.*

Me: *And in case I'm not being clear, no.*

Me: *Also, no.*

I put my phone down. It buzzed again, but I ignored it. He'd get distracted by something shiny—his ridiculous Instagram groupies or his equally douchey club-hopping friends.

"Trouble in paradise?" Valentina asked, wielding a makeup brush. "Close your eyes."

I did as I was told. "No, just Bobby Spencer."

"Ugh, that guy. I heard he got blacklisted by both Liv and Wall Lounge."

"Barred from Miami's hottest clubs? Such a shame."

Valentina snorted. "Almost done. You just need mascara and another layer of hairspray."

She finished caking on my makeup, then covered me in a cloud of high-hold spray. I bit my lip with excitement while she sprayed the back of my hair, waiting to get a glimpse of her magic. Eighties night couldn't have come at a better time. I desperately needed the distraction, and I had a shameless love of eighties music. If they broke out the karaoke machine, I was going to dominate. I could rock anything by Pat Benatar.

"Okay, gorgeous, take a look."

I spun around and giggled. I looked like a ginger version of Jem from Jem and the Holograms. My green and gold eyeshadow went all the way to my sculpted eyebrows. She'd painted sparkling gold stars at the corners of my eyes and dramatic peach blush highlighted my cheekbones. The lipstick she'd chosen was a darker peach and so shiny it almost looked like glitter. My hair was southern-beauty-queen huge, a mass of teased-out waves that gave me at least another four inches of height.

It was perfect.

"You're a goddess," I said. "I look ridiculous."

"Ridiculous but still hot," she said. "I keep trying to make you ugly and it never works. Your outfit is on the bed."

I laughed. "Thanks, Val."

I'd mused many times that money couldn't buy happiness. But today it had gotten me a brand-new king-size memory foam mattress and my favorite luxury high-thread-count sheets delivered same day. Between the new bed and the fresh air coming in through the open glass doors, any hint of fish smell was gone.

I changed into the outfit Valentina had selected for me. Black bra with a slouchy peach shirt that draped off one shoulder. Black leggings with a bit of shine to them and a pair of sparkly gold legwarmers that brought me more joy than was strictly healthy. Because she was amazing, she'd paired the whole thing with huge hoop earrings and garish gold heels.

Perfect.

She gave me a final once-over, declared me fit to be seen, and carted her things downstairs.

I put my phone and the touch-up kit Valentina had left in a lime green clutch, rubbed my lips together one last time, and went down to find Jude.

He wasn't in the breakfast nook—a space off the kitchen with a view of the water—where he'd set up his laptop and two additional travel monitors. I opened the door to the terrace and poked my head into the warm evening air.

"Jude?"

His voice came from inside, behind me. "Ready to go?"

I spun around and my mouth dropped wide open. Jude stood in my kitchen dressed in a sleeveless mesh half-shirt —putting his huge arms and chiseled abs on full display— and a pair of gold and black parachute pants.

"Oh my god." I shut the door and moved closer. "Where did you get that?"

His hands were in his pockets, his posture casual, like there was nothing abnormal about the way he was dressed. "You said eighties night and people would dress to the theme. I'll blend in this way."

"But where did you get that outfit? Did you leave while Valentina was doing my hair?"

He glanced down at his clothes. "No. I brought it from home."

"You just had that in your closet."

"Yes."

"Are you serious? Did you dress up for Halloween recently?"

"No."

It was hard to keep from laughing. "Then why do you have those? Some weird undercover mission?"

"If I told you, I'd have to kill you," he deadpanned.

"Fair enough. How do I look?"

He finally cracked a small smile. "You look really terrible."

"Thank you," I said, patting my stiff hair.

The door opened behind me and Nicholas and Inda came inside. Inda was dressed in a lavender tank top and cropped leggings, her hair in her usual ponytail. Nicholas wore a plain t-shirt and tapered sweats.

Nicholas snickered until his eyes moved to Jude. He stopped and cleared his throat.

"Wow," Inda said. "You both went all in."

"Are you sure you don't want to come?" I asked. "You're more than welcome, and we can wait for you to get ready."

Nicholas gave his wife an alarmed glance, but she shook her head.

"No, thanks. We'll stay here and make sure no one else breaks in."

"Okay, thanks."

"Go have fun, crazy kids," she said, waving us away.

Jude followed me out to the garage where I kept my tricked-out golf cart. The best way to travel around Bluewater was by golf cart, and I'd added aerodynamic spoilers, ventilated seats, and a fringe of neon-lighted tassels that hung from the roof. I'd wanted to beef up the electric engine, but I hadn't found the time to do more extensive modifications.

I sat down and hit the remote for the garage. The tassels lit up as soon as I turned the cart on.

"Did you have this decorated for tonight?" Jude asked, settling into the passenger's seat.

"Nope. This is my standard mode of transportation."

"The aerospace CEO has a golf cart with hanging neon lights. Because of course she does."

I pressed the horn and it played a verse from Rick Astley's "Never Gonna Give You Up."

Jude just shook his head.

I drove us out of the garage and paused while Jude looked back to watch the garage door go down—I could tell he wanted to make sure it closed fully—then took the closest paved trail over the bridge and toward Bluewater's charming downtown village.

I'd done a lot of things that I was proud of in my life so far, but few were quite as special as Bluewater. The four of us—Daisy, Luna, Emily, and myself—had developed it on our own, transforming twenty-five hundred acres of swamp into a thriving micro-community. It also happened to look a lot like a female reproductive system when viewed from the air, a joke that had yet to get old. Daisy,

Luna, Emily, and I had built our respective homes on one ovary.

Considering the four of us founders were weirder than we often appeared to the outside world—Daisy excluded, who was nothing if not wildly authentic, even in public—it shouldn't have been a surprise that the Bluewater enclave had grown into a haven of the quirky and eclectic in Miami.

Which was probably why our nightclub had been renamed the Bluewater Disco at a town hall meeting earlier in the year. And sported an eight-foot carved parrot next to an equally massive rooster statue outside.

Why? Because Bluewater.

I parked my golf cart among the dozen or so already here. The faint thump of music carried from inside and a neon sign in the window announced the Bluewater Disco in shades of pink and electric blue.

"Are you ready to enjoy the best music ever made?" I asked.

"That's debatable, but I think you could use a win, so I'll just agree and say yes."

"How magnanimous of you." My eyes flicked up and down his large frame. His outfit should have been hideous, but he made it look so damn good.

He tilted his head slightly. "Cameron, am I your bodyguard tonight? Or your date?"

The hint of vulnerability in his voice made my breath catch. I knew if I answered wrong, I'd risk doing permanent damage to whatever was happening between us.

"Can the bodyguard take a night off for a date?"

He stepped closer and slipped his hands around my waist. "I'll still be watching out for you."

I nodded, smiling as he leaned down to brush my lips with a kiss.

God, my friends were going to go nuts. But fuck it. Jude made me happy.

I slipped my hand in his, twining our fingers together, and we went inside.

The Bluewater Disco had been transformed into a garish—and fabulous—parody of the nineteen-eighties. Brightly colored balloons decorated the bar and neon lights flashed over the dance floor. A vintage Ms. Pac Man game stood near the hall that led to the restrooms, and giant Rubik's cubes provided seating and places to set drinks. An eighties tribute band played on the stage at the far end of the room.

I squeezed Jude's hand. It was dark and the place was packed. It didn't make me nervous—these were my friends and neighbors—but I noticed Jude visually marking the exits. I wondered what else was going on in that strategic brain of his.

"Do you need to do a lap to make sure it's safe?" I asked, raising my voice to be heard above the music.

He squeezed my hand back. "Just stay with me."

"I planned on it, big guy. Let's go have some fun."

Emily spotted us and waved. She'd gone all out with a shiny pink jacket—complete with shoulder pads— matching mini skirt, huge teal earrings, and blue eyeshadow that didn't do anything to diminish her beauty. Her blond hair was teased high and she held a bright pink cocktail.

"You look amazing," she said. "Wow, Jude. Nice outfit."

Derek sauntered over, dressed in a more subdued version of eighties menswear—a pastel polo with the collar popped and a pair of well-tailored slacks. He took one look at Jude and burst out laughing.

"Jealous?" Jude asked.

"Dear god, no," Derek said.

I slipped my hands around his waist, indulging in a little trace of his abs with my fingers. "I think he looks radical."

Emily's eyebrows shot up and her mouth popped open. I gave her a smug smile while Jude put his arm around me.

"Well," Derek said, draping a casual arm around Emily's shoulders. "Isn't this interesting."

Jude glanced down at me. "Drink?"

"Definitely."

We had to pause for introductions every few feet on our way to the bar. It seemed like most of Bluewater was here. Jude met the secretive Mr. Joneses, who claimed to be retired business executives, but we had other suspicions. I half expected Jude to recognize one or both of them, but if they'd ever encountered each other in their murky pasts, none of them hinted at it.

Then it was three of the WWs, decked out in swaths of neon and cheap plastic jewelry. They fawned over Jude, complimenting his arms and his abs. Next came Mr. Zabrinski, one of our tech geniuses. I had to pry Jude away before we got roped into a lengthy and intricately detailed discussion on the benefits and dangers of artificial intelligence.

The band started another song—"Jessie's Girl"—and the crowd cheered. We stopped again as Luna spun around in front of us, clasping her hands to her chest. She looked adorable in a slouchy pink shirt and leggings, a wide headband in her mass of dark hair.

"Look at you," Luna said, her eyes bright with enthusiasm.

Daisy was standing with her, decked out in a black bustier, black and pink tulle skirt, and lace gloves. Her hair was a surprisingly normal shade of dirty blond, but it was crimped into beautiful frizzy chaos.

"Holy shit," Daisy said, looking Jude up and down. She had a neon pink cocktail in her hand. "This is fucking epic."

Jude attempted to brush my hair back over my shoulder, but it was cemented in place. "Do you want me to get you a drink?"

"Sure."

He nodded and went to the bar.

"Please tell me you're fucking that glorious hunk of man meat," Daisy said.

Luna shook her head at our blunt friend.

"You guys, I don't know what I'm doing with him," I said. "It's so inappropriate."

"And unprofessional?" Daisy asked.

"Yes."

"Good," she said. "You need some inappropriate in your life."

I smiled. "I guess so. And we were very, very inappropriate."

"You look happy," Luna said. "And refreshed. I'm glad for you."

"Thanks."

Jude came back with a neon orange cocktail. He and I wandered around a little, chatting with people. Enjoying the music. It felt good. Relaxed. Fun. Jude even smiled.

The band started one of my favorite cheesy love songs —"Lost in Your Eyes." I glanced at Jude and gave the dance floor a pointed look. He smiled at me, acquiescing with a subtle shrug, and took me out to the dance floor.

He held one hand and wrapped the other around my waist while we swayed to the music. Mrs. Chang, one of the WWs, danced with Reggie Drinkwater, a hotelier and recent addition to Bluewater. Emily and Derek embraced nearby. Daisy and Luna did a giggling impression of awkward middle schoolers attempting to slow dance, and other couples crowded around, their brightly colored clothes sparkling in the neon lights.

I rested my head against Jude's chest. And in that moment, wearing garish makeup and gold leg warmers, dancing to a cover band's rendition of Debbie Gibson, I fell a little bit in love with Jude Ellis.

23

JUDE

I slept better with Cameron mere inches away. I'd put my things in a guest room—not wanting to assume that I'd been invited to share her bedroom—but she came out of her home office every night and asked if I'd come to bed with her.

Of course the answer was yes. I couldn't get enough of her.

After only a few days, we'd already settled into a comfortable routine. We were both early risers, so we'd get up and hit her gym first thing. Inda knew her shit. She worked Cameron hard, and she had some good suggestions for me to keep my shoulder joints healthy—a common place for a big guy like me to have problems.

Then coffee and a light breakfast with a view of the bay, marred only once by the appearance of horny dolphins engaging in some very explicit behavior.

We'd get ready for work and drive to her office. Evenings were spent chatting about our day over dinner, catching up on more work, and watching TV in bed together. Turned out she liked cooking shows as much as I did.

Some of it felt so normal, a tempting version of the ordinary life I kept telling myself I needed. And it scared me a bit to realize how quickly we'd molded our lives and routines around each other. It had been effortless, like we'd been living and working together for years, not days.

But much of it was anything but ordinary. Cameron's life was filled with decisions that affected the lives of thousands of people. With steering the vision of an aerospace empire. She'd always be subjected to a high degree of scrutiny. Always exist at least partially in the spotlight.

Always need someone like me.

Dangerous thoughts to be having just days after realizing my infatuation with her wasn't one-sided.

But I still had a job to do. I'd spent the last few evenings making modifications to her home security—adding cameras and more motion detectors, as well as adjusting the angles to eliminate blind spots. As expected, the police didn't have any leads on the break-in. No fingerprints. There were too many places to buy red snapper in Miami to trace the origin of the fish.

I was frustrated as hell.

Still dressed in a sweaty tank top and shorts after a morning workout—Cameron was showering upstairs—I rooted through her kitchen cupboards. One of these days, I was going to slip into that enormous walk-in shower with her. But today she had an eight-thirty meeting, so I ignored the pressure of my unwanted hard-on and found some protein powder.

Nicholas came in the back door, dressed in a pink hibiscus shirt, his hair damp, his beard neatly trimmed.

"Morning," he said with a friendly smile.

"Morning."

I liked Nicholas. Usually I didn't trust people who

smiled a lot, but he just seemed like a contented dude. Maybe it had something to do with being happily married. He and Inda were an odd-looking couple—she was athletic and fit, and he had a bit of a dad bod—but they were obviously crazy about each other.

I pulled the blender from under the cabinet and opened the protein powder.

"I'd be careful with that," Nicholas said.

"With the blender?"

"Cameron modified it. I'm pretty sure that thing could puree a chunk of marble. Stick to the lowest setting."

I dumped in a cup of ice and a scoop of protein. "What do you mean she modified it?"

He shrugged and started getting pans out of a cupboard. "She has a workshop off the garage. She takes stuff apart and when she puts it back together, you need goggles and a hard hat to handle it safely."

A workshop? I'd noticed a room with tools and a large worktable, but she'd never mentioned anything about it.

"Thanks for the warning."

I added a few more things, secured the lid, and pressed blend.

It sounded like a jet engine gearing up for takeoff. I held the blender down, worried it was going to vibrate off the counter. A few seconds later, I turned it off.

"Told you," Nicholas said.

I glanced around the kitchen. "What else has she modified?"

"The garbage disposal could probably chew your arm off, the electric mixer sounds terrifying but it whips heavy cream in about half the time, and I'd avoid the toaster altogether. We talked her out of taking apart the microwave, and

I covertly got rid of the popcorn maker. Everything else is more or less normal."

"Good to know."

Cameron came downstairs with wet hair, dressed in a silky robe, her long legs on display. God, she was gorgeous. I wanted to toss her over my shoulder and haul her upstairs so I could devour every inch of her.

"Morning, Nicholas. Meal prep day?"

"Indeed it is," he said, unloading an armful of produce onto the counter.

She sidled up to me and lifted onto her tiptoes to brush a soft kiss across my lips. "Shower's all yours."

I kissed her back. "Thanks."

She glanced around, then leaned closer to Nicholas. "Will I find anything naughty hidden in the back of the fridge when you're done?"

"You know Inda wants me to stick to the meal plan she made for you."

"I know, but if you accidentally make a key lime tart or two, I promise I won't tell."

Nicholas grinned. "Don't get me in trouble."

"It's our little secret."

She winked at me. I smiled back, then took my protein shake upstairs to get ready for work.

CAMERON'S SCHEDULE WAS PACKED, as usual, which kept me busy. I shadowed her as she went about her day and checked the security feeds from her house regularly. We were keeping things strictly professional in her office. Nothing but occasional lingering eye contact and a stolen kiss or two. The people in Cameron's personal life knew about us, and she'd told Brandy. But as far as everyone else at Spencer knew, I was still just Cameron's personal security.

She'd been in her office for about an hour when the back of my neck tingled. I shifted my shoulders to rub my collar against it. That was odd. It was rare that something riled up my instincts here in Cameron's office. I still got the subtle sense that she was in danger, but that was a feeling I'd relegated to the background. It wasn't exactly useful at this point—we already knew.

But her office was reasonably safe. I stayed with her during the day because she often had meetings and appointments off-site, and to send the message that she was well-protected.

My top four exit strategies ran through my mind like a reflex.

Noelle Olson walked into the office, dressed in a cream blouse with a wide collar and navy slacks. Her dark hair was pulled back in a sleek bun, making her high-cheekboned face look particularly severe. I'd been in meetings with most of Spencer's executive team, and where the rest of them were cordial, Noelle pretended like I didn't exist.

She paused near my desk and glanced toward Cameron's half-open door. She was walking slowly around her office on a phone call. Brandy shifted to the edge of her seat, poised to intercept Noelle if she tried to walk in on her boss unannounced.

"Is there anything I can help you with, Noelle?" Brandy asked.

Noelle gave Brandy an annoyed glance. "I'll come back."

I watched her walk down the hall toward her office. Her dislike of Cameron was well-known. Everyone from accounting to the engineers to the receptionists knew the COO had wanted Cameron's job. The apparently random nature of the threats against Cameron could be Noelle's way of keeping suspicion at bay. Who would assume a high-level executive would leave a fish in her rival's bed?

It was tempting to follow Noelle to her office and ask a few well-placed questions. But my instincts told me it was better if I stayed Cameron's invisible bodyguard—just the muscle—for now.

"Bobby, you can't just go back there."

The front receptionist followed Bobby through the small hallway behind the reception desk. He wore dark sunglasses —the Dolce & Gabanna logo on full display—a polo that said Versace across the front, and a belt with a large gold Gucci logo for a buckle. The only thing that didn't declare its designer—and therefore its expense—were his shoes, a pair of black leather sneakers.

I glanced again. I was wrong. They were embossed with a Fendi logo on the toe. It was surprisingly subtle, considering the rest of his clothes looked like a commercial for lifestyles of the gaudy and pretentious.

"Sorry," the receptionist said.

"It's okay," Brandy said, and scowled at Bobby when he casually leaned against her desk.

"What's the boss lady up to?" he asked. Like the douche he was, he didn't take off his sunglasses.

"She's busy," Brandy said.

I couldn't see his eyes behind his sunglasses, but I could tell when he glanced at me. He swallowed and rubbed his palms against his thighs. I made him nervous. Good.

"No big deal. Just be a doll and put dinner with me on her schedule for tonight."

"Her schedule's full," I said.

I could see Bobby at war with himself. He was used to feeling like the alpha here. Not that it was true, but most people in his father's company tried to stay out of his way rather than stand up to him. I challenged his perceived dominance.

But unlike a true alpha male, he was weak—protected by wealth and his last name, with nothing to back up his unearned swagger.

Would he argue with me in an attempt to reestablish his dominance, or back down?

My money was on back down, but you never knew with a guy like him.

Cameron came out of her office and crossed her arms. Her legs looked fantastic in her sleek skirt and her snake-skin heels made her look like the badass she was.

"Cami," he said, swiping off his sunglasses. "You're looking especially hot today."

"Bobby, I have a company to run. If you're here to invite me to party with you, the answer is no. And if you just came up here to brag about last night's ten-thousand-dollar bottle service, save it for your Instagram followers."

"My fans do love my club pics," he said. "But that's not why I'm here. I heard somebody broke into your house."

A hint of alarm flashed across Cameron's face, replaced quickly by her calm and cool CEO expression. "Where did you hear that?"

He pulled out his phone. "It's on a couple of blogs. You'd think it would have had better coverage by now. That's a bold move, getting into Bluewater and breaking into your house like that. Guy must have some balls."

Brandy was already typing and by the way her eyes widened, I could tell she'd found something. She met Cameron's gaze and nodded.

"Is this an issue?" Cameron asked.

"The spin isn't great," Brandy said.

"If you need help with this, Cami, say the word. Or if you need a distraction, I can do that too." He wiggled his eyebrows at her.

This guy was such a joke, I didn't even bother growling at him.

"Get Derek Price on the phone." Cameron turned and went back into her office.

Bobby cast a nervous glance at me, then put on his sunglasses. "I'll just text her later."

Through narrowed eyes, I watched him go.

Brandy was already in Cameron's office. I googled, wincing at the headlines. The media could be a fucking circus. There wasn't much I could to do protect Cameron from this kind of problem. She had a good PR team and Derek Price was the best at what he did. He'd help her sort this out.

I didn't like feeling helpless, especially when it came to her. But maybe there were other ways I could take care of the boss lady.

24

CAMERON

My schedule, at least until tonight, had gone out the window. Brandy had scrambled to rearrange my afternoon while I'd met with Derek Price and Spencer's PR team to talk damage control.

The problem wasn't that the media had reported the break-in. That might have caused a little drama at the next Bluewater Town Hall—if enough of the residents decided it meant we had a security problem in the enclave. But that would have been easy to address, and certainly not a reason to bring in a corporate fixer.

The problem was the spin. Apparently a story about a home invasion wasn't salacious enough. The media glossing over the fact that I'd been the victim, and was portraying me as a power-hungry backstabber who'd made enemies on her rise to the top. The break-in was being touted as a revenge move.

Speculation as to what I'd done to cause this—the blame-shifting made me furious—ranged from sleeping with Spencer executives to get my job, to stealing ideas from fellow engineers early in my career and refusing to give them credit.

The worst was a lengthy article by gossip blogger Sydney Phillips. She'd dug into my past enough to know Milton Spencer had paid my private school tuition. She claimed I'd turned on my benefactor and bullied him into retiring. Her article also referred to my numerous enemies in the aerospace industry—without actually naming any—and painted Spencer Aeronautics as a company on the brink of revolt against its CEO.

It almost sounded too outlandish to do real PR damage, but there was just enough truth woven among the wild speculation to give Sydney's article an air of credibility. As did the one Spencer executive she did have on record. Noelle Olson.

She'd quoted Noelle as saying, "Cameron Whitbury is reckless, taking unnecessary risks with Spencer's resources in order to indulge her personal ambitions."

It was a shitty thing for Noelle to say, especially to a gossip blogger, but not surprising. She'd said similar things to my face, although cloaked in more diplomatic language. But Sydney had run with it. I'd wanted to march down to Noelle's office and confront her, but Jude had stopped me. If she was behind the other incidents, this was probably part of her larger plan to discredit me. An angry confrontation wouldn't help.

The worst part was how much time and attention this was going to take. I already had enough on my plate without trying to counteract crappy news coverage. I had a fucking company to run. Thousands of jobs fell under my responsibility and this was a distraction I didn't need.

I picked up my phone to check the group chat that Daisy had named Vagillionaires.

Daisy: *I'm so fucking angry right now. That article is bullshit.*

Luna: *It's very troubling. How can this woman get away with lying about Cam?*

Emily: *Spin. We all know it can happen. Sensationalism sells.*

Luna: *Cam, check in when you can.*

Daisy: *Where are we drinking tonight? I have a bottle of Luna's favorite organic vodka ready.*

Luna: *I love your generous heart.*

Daisy: *Let's just gather at my place. Cam needs a dip in the D.*

Despite everything, I couldn't help but laugh. Daisy's pool was shaped like a dick and balls. Because of course it was. This was Daisy.

Emily: *To be fair, she's probably getting the D.*

Luna: *Meditative sexual experiences can be very cleansing and good for stress. Cam, I have a book you can borrow if you want it.*

Daisy: *Speaking of the D, I need to know if Jude is proportionate. Because if he is, Cam's a lucky bitch.*

Me: *I'm a lucky bitch.*

I grinned while the three of them sent me a series of emojis—shock face, happy face, and heart eyes, interspersed with eggplants.

Me: *Serious note. Derek and my PR team are on it. I'm pissed but we'll handle it. Not sure about drinking in the dick pool tonight. I'll get back to you. Love you guys.*

Jude pushed my office door open. He'd been somewhat on the sidelines today. There wasn't a lot he could do against this kind of attack. But his presence here had made such a difference. Knowing he was nearby had kept me from completely losing my mind.

"Hey," he said.

That little smile of his made me feel melty inside. "Hey."

"Why don't we get out of here?" he asked. "Let me take you out. Get your mind off everything. It'll still be here in the morning."

"Like a date?" I asked.

"Exactly like a date. In fact, I was thinking an actual date."

"Yeah?"

"Why do you seem surprised?" he asked.

I shrugged. "I don't know. We're not really following the pattern. You already moved in."

"Extenuating circumstances. And it doesn't mean I'm skipping the part where I date you, Cameron."

Those heart eyes emojis danced in front of my face. "I'd love to. Where are we going? Do I need to change?"

"No. It's a little hole in the wall not far from my place. But trust me, the food's amazing."

"Sounds perfect."

I sent my friends a quick text telling them I had a date. They replied with more emojis. I really loved those weirdos.

We left the mostly empty office and Jude drove us to a little restaurant housed in a building with chipping paint and a pink flamingo painted on the outside wall.

Inside the restaurant looked worn, but in a way that made it look well-loved rather than neglected. Rectangular tables were surrounded by mismatched painted wood chairs, and an eclectic mix of colorful art decorated the walls. Several of the tables had small groups enjoying their meals and a few servers bustled around the dining room.

We seated ourselves and a server brought us menus.

"Their specialty is seafood," Jude said. "But I've never had anything here that isn't amazing."

I browsed the menu, but everything sounded good. I felt a little sheepish for how long it had been since I'd been to a little family-run restaurant like this. Usually my meals out were for business. This was the kind of neighborhood favorite that reminded me of a place my grandparents had taken me as a kid. We hadn't eaten out often, so when we had, it had been a treat.

"What do you suggest?" I asked.

"I always get the ceviche."

I closed my menu. "Sounds good to me."

The server came back and took our orders. I asked for a glass of Salishan Cellars white wine and she brought it a few minutes later.

I leaned back in my chair and took a sip. My shoulders were knotted with tension, but for the first time today, I felt myself begin to relax.

"How are you holding up?" he asked.

"I'm all right. I think. Today was a shit show."

"It was. But Derek is the best at what he does."

I nodded and set my glass down. "In the long run, this will probably be fine. It's just hard to remember that when you're in the thick of a crisis."

Something crossed his expression so fast, I almost didn't see it. Was it sadness? It was hard to be sure.

"This is perfect, though," I continued. "I didn't realize how much I needed to get out of the office."

"A good meal always helps. Oh, this was supposed to be a surprise, but Nicholas texted me something earlier." He held up his phone. Two perfectly beautiful key lime tarts sitting on my kitchen counter.

"That's the best news I've had all day."

Our food came out remarkably fast—the ceviche was indeed delicious—and Jude and I fell into easy conversation. We didn't talk about anything serious. Not the media shitstorm. Not Noelle or Aldrich or corporate espionage or whether we were going to find something creepy on my bed again.

We talked about motorcycles and the merits of various makes and models. About the challenge of restoring old cars and the satisfying way a motor rumbled when it was in good condition. We talked about beaches and swimming. About animals we were afraid of—sharks for me, raccoons for him, although it wasn't so much fear as vague distrust.

By the time we'd finished most of our meal, I felt considerably better. My problems hadn't gone anywhere, but at least I'd set them aside for a little while.

A group of three men came in and took the table next to us. They were dressed casually in dark shirts and jeans. They leaned close to each other, speaking in low voices. It sounded like Russian.

I could see Jude's awareness of not just them, but everything in the room. He was constantly vigilant, his eyes taking in every detail. It wouldn't have surprised me to find out he'd mentally mapped out several different ways to get to an exit in case of an emergency.

"Finished?" Jude asked.

I put my napkin on the table. "Yes. That was amazing."

"Did you save room for key lime tart?"

"I always have room for key lime tart."

Jude leaned closer and lowered his voice. "Good. Because I was thinking about ways I could eat it off you."

I bit my lip at the rush of heat between my legs. My pleasant evening was about to get even better.

One of the men looked over at me and said something to his friend. The second man chuckled and replied, his eyes tracing me up and down. Although I couldn't understand what they were saying, I had a pretty good idea.

I was about to say that just because I didn't speak their language didn't mean they could be assholes, but Jude's face went stony. He slowly turned to face their table. When he spoke, his voice was dangerously low and he said something I couldn't understand.

In Russian.

All three men went pale. They cast each other worried glances. Jude said something else, then turned back toward me.

The first man rose from his seat and nodded at me. "So sorry. Have a nice evening."

The other two followed suit, rising from their table and mumbling apologies. They put their heads down and walked out the front door.

I gaped at Jude. "What was that?"

"They were being rude."

"You speak Russian?"

"Yes."

"What did you say to them?"

He shrugged. "I told them not to talk like that in front of a lady, especially when she's my lady."

"Is that all?"

"And I told them to apologize."

I narrowed my eyes at him. He must have said something else to intimidate them so easily. "Did you threaten them?"

He smirked, all cool casual confidence. "I wasn't serious."

"Is that why they left?"

Another shrug.

"How do you know Russian?"

"Mostly YouTube."

I stared at him for a long moment. "Who are you?"

"No one of consequence."

Shaking my head, I smiled. This man.

I wondered if I'd ever discover everything there was to know about the mysterious Jude Ellis. Probably not.

But for now, we had key lime tarts to get home to.

25

CAMERON

*D*erek and my PR team had come up with a comprehensive plan to counter the bad press. Our small board of directors made a public statement indicating their support, and several of our executives did the same. I released a brief statement noting the glaring inaccuracies and lack of fact-checking.

My PR team was still trying to reach Milton—he was on his yacht somewhere in the Caribbean—but I hoped a statement from the founder would help discredit Sydney's article. Noelle was conveniently out of the office, so I hadn't been able to confront her about her part in all this. For all I knew, she was behind everything.

Part two of the plan was very similar to what we'd done when I'd first hired Jude. I needed to be seen in public as if nothing was amiss. Business as usual.

Which meant tonight, I was attending the Southeast Aerospace Association dinner at the Intercontinental Hotel.

I'd gotten a saucy look from Valentina when I'd told her that as much as I loved the long evening gown she'd chosen for me to wear tonight, I was going with something a little less predictable. A pale peach dress with silver mermaid-scale accents that was just long enough to be appropriate on my tall frame—and only just.

We'd agreed on a pair of glittery Louboutins. Their shimmer was understated, yet sexy. The whole outfit—along with Valentina's expert hair and makeup treatment—made me feel confident despite the media debacle.

Jude looked utterly charming in his tux. I didn't bother asking why he had a custom-tailored tux on hand. I had a feeling he wouldn't give me a straight answer if I did. So I simply enjoyed how delicious he looked and hoped we'd be able to manage an early exit. As good as his clothes looked, I wanted to slowly strip him out of them.

The dinner was uneventful. Good food. Industry chat with other aerospace executives. No one mentioned my bad press. Most of the attendees were either high-level executives—many of whom had faced something similar in their careers—or engineers who either didn't pay attention or didn't care about that sort of gossip.

Three attendees, however, were not industry people. They were journalists.

And they were here for me. I could tell by the way they watched me.

I'd noticed them just after the keynote speech. I stood with Jude near the bar, feeling like a gazelle being circled by a pack of hyenas. None of them had come close yet, but I knew as soon as one did, the rest would dart in to attack.

"How did they get in here?" I asked. It was mostly a rhetorical question. But typically these regional industry events didn't draw much in the way of mainstream media. Representatives from *Aviation Week* or *Aerospace Manufacturing Magazine*, perhaps. But those publications were interested in industry news, not in stirring up fabricated CEO scandals.

Those three weren't industry reporters. And by the predatory looks on their faces, they were out for blood.

"I'd say they aren't here for you, but they're obviously here for you," he said.

"I should have worn sassier shoes."

"We can go," Jude said.

I took a casual sip of my champagne, pretending I hadn't noticed them. "They'll follow us out."

"I'll have Joe meet us out back."

"Yeah, but they'll still follow us. And I really don't want to talk to them tonight."

"They won't follow."

"Why?"

He took my drink and set it on the bar, then grabbed my hand. "Because we're going to lose them."

How he could appear so casual and still hurry us toward the hotel ballroom entrance, I had no idea. He was slick like ice, people's gazes sliding right over him. He led me toward the lobby and sure enough, the three reporters followed.

"See?" I whispered.

"Just don't trip."

"I wear heels almost every day, I won't trip."

He squeezed my hand and we took a sharp turn down an adjacent hallway.

"Excuse me, Ms. Whitbury?"

"You can't hear them," Jude whispered.

I kept walking, eyes straight ahead.

"Ms. Whitbury, is it true you essentially staged a hostile takeover of Spencer Aeronautics?" she asked, raising her voice.

"She's getting closer," I hissed. "And where are the others?"

"Trust me," he said.

The hallway came to a T up ahead. Jude turned us left, but one of the other journalists was closing in from that direction.

"Shit," he muttered.

We spun around and quick-walked in the other direction, passing a bank of elevators. Without warning, he pushed open the door to a stairwell.

Thankful for every leg day I'd endured with Inda, I charged up the stairs with Jude's huge hand still engulfing mine. He pushed open the door to the second floor, took one quick look up and down the hallway, and chose a direction.

The hall was lined with room doors and for a second I wondered if he knew how to hack an electronic lock. My heart raced—both from the trip up the stairs and the odd excitement of fleeing—and I almost laughed out loud. At least no one was trying to run over me. They just wanted to ask awkward questions and possibly take anything I said out of context. Running from them was so silly, and yet Jude hadn't hesitated to get me out of there.

My heart went from racing to fluttering.

I was afraid to look back. One of the reporters had to be about to burst onto the second floor. The elevator dinged behind us. Had one of them taken it? And where had the third gone?

"In here," Jude said, pulling open a door.

He went first and, in the same movement, wrapped his arm around my waist and hauled me in with him. The sliver of light from the hallway disappeared as he silently shut the door, shrouding us in darkness.

Jude stood so close behind me that my body pressed against him. I blinked a few times, trying to adjust to the darkness.

"Where—"

"Shh."

He kept his arm around me, and I wondered why he wasn't moving us away from the door. Dim shapes came into focus. Shelves. Cleaning supplies. I glanced down and made out what was probably a bucket near my feet.

We were in a supply closet.

I almost started laughing again. I could just see the headlines.

BILLIONAIRE CEO CAMERON WHITBURY attempts to escape press by hiding in mop closet.

JUDE LOOSENED his hold on me and slid his arm so his hand rested on my hip. That subtle movement made me keenly aware of his muscular body behind me. My back against his chest. The soft sound of his breath near my ear. And was that his...

Oh god, yes. Yes, it most certainly was.

I moved just enough to press against his hard-on. "Is that a gun in your pocket, or are you just happy to—"

He clapped a hand over my mouth.

"Shh," he whispered next to my ear. It wasn't an urgent plea to be quiet. It was a soft command, delivered with a slight thrust of his hips.

He was about to melt my La Perla thong right off me.

The hallway outside was silent. No footsteps. Nothing.

With his hand still covering my mouth, he pressed his

lips to my neck. My back arched and I rubbed against his erection. His low growl was almost silent—just enough to send the vibration down my spine.

His hand slid from my hip down to the hem of my dress and he pulled it up. He traced across the front of my thigh. My eyes fluttered as his fingers brushed my thong. Damn that stupid scrap of fabric.

My clit throbbed with sudden need. I didn't care where we were, his soft teasing strokes made me whimper against his hand.

"Shh," he whispered again. "You have to stay quiet. They'll hear us."

I'd never been one for sex in odd places. But Jude slipping his fingers into my panties and fingering my swollen clit in a hotel closet while we hid from reporters set me on fucking fire.

I felt free. Wanted. And god, it felt good.

Shifting my feet, I widened my stance, inviting him to continue. He didn't take his hand off my mouth, and I didn't want him to. He was in control of my body, playing me like an instrument. His fingers traced my seam, gently dipping inside. I arched harder against his cock, rubbing my ass against him.

The reporters had probably abandoned the chase. But neither of us made any move to leave. Or stop what we were doing.

His fingers worked magic between my legs. Unabashedly, I rocked my hips to ride his hand. His fingers slid in deeper and I tried not to moan.

He thrust his hips against my ass, pushing that thick erection against me. He was proportionate, thank you very much, and right now, I wanted that glorious cock deep inside me.

I only pondered for a second. We didn't have a room in the hotel to run to. Home was too far. The car was too far. The closet was crazy and maybe even stupid, but fuck it, I wanted to get crazy and stupid with Jude.

I wanted to let go again. It felt so good to let go.

Reaching behind me, I gripped his cock through his pants. He grunted softly and loosened his hand on my mouth.

"Here?" he whispered.

"Can you make it work?" I whispered back.

"Are you kidding?" He tightened his hand over my mouth again and drew my head back, baring my neck. "You want to get fucked in this closet, I'll fuck the shit out of you right here."

Oh my god yes please.

"No condom," he whispered and loosened his hand so I could talk again.

"Baby, I'm as clean as a fucking virgin."

"Fuck, Cameron," he growled. "Put your hands on the door frame."

I happily complied, leaning forward to brace myself, and spread my legs wider. He pushed my dress up over my backside, grabbed my thong, and tore it in two with his bare hands.

Holy shit. I was so turned on I thought I might die.

The sound of his zipper and the shift of fabric as he pulled out his cock in the dark was insanely erotic. He ran his fingers up and down my slit, then I felt the head of his cock do the same.

"Don't make a sound," he whispered, then grabbed my hips and slid inside.

His command was almost impossible to obey. His thick length stretched me open, giving me the intense pressure I desperately craved. He moved in and out a few times, as if testing our positioning. Then he started a slow but determined rhythm.

Hard thrust in. Slow slide out. I held onto the door frame, arching my back, and let him have me. He drove into me, his hands gripping me tight, fingers digging into my hips. Neither of us was going to last long. My inner walls already trembled with ready-to-explode tension and his cock seemed to thicken, pressing against my walls even as it dragged through my wetness.

His barely controlled cadence made the pressure between my legs intensify. He grunted softly behind me, a low noise in his throat with every thrust. I arched harder, pressing into him, trying to take him deeper.

I wanted more.

I wanted all of him.

Suddenly he stopped, his hands still gripping me tight, his thick cock buried to the hilt. I froze, scarcely daring to breathe. At first, I didn't hear a sound. Just the blood pounding in my ears as my heart raced. A second later, muffled voices. They grew louder, as did the sound of footsteps.

How had he heard that? Especially while he was...

The voices gradually quieted. Then the distant click of a door.

Jude slid out and thrust into me again—hard. It was all I could do to keep from crying out.

His rhythm was faster now. Aggressive. I held myself in place, feet planted, back arched. He reached around, still fucking me hard, and his fingers found my clit.

Oh holy fuck yes.

With his fingers rubbing my clit and his thick cock driving in and out of me, I was ready to come apart. Almost.

So.

Very.

Close.

"Come," he whispered.

My body exploded with obedience to his quietly uttered command. My pussy tightened around him, hugging his cock with rhythmic pulses. The orgasm swept through me, making my eyes roll back and my legs shake.

Just when I thought I couldn't take anymore—and I'd simply collapse onto the floor—he grabbed my hair with one hand, held my hip with the other, and started to come.

He barely pulled out between thrusts, keeping his throbbing cock buried deep. The pressure sent me tumbling over the edge again, my almost-finished orgasm ramping up to new heights. He yanked on my hair as he unloaded into me —I'd never let anyone do that before—and the thrill of his aggression made me come even harder.

Eventually, he stopped, letting his cock slide out. I straightened and he loosened his grip on my hair. His fingers massaged my scalp while he wrapped his other arm around my waist, and I sagged against him.

He gently kissed my neck. I closed my eyes, catching my breath. Jude had just fucked me senseless in a closet and I'd never felt so alive.

We fixed our clothes as best we could in the small, dark space. My panties were ruined, my inner thighs wet, but I was too euphoric to care. Jude listened at the door for a moment, then we slipped out into the empty hallway.

He winked at me while he tucked my ripped panties into the inside pocket of his jacket.

"It's obvious on me, isn't it?" I asked, checking my dress to make sure it was all where it was supposed to be.

One corner of his mouth hooked in a grin. He ran his

fingers through my hair and smoothed down the back. "Little bit."

There wasn't much I could do about it here. He placed a soft kiss on my lips, then took my hand and led me back to the stairwell. And despite everything else, I couldn't remember the last time I'd felt this good.

26

JUDE

The sheets stirred, sliding across my chest. I was awake in an instant, but it was just Cameron turning over in her sleep. The sky outside was still dark and I could just make out the curve of her body. Her soft hair falling across the pillow.

I ran my hand down her hip and over her fantastic ass. She stirred, making a sweet sound in her throat. The alarm would go off soon, but I hooked my arm around her waist and hauled her closer. Felt her warm body relax against me, her ass nuzzling against my groin.

That was really waking me up.

Life had taken some unexpected turns since the day Derek had asked me to do a favor for Emily's friend. I'd been set on retiring. Never taking another security job. But thank fuck he'd talked me into it.

I was going to get to the bottom of everything—it was my job and failure wasn't an option—but an unsettling thought lingered in the background. What came next?

What would I do when Cameron didn't need me here twenty-four/seven? Would I go back to my place? Live alone again? See her in her off hours... if she still wanted to date me when I wasn't shoved in her face all the time?

I'd lived alone for a long time. I was used to being on my own. My parents lived in Minnesota and once every couple of years I went out there to visit. But we'd never been a close family and they had their own life. I hadn't been a big part of it since I'd left home at eighteen. Five years ago, I'd walked away from the CIA. Felt like I had to cut ties in order to move on.

And what did I have now? A couple of friends. A loft I'd never meant to keep. A second career I'd never meant to start. A life I couldn't seem to figure out.

Until Cameron.

I breathed in the scent of her hair. Felt her curl up against me. I'd been searching for something since moving to Miami. Purpose. Direction. A new focus for my life. I hadn't expected to find it in the form of a tall redhead with a sharp wit and a weakness for sexy shoes and key lime desserts.

But somehow, I had.

The alarm buzzed on the bedside table and Cameron stretched her long limbs. I rested my hand against her stomach while she took a deep breath. She glanced over her shoulder at me, her eyelashes fluttering.

"Morning."

I kissed the tip of her nose. "Morning."

This was good. It felt right. And a twinge of fear took root in the pit of my stomach. The fear of losing her.

That was decidedly uncomfortable. There weren't many things that scared me. I was cool under pressure—an essential skill in my former line of work—but this wasn't the kind of fear that made people hesitant to cross a bridge or swim in the ocean or walk into a meeting surrounded by armed men liable to shoot first and not ask questions in a foreign country where you didn't have diplomatic immunity.

That last one was probably just me.

But this fear was different. Deeper.

"I guess we should get moving," she said, her voice still sleepy.

"Yeah."

Pushing that little knot of fear aside, I reluctantly let her go so we could get ready for the day. She met Inda for an early workout. I did some cardio and enjoyed the view—Cameron, not the sparkling waters of the bay. We showered, dressed, grabbed a quick breakfast, and headed to her office.

I drove her Tesla. The seat went back just far enough to accommodate my height. It was early enough that there wasn't a lot of traffic, and an overnight rainstorm had left everything looking fresh.

Cameron was already working, flipping through emails on her phone. Her hair was up and her beige suit was tailored perfectly to her beautiful frame. She wore a pair of nude heels—subdued, but sleek and professional.

The back of my neck prickled, and I shifted my shoulders, rubbing my shirt collar against it.

"Something wrong?" she asked.

I checked the rear-view mirror. "Why?"

"You did the neck thing."

"Neck thing?"

"Yeah. You move your shoulders and kind of stretch your neck a little. It usually means you're concerned about something."

My eyes kept darting to the mirrors. Something felt off. "I guess you're figuring me out."

She smiled. "I guess so."

An SUV followed a few car lengths behind us. It had

been there almost since we'd left Bluewater. Maybe that's what was bothering me.

"It's probably nothing, but a car back there looks like it might be following us."

"What makes you think so?"

"Because if I was following someone, I'd do exactly what they're doing."

There was one way to find out.

I changed lanes and took the next exit, my eyes flicking to the mirrors to see if the SUV would take the same route.

They did.

Keeping an eye on the SUV, I changed lanes again and took a series of right turns, effectively driving us in a circle. The SUV did the same.

We were definitely being followed.

"Are they still back there?" Cameron asked.

I nodded, my mind shifting to evasion tactics. Instead of speeding or darting around other cars—standing out made it harder to lose a tail—I kept with the flow of traffic and looked for potential visual barriers.

Cameron stayed silent while I took a winding route through the city. The SUV didn't approach or make any aggressive moves. Just followed a short distance behind.

"Hold on."

I took a hard right onto an empty street and accelerated. Cameron braced herself against the door as I whipped around another corner. The SUV didn't make the turn.

But then I realized it wasn't the only car.

A small dark sedan was right behind the SUV, and it took the corner easily.

Fuck. These guys were good. Scary good. That sedan had been tucked behind the SUV, out of my sight.

I needed to lose these guys.

Cameron's phone rang but she declined the call. I headed for the freeway. The SUV was nowhere to be seen, but the sedan followed up the ramp. I took advantage of her car's quick acceleration and darted through the slower moving traffic.

The sedan kept pace. I moved to the left lane and watched the cars ahead of me, mentally mapping my next move. Just before an exit, the opportunity came. A gap in the traffic. I cut across the lanes and flew down the off-ramp.

Without hesitating to see if the sedan would make the exit, I took a sharp left, then went around a white delivery truck. Using the truck as cover, I drove a few more blocks before making another turn.

No sign of the sedan. Or the SUV.

"They're gone," I said when I was sure.

Cameron took a deep breath and laid her hand on her chest. "My heart's beating so hard. What was that?"

"They were tailing you. Two of them. I didn't see the second one at first."

"Why?"

"I don't know." I kept driving, taking a roundabout route to Cameron's office. "Tracking your routine, maybe. Looking for an opportunity to make you pull over or force you off the road. Or just keeping eyes on you. It's hard to say."

"God, that was scarier than the hit and run."

I reached over and took her hand. "It's okay. I've got you."

She squeezed back. "I know you do."

I checked the mirrors again. Something still felt off, like the wind had shifted. The air buzzed with a heightened sense of danger.

Those had been professionals.

"You don't happen to have secret dealings with a mafia group that you've been keeping from me, do you?"

She laughed softly. "No. Definitely nothing like that."

I cracked a smile.

Her phone rang again. "Hi, Brandy, sorry, we were —what?"

The alarm in her voice sent another hit of adrenaline running through my veins.

"Oh my god," she said, her eyes darting to me. "Someone broke into my office. We'll be there soon. Be careful."

Oh shit.

"What did she say?"

"Someone was in my office. The door was closed so she didn't realize it right away, but she went in and it's trashed."

"Well, that escalated quickly," I said, making another turn toward her office building.

"I can't believe this is happening."

I took her hand again and squeezed. "It's going to be okay, Cameron. I swear."

She nodded, but her eyes shone with fear.

27

CAMERON

*M*y office was a disaster. Papers strewn everywhere. Monitor on the floor, the screen cracked. Drawers emptied of their contents. My favorite *lady boss* coffee mug smashed.

IT had already taken my PC to examine it for signs of tampering. They'd locked down the network and sent a team to check all the computers on this floor.

Two police officers had already come and gone. I'd sent out a company email to keep everyone informed and sent most of the employees on this floor home early.

No one had seen anything. The intruders had tampered with the security cameras. Gotten in and out sometime overnight. Brandy had found the mess when she'd opened my office door, and called me while Jude and I were being followed.

It was early afternoon, and I'd already been tailed on the way to work and found my office trashed. But apparently that was my life now.

"This is fucked up," I said, staring at the mess.

Jude picked through the debris, carefully inspecting

everything. He'd already gone through the whole room with some kind of handheld scanner he'd produced from his backpack. "Fucked up, indeed."

"What are you looking for?"

"Trying to find the reason they did this."

"The police said they were probably looking for something."

He put his hand inside a file cabinet drawer and felt around. "That's one possibility."

"What's the possibility you're looking for?"

"I'll tell you when I find it."

I glanced at Brandy. She stood leaning against her desk, her arms crossed.

"You should go home."

"I'm fine. I can stay."

"Really. The only thing I need you to do is touch base with Everly to see how things are going in Seattle. You can do that from home."

"But you have a meeting with Derek Price and the PR team, not to mention—"

"Brandy. Do I have to fire you?"

She tilted her head and gave me a wry look.

"You're fired until morning," I said. "Go home. Hug your son. Make out with your husband."

"You know, one of these days you're going to fire me for real and I won't know the difference," she said with a grin.

"Not going to happen." I narrowed my eyes. "Unless you're really the mastermind behind everything and you're out to destroy me."

"You see right through me, Whitbury." She grabbed her purse. "I'll touch base with you tonight or first thing in the morning."

"Thanks, Brandy."

She gathered the rest of her things and left.

I leaned against the doorway to my office, my arms crossed. Jude was still searching.

He pulled his hand out of one of my desk drawers and put his finger to his lips, then came out to his desk. He stretched out his hand, revealing a tiny device sitting in his palm. It was smaller than a dime with a one-inch wire sticking out.

He turned the device over and popped off the backing, then took out the disc-shaped three-volt battery.

"This is what I was looking for," he said, picking up the device between his thumb and forefinger.

"Is that a bug?"

"Yep." He eyed it carefully, turning it so he could see both sides.

"And you took the battery off so they can't hear us now."

"Exactly. Unless there are more, but I've checked everywhere. I didn't find any camera lenses, either, but we'll want to get a team in here to search the floor. I know a guy who can handle that kind of sweep and get it done fast."

"Good, let's schedule it."

Jude narrowed his eyes, still inspecting the bug.

"What?" I asked.

"This is sophisticated. It fooled my radiofrequency detector."

"Should I even ask why you carry a radiofrequency detector with you?"

He put the bug down. "Old habit."

A voice behind me nearly made me jump. "Cameron, what's going on in here?"

I closed my eyes for a second. Noelle Olson. My day just kept getting better and better.

"Someone broke into my office," I said, turning to face her. "Police have been here. We don't know who did it yet."

"This is getting out of control," she said. Her hair was in that bun she always wore, her pantsuit well-tailored and practical.

"I couldn't agree more. Just when I thought my biggest issue was predatory journalism."

She pinched her lips together in a thin line. "That reporter took my comments completely out of context."

"I'm sure she did." I was inches away from telling Noelle exactly what I thought of her. But Jude put a calming hand on my shoulder, and I bit back my rant. "We're taking every precaution to ensure the office is safe. If you'd like to speak with the head of security or the police who are investigating, you're more than welcome."

Her eyes flicked up and down, her judgmental gaze scathing. "I'll be working from home."

I nodded once and she walked down the hall to her office.

"All I need now is for Bobby the douchebag to show up and my day will be complete," I said, shaking my head. "I'm surprised he's not blowing up my phone with texts already."

"Why?"

"I don't know, it seems like every time I'm dealing with one of these incidents, Bobby either starts texting me or shows up. It's like the universe keeps trying to add insult to injury when I've already had one hell of a day."

"If he shows up, just let me deal with him."

"That would be very entertaining to watch." I tucked a loose tendril of hair behind my ear and lowered my voice. "If Noelle is trying to get me fired, it could explain the bug. But who were those guys following us?"

"Whoever did this hired professionals."

A shiver of fear ran down my spine. "Maybe we should just get out of town. I have a plane. Two, in fact."

"It's an option I'm considering."

Even though I'd said it, I hated that idea. I didn't want whoever this was to have that kind of power over me. To make me leave my home and my company, even temporarily.

"Running is a last resort."

"Agreed," he said.

"What do we do now?"

He traced his fingers down the curve of my neck and laid his big hand on my shoulder. An intimate gesture here in my office, and one I appreciated. "We go back to Bluewater. Your physical space is easier for me to control there. And I have some calls to make."

I took a deep breath and nodded.

Vagillionaires

Daisy: *What's happening over there? I'm in Milan. Do I need to fly home?*

Emily: *Someone broke into Cameron's office. Trashed it. Planted a bug.*

Daisy: *WHAT THE FUCK*

Luna: *Cam, are you okay?*

Me: *I'm fine. Nothing a stiff drink and a good fuck won't cure.*

Daisy: *She's not wrong.*

Emily: *I'm at the lab, but I'll come over as soon as I can.*

Luna: *Let me know if you need anything.*

Me: *Thanks. I'll be fine. Just one more thing to handle.*

Emily: *Be careful.*

Daisy: *Kick their asses, lady boss.*

Me: *Love you bitches.*

28

JUDE

No sign of a tail on the way back to Bluewater, but that didn't make me feel better. Why had someone followed us this morning but not now? Had it been a message? A sign that they were watching? They couldn't have been following this morning simply to find out where she worked. Locating Spencer's headquarters was as simple as a quick Google search.

And just as importantly, who were they?

The tail this morning and the bug in her office gave me an important new piece of information. Like I'd told Cameron, these were professionals. They represented a new angle and new tactics. Which probably meant they'd been hired recently.

Find out who they were, and I could find out who'd hired them.

There weren't an unlimited number of options when it came to hiring this kind of team. Fortunately, I was acquainted with several of them. Unfortunately, I'd been at odds with most of them at some point in the last five years. But just because they didn't like me didn't mean they didn't respect—and maybe even fear—me. I could work with fear and respect.

When we got to Cameron's house I did a sweep looking for camera lenses, bugs, and any evidence of tampering—particularly in her office and bedroom. Checked for errant radio and wifi signals. I'd need to get my guy in here for a more thorough search, but so far, her house seemed clean.

Derek arrived, dressed in a tailored suit, no tie. Cameron was busy in her office, so I let him in the front.

"Some excitement today, I take it?" he asked, strolling casually into the foyer.

"You could say that."

He paused and narrowed his eyes. "You sound... concerned."

"I shook a tail this morning. Two of them, actually. They were good. And Cameron's office was trashed. I think it was mostly for show, and to hide the fact that they planted a bug." I took the bug out of my pocket and dropped it into his outstretched palm.

He held it up, pinched between his thumb and forefinger. "Emily told me. This wasn't made by some kid watching a YouTube video, was it?"

"Nope." I took it back and slipped it into my pocket.

"Anyone you know?"

"Might be. This isn't CIA issue. Or it wasn't five years ago. But it could still be an ex-spook gone private. And there are a few groups who could have access to this kind of tech. The Cubans. The Russians. Italians. There's no shortage of organized crime down here."

"But what would the mob want with Cameron?"

"I don't think they want her at all. Not directly. I think someone hired a team, though, and one of the ways to find that kind of talent is to go to one of the families."

"They'd need a big set of brass balls for that. Not to mention a hefty bank account."

"Which doesn't really narrow it down," I said. "Anyone with a reason to go after Cameron has the funds to pull this off."

"True." He checked his watch. "I need to get to my meeting with the lovely Ms. Whitbury. Maybe a little reputation-fixing will take her mind off everything else."

I shook my head. This was such a clusterfuck. "Please tell me there's not more bad news on your end."

"Nothing new yet, but we're planning for the worst when it gets out that someone broke in to Spencer headquarters and ransacked the CEO's office."

"Thanks for helping her with this," I said.

"Of course," Derek said. "Just doing my job."

"Aren't we all."

Derek disappeared inside for his meeting with Cameron, so I went out front to make a few phone calls.

I knew a guy over in Little Havana who always had his ear to the ground. If someone had been asking around for a team who could break into a highly secured building and plant a bug, he might know about it.

Unfortunately, he didn't.

I made a few more calls. Some friendlier than others. But they either didn't know, or weren't going to tell me without additional motivation. There was only so much I could do over the phone.

What I needed was access to both Aldrich and Noelle's phone records. From there I could trace if either of them had been in contact with anyone connected to one of the crime syndicates. But I couldn't do that legally. I had a guy who might be able to swing it for me, but it would probably take him a couple of days.

I swiped through my contacts to find his number, but Emily pulled up in her golf cart.

"I just got back from the lab," she said, jumping down. She was dressed in a lavender blouse and slacks. "Is Cam okay?"

"She's handling everything like a badass." I slipped my phone in my pocket. "Derek's meeting with her now."

"Good. I swear to god, I hope you find the asshole who's doing this to her so we can crush them."

"We will." My voice was flat, but she had no idea how much rage simmered inside. Crushing them was only the beginning of what I wanted to do to whoever was behind this.

"Was there really a bug planted in her office?"

"Yeah, a sophisticated one."

She folded her arms across her chest. "Corporate espionage?"

"Could be. Her IT people are looking for breaches, anything that might indicate stolen information. But I don't know. My gut tells me this is personal."

"Cam said her COO is a suspect. It makes sense. Or Aldrich?"

I nodded.

"Before the sex tape thing, I never would have thought Aldrich would do something like this. I didn't think he was good for Cam, and I was glad when she left him, but I didn't think he was the type to go psycho ex-boyfriend. But now?" She shrugged.

My brow furrowed. Had she just said *sex tape*? Had I heard that correctly? "You never would have thought Aldrich would do this before what?"

"Before the sex tape," she said.

I raised my eyebrows.

"Oh my god, Cam didn't tell you?"

I shook my head slowly.

"Oh no. I assumed you knew."

My heart beat too fast and my eye twitched. "What sex tape?"

"Maybe Cam should—"

"Emily. Please."

She took a breath. "Aldrich had a video of them. He assured her he'd deleted it, but she found out from a mutual friend that he'd shared it with some of his buddies."

"When? How long has she known?"

"It was around the time that guy tried to attack her in the parking garage."

I ground my teeth together and glanced away. Why the fuck hadn't she told me?

"Look, Jude, I know her. Doing something like that is very out of character for her. She really regretted it."

I didn't say anything. Just nodded. I was too busy trying to process this new piece of information. See where it fit. How it changed things.

But mostly I was fucking furious that she hadn't told me.

"I'm sorry, I didn't mean to make things worse," she said. "I just figured—"

"Not your fault," I said. "She should have told me."

Emily nodded, then walked up the porch stairs and went inside.

I took a few deep breaths to get my shit under control. I couldn't afford to be compromised right now. Had to stay focused. Stay sharp.

Although I didn't like the idea that a video of Cameron —my fucking Cameron—having sex with another man existed, that wasn't what had my guts twisted in a knot. It wasn't even that it cast further suspicion on her ex, nor that it introduced the question of why he'd choose to keep it quiet if his intent was to hurt her.

What really got me was wondering why. Why hadn't she trusted me enough to tell me?

I still had a job to do, and I was going to see it through. But I was also going to find out why the hell she'd kept this from me—and what else she was hiding.

29

CAMERON

*D*erek and I finished up our call with my PR team. We had a plan of action for handling any negative spin as a result of the break-in at headquarters. We were taking a proactive approach, releasing a statement in an attempt to get ahead of things.

But at this point, bad press wasn't my biggest worry. Not by a long shot.

This morning's events had left me shaken. But more than that, I was frustrated. Stressed. And angry.

I was pissed at whoever was doing this to me. Pissed at the people they'd hired. Pissed that I couldn't be in my office, working on forecasts and planning for next year. I wanted to get back to normal.

I wanted my fucking life back.

Emily was in the kitchen waiting for Derek when we came out of my office. She pointed to her phone and mouthed *we'll talk later* before heading for the front. I grabbed my phone and checked my messages.

Emily: *I didn't realize Jude didn't know about the sex tape. I'm so sorry.*

A sickening sense of dread poured through my stomach. Oh god. He knew.

It had been stupid of me to hope he'd never have to know, but damn it, I'd held onto that hope like a little kid clinging to belief in Santa Claus. It felt like Jude finding out the video existed would be as bad as him actually seeing it. And I'd been desperate to avoid that.

Fuck.

I found him on the back terrace. He leaned forward against the railing, facing the water. The blue waves of the bay sparkled in the sunlight and the marine breeze had cut the humidity. Under any other circumstances, it would have been a gloriously beautiful afternoon.

Any hope I'd had that he wasn't angry with me burned away to ash as I took in his posture. I already knew him so well. The man I'd thought was a brick-wall—so adept at hiding his emotions—communicated volumes with every little movement and gesture. With the way he stood with one foot crossed over the other—seemingly casual but ready to whip around in an instant. With the way he leaned his forearms on the railing, his head lowered. I could see that he was angry in the way his shoulders bunched, his thick muscle knotting.

"Jude, I know I should have told you about Aldrich, but—"

"But?" he asked, cutting me off. He turned to face me. "Yes, you should have. Full stop."

"You're not going to give me a chance to explain myself?"

"No, I am going to give you the chance to explain yourself," he said, his voice ice cold. "But first, I'm going to explain something to you. You hired me to do a job. And in order to do my job, I need all the relevant information. Without that, things get missed. People get hurt. Now I need you to listen to me very carefully, Cameron. What else haven't you told me?"

"Nothing."

His expression didn't change. He was back to stone-cold bodyguard. Worse than stone-cold bodyguard. His eyes were like razors digging into my soul.

"Don't lie to me."

"I'm not lying."

"I asked you repeatedly if there was anything else I needed to be aware of. You're a smart woman. You can't tell me you didn't realize the fact that your ex has an unauthorized video of the two of you having sex is something I should know."

I clenched my teeth, my defenses going up at the way he'd phrased that. Not *sex tape*. He'd specifically said *a video of the two of you having sex*. Like he needed to emphasize what it was. What I'd done.

"What good would it have done if I had? Given you one more checkmark on the list of reasons my ex is a prick? We already knew that."

"What else are you hiding?"

"I told you, I'm not hiding anything."

"Why didn't you tell me about your workshop?" he asked.

"What about it?" I asked, drawing my eyebrows together. "And how is that even relevant?"

He crossed his arms. "Nicholas had to warn me about the blender."

"There's nothing wrong with the blender. It works great."

"You should probably need a license to operate it."

"Are you trying to be funny right now?" I asked. "Because I don't know what this has to do with anything."

"I'm just realizing how much I don't know about you."

"What are you talking about? You know plenty about me."

He raised his eyebrows. "Do I? I know your work history. I know things that anyone could discover if they did some research. Other than that, all I know are things you accidentally let slip in a moment of weakness, or things you had to tell me because I asked direct questions. Even then you can be evasive."

"*I'm* evasive?" I could feel my cheeks flushing and it had nothing to do with the sun. He couldn't be serious. "That's rich, coming from you."

"That's different."

"Why?"

"Because I'm not the one in danger," he said. "And because there are some things I can't tell you."

I put my hands on my hips. "That's very convenient, don't you think? I know you speak Russian and own a six-thousand-dollar custom tailored tux, but I have no idea how or why."

"It cost four."

"That's a good deal, it's beautiful. And also beside the point. I think your number one skill is question evasion."

"I told you, I can't always answer questions."

"Of course—murky past. Top secret. Things you can't reveal to anyone or you'd have to kill them."

"Look, Cameron, you're my client. And as my client, I thought we had an understanding."

I knew he was right. I was his client, and I should have told him. But I was at the tail end of a day that had included scary people following me, a trashed office, a high-tech spy gadget, and the continuation of a PR fiasco. And he'd just poked at one of my deepest private insecurities.

Other than my three friends, the only people around me were employees. I was alone.

"Right, your client."

"Yes."

"And that's why you're here. To do a job."

His eyes narrowed slightly. He probably sensed danger. And I could have stopped there, but instead, I snapped.

"You didn't even want this job. You're supposed to be retired, not shadowing a bitchy CEO in and out of meetings all day."

"Cameron—"

"And because some psycho broke in to my house, suddenly we're sleeping together. I'm in the middle of a PR nightmare, my office is trashed, and someone's trying to either get rid of me or hurt me, or both. And here we are, playing house, watching Food Network in my bedroom and fucking in a hotel closet. We still don't know who's behind all this shit, and now the whole thing is fucking complicated."

"Well, maybe we should have kept it professional."

His words stung, but I refused to let it show. Fought back those traitorous tears threatening to form in the corners of my eyes. "Apparently so."

A flash of emotion crossed his face, but it was gone as quickly as it had come. "I still have a job to do."

"Fine. Do your job. I'll sit here on house arrest so the big bad wolf doesn't eat me. And I'm not hiding anything from you, so you can drop the interrogation."

I turned and walked back inside. I didn't stomp. I didn't try to slam the door. I didn't clench my hands into fists or whip my hair around in a show of anger.

I stayed cool and collected. The consummate professional. If he wanted to be a brick wall bodyguard, I'd be the unflappable CEO.

It didn't matter that I was crumbling on the inside. I didn't have time to crumble. There were too many people who depended on me. Too many responsibilities for me to see to. I'd hold myself together, like I always did. Keep a tight grip on my feelings and face each problem as it came. As the saying went, I'd put my hair up, put on some gangsta rap—or maybe some eighties pop—and handle it.

I couldn't afford to be more vulnerable right now.

30

JUDE

*C*ameron walked away like she'd just left an R&D debriefing. I could imagine her strolling calmly to her office to catch up on emails. Maybe taking her laptop out to the upper balcony so she could sit in the shade of an umbrella and get some work done.

Like she didn't care.

Like I was just another employee.

An employee who'd been dismissed.

Fuck this.

For the first time in five years, I was quitting a job. I didn't need this shit. She was the one who'd kept information from me. And she had the audacity to get defensive? I was trying to keep her safe—keep someone from screwing up her life, or worse. So much worse.

And she wanted to argue about who was keeping secrets. Who was being guarded.

Yeah, I was fucking guarded. I kept secrets. A fuck ton of them. But that was the nature of my life. I didn't say the actual words very often because it tended to freak people out, but *I'd been a spy*. A spook. People thought they knew what that meant because of movies and spy dramas. But they didn't know. They had no fucking idea.

I went inside, ignoring the prickly sensation that crawled across my skin. Grabbed my motorcycle helmet from where I'd stashed it in a closet. Walked out the front door.

I still stopped and made sure it locked and the alarm set.

But that was it. I was done.

My bike was out front. I jammed my helmet down—why did it feel hard to put on?—gripped the handlebars, and swung my leg over. Turned it on and the engine roared to life.

The muscles in my back knotted and my chest ached. I felt hollow and raw. But I pushed it all aside and tore down her driveway.

Because fuck this.

I skidded to a stop at the first golf cart crossing. It was empty, but I didn't want to hit anyone on my way out. I paused, checking right, then left. Making sure it was clear.

There wasn't anyone there. No group of seniors in bright tracksuits doing their walking jazzercise routine, complete with a peppy trainer carrying a boombox on his shoulder. No Mrs. Montecito swerving in her golf cart after too many margaritas down at Bluewater's beach bar.

I accelerated again, driving by the canal, but slowed, wondering if anyone had fed Steve recently. With all the chaos, Cameron might have missed her turn.

Why the hell did I care if a three-legged alligator missed a meal?

I groaned and pulled to a stop. I shouldn't care. But if Dr. Whittaker let Schnitzel, her miniature dachshund, too close to the water, and Steve hadn't been properly fed...

I flipped to my calendar—I'd synced the Bluewater

events calendar to mine—but Cameron's turn wasn't for another few weeks. Steve probably had a belly full of rotisserie chicken. Schnitzel the wiener dog was safe.

My neck prickled uncomfortably, and I felt like I was going to crawl out of my skin. A delivery van drove by, reminding me that I was sitting in the middle of the road. What the fuck was wrong with me?

Cameron was what was wrong with me. I never should have taken this job.

I kept going, well aware of how slow I was driving. Took a right I didn't need to take. Cruised toward the marina, not the Bluewater gate. Because if I left, then what?

She'd be alone.

My stomach was doing uncomfortable things, and it wasn't like that time I'd gotten some questionable tacos down at the beach. The ache in my chest grew with every inch of ground my motorcycle ate up beneath me.

Maybe we should have kept it professional.

I'd said that. Thrown it in her face when she'd said things had gotten complicated. I still wanted to know why she hadn't trusted me enough to tell me about the sex tape. But saying that had been a dick move on my part. No wonder she'd walked away.

And that cool businesswoman thing she'd done? I knew that act. It was as fake as her friend Daisy's turquoise wig had been the other night. She hadn't walked away from me all calm and collected because she felt that way. She'd done it because she was trying to convince me—and maybe herself—that she was fine. But I knew her. I didn't need to know why she turned her blender into a jet engine or where she'd grown up or whether she had any family to know her.

She'd been hiding. Trying not to let me see that she was hurt.

Hell, I'd been doing the same thing during that entire stupid fight on the terrace.

Somehow I'd circled around and the Bluewater entrance was up ahead. I could keep going. Drive right on out of here. Abandon my mission. I could leave Cameron to her own devices. She could hire any private security team she wanted. It wasn't like she didn't have the money.

I stopped again, staring at the entrance gate. At the road beyond and where it led.

God, I was being an idiot. Of course I wasn't going to leave her. I couldn't. And it wasn't about the job. It wasn't because I knew she was in danger. There were other people who could protect her.

But there wasn't anyone else who was going to love her.

Not like I did. Because holy shit, I loved her like fucking crazy.

I turned my bike around and cruised back toward her house. She did owe me an apology, but this time I'd stop acting like a jackass and give her a chance to explain. And I'd apologize for what I'd said to her. I hadn't meant it.

And she'd had one hell of a day. I really should have cut her some slack.

One hell of a day. She'd said something like that back at the office earlier and now it tickled my brain like a feather. Something about Bobby. She'd said he always texted or showed up right after she was dealing with one of the incidents. Like the universe was adding insult to injury.

She was right.

I didn't know about the parking garage attack. I hadn't been there. But after the hit and run, he'd tried to call her. I remembered her ignoring his call when we were drinking bourbon in her kitchen.

He'd texted her the day after the break-in at her house.

Something about inviting her to a party on his stripper plane. And he'd shown up at her office right when the media shit storm had started. He'd claimed that was how he knew.

I drove up Cameron's driveway and stopped in front of her house. Both she and Brandy had dismissed Bobby as a suspect. They didn't think he had a motive. He had a trust fund that would enable him to keep living his best life without ever having to work.

But what if he didn't?

Cameron had sarcastically referred to his stripper plane as another brilliant business idea that had wasted a bunch of his trust fund. *Another*. That meant there'd been more than one. And she'd said it casually, like it was a regular occurrence.

Maybe Bobby didn't have an endless supply of money like Cameron thought. Maybe he'd spent too much on so-called businesses that were really just excuses for him to show off in front of his friends and Instagram followers.

And now Cameron was poised to buy a majority share in the company his father had founded. A company he might have always assumed he'd inherit. After all, it had his last name.

But if he'd discovered he wouldn't—that Cameron Whitbury was gradually buying out the Spencer family...

I yanked my helmet off and ran up the front porch. Jammed in the code to unlock the door. I needed to see the security footage from the night of the break-in here.

If Bobby was behind everything, he could have hired someone to break in to Cameron's house. But my instincts were screaming at me; it felt like my brain was on fire. I had a feeling it was him. That he'd want to do it himself, just to get into Cameron's private space.

Ignoring Nicholas, busy starting dinner in the kitchen, I went to my temporary desk in the breakfast nook.

Still standing, I powered on my laptop. Opened the video. The intruder walked up to the front door, head down, hood up. Dark clothing, down to the shoes. Unlike Bobby, no designer labels.

But even Bobby Spencer had to be smart enough to know Cameron had security cameras. And if he wore something recognizable, he'd get caught.

I clicked through the frames, pausing, looking for the right angle. There had to be a moment when I could see the intruder from head to toe.

Finally, I found it. I isolated a spot and zoomed in.

There it was. The embossed Fendi logo on the toe of his black leather sneakers. The same sneakers he'd been wearing when he'd come into the office after the break-in. The ones that had seemed subdued compared to the rest of his clothes.

That little fucker.

"Cameron," I shouted, saving the image. "Cameron, are you in your office?"

"She's not here," Nicholas said without looking up from the vegetables he was slicing.

I straightened, my back going stiff, a hit of adrenaline racing through my veins. "What?"

"I don't want to make it weird, but we heard you guys fighting. Inda went upstairs to talk to her and a couple minutes later, they left."

"Where the fuck did they go?"

"Just down to the village to get a drink. They're in Cameron's golf cart. They won't leave Bluewater."

"Fuck." I pulled my phone out of my pocket and checked Cameron's GPS. Her little dot was right on top of mine. That meant she was in the house. "No, she's here. Maybe they came back."

"Maybe," he said, still slicing.

I pocketed my phone and went to check the garage. I glanced in her office on my way, but it was empty. And regardless of where Nicholas had said she'd gone, my instincts were going crazy. Something was wrong.

"Cameron?"

Her Tesla was parked in its spot. But her golf cart was gone.

My heart thumped hard in my chest. She could have parked it outside. I ran around to check, racing down the porch steps, but the only thing in her driveway was my bike.

I darted back inside and pulled out my phone to call her. It rang once.

"Come on, Cameron."

Twice. I ran halfway up the curved staircase, willing her to answer. To be upstairs in the shower or out on her balcony.

Three times.

"Cameron, where the fuck are you?"

On the fourth ring I stopped, listening. Held my breath. A faint noise came from the second floor.

Her voicemail picked up and I bolted, taking the rest of the stairs two at a time. Rushed down the hallway to her master bedroom.

And found her phone sitting in a depression in the fluffy white comforter on her bed.

31

CAMERON

*M*y cool CEO act lasted all the way to the bottom of the stairs.

Then the stomping started.

The fist clenching.

And when I got to my bedroom, a good old-fashioned door slam.

I took my phone out of my pocket and tossed it on the bed, then paced to the window and back. I was considering doing something I almost never did—letting the tears that stung my eyes fall—when Inda knocked gently, opening my door enough to poke her head inside.

"Hey, you."

I swiped beneath my eyes in case any wetness had already leaked out. "Hi."

"Sorry to bother you, but I kind of heard everything. I came up to see if you're okay."

"Of course I'm okay," I said, but ruined my attempt at composure by sniffing hard.

"I know you're not," she said. "And it's okay if you're not."

I shook my head. "No, I'm not."

She came in and sat down on the edge of my bed. "Do you want to talk about it?"

"I don't know." I wandered toward the huge windows.

She was quiet for a long moment while I stared out at the water, a potent mix of emotions swirling through me.

"Come on," she said, standing. "Let's go."

"Where?"

"Down to the village to get a drink."

I glanced at her. "Tempting, but I'd have to bring the muscle. You know I can't go anywhere alone."

"We won't leave Bluewater," she said. "And you won't be alone. You'll have me."

Inda had served in the Israel Defense Forces before she'd met and married Nicholas. She was a legitimate badass.

"Okay, well, that means you're on bodyguard duty," I said. "But if we get in a high-speed chase with another golf cart, leave the driving to me."

"Sounds like a plan," she said with a smile.

I glanced down at my feet. I was still wearing the shoes I'd worn to work this morning. They were nice—a classy pair of nude Saint Laurent pumps.

But I was in a mood. I needed sassier shoes.

"Hang on, let me change my shoes."

I went into my walk-in closet and stepped out of my pumps. I scanned my collection for a second before finding the ones I wanted. Those red suede and crystal Jimmy Choos that I'd bought when I went shopping with Jude.

Hell yes.

I slipped them on my feet. Took a quick look in the full-length mirror. They complemented my beige tailored suit quite well. A pop of red sparkle on the sleek CEO.

A sassy pair of shoes didn't do anything to help my situation, but they made me feel a bit better. And after the day I'd had, I'd take the tiniest improvement.

Inda said a quick goodbye to Nicholas, and we left out the garage. The lighted tassels on my golf cart glowed happily as I drove us toward the nearest path that led to the village.

Something in my driveway caught my attention—or rather a lack of something. I stopped and twisted in my seat to look behind me.

"Was Jude's bike in the garage?"

"I don't know. It might have been. I wasn't looking for it, so I'm not sure."

It wasn't in front of my house, and I'd thought he'd left it there. I didn't remember seeing it in the garage, but maybe I just hadn't noticed it.

His things among mine had already become so commonplace, I didn't think about them anymore.

With a sigh, I kept going. We bumped along the path, meandering our way toward the village. The path arched over a wooden bridge to cross the canal and I stopped at the peak.

The dark water flowed below us. We were surrounded by lush landscaping and the breeze coming off the bay was cool and refreshing.

"I kept something from him," I said, breaking the silence. "You already heard us, but Aldrich—"

"Has a sex tape."

I rolled my eyes. "Yes. And I didn't tell Jude."

"That's why he was angry."

"He's right, I should have told him."

"Why didn't you?"

"I'm embarrassed," I admitted. "Not just because it's a video of me having sex. And yes, I've seen the stupid thing, he wanted me to watch it with him afterward. And yes, you can see my face."

"I wasn't going to ask for details."

I tucked my hair behind my ear. "Yeah, well... I'm embarrassed because it was bad judgment to let him record it in the first place. It makes me feel stupid. And I really, really hate feeling stupid."

"You're not stupid, Cameron. You're human. We all make mistakes."

"I know."

Inda shifted in her seat so she was partially facing me. "Can I speak candidly?"

"Of course."

"I don't think you were really fighting about whether or not you should have told him about the video."

"No?"

"That was part of it. But I think you're both struggling to trust each other. And wondering whether or not you're trusted."

"I trust him."

"Maybe you do, and he's just not certain of it," she said. "Or maybe you trust him in some ways, but not others. But I've known you for what, four years? I know that trust doesn't come easily to you."

"I've trusted Jude in some very serious ways," I said.

"Well, yes, you trust him as your bodyguard."

"Not just that. Inda, we had sex in a closet at the Intercontinental Hotel. That's some serious trust."

Inda raised her eyebrows. "Wow. That's bold."

"Exactly. I'd never take a risk like that with someone I didn't trust."

"True," she said, nodding. "But what about other risks?"

"Like what?"

"Jude said he doesn't know very much about you. Neither do I, to be honest. I know the things anyone could know. Or things I've picked up on over the last few years. But you don't share a lot of personal stories with others."

I stared out the front of the cart, not really seeing anything. She was hitting a bit too close to the truth.

"Listen, you don't act like you're better than other people because of your job or your money, and I admire that about you. You're easy to talk to. But when was the last time you shared something deeply personal with another person?"

"Does my vagina count? That's deeply personal."

She laughed. "Not something physical."

"I don't know. It's easier to talk about work. Or Bluewater."

She patted my leg. "It's just something to think about if you and Jude decide to get serious."

"Yeah. Thanks, Inda."

Gripping the steering wheel again, I accelerated down the slope of the bridge. She wasn't wrong. I had a hard time letting people get close to me. Probably because I knew how much it hurt to lose them.

Hazard of growing up an orphan.

Things had been happening so fast. I hadn't approached this relationship like I usually did. No lengthy period of dinner dates and appearing in public together at events and galas. No careful consideration as to lifestyle compatibility. No analysis of goals and schedules and logistics.

God, that made dating me sound like a nightmare.

With Jude, I'd given into my feelings. My desires. The things my body—and my heart—wanted without over-analyzing the potential consequences. I'd started to let him in—really let him see me—but stopped just short of taking the full risk.

We came out onto the road, the village up ahead, but I stopped. "I should go back and talk to him. I handled that so badly and he doesn't deserve to be my punching bag because I'm stressed."

"No, but I'm sure he'll forgive you."

Those tears threatened to well up again and a lump rose in my throat. Would he forgive me? God, I hoped so. Because suddenly all I could think about was how empty my life would be without him. About how much I needed him. I didn't want to need anybody—not like this— because that was a surefire way to get hurt, but damn it, I did.

I didn't just need him. I loved him.

Oh my god, I loved that big, gigantic, mysterious, infuriating, gentle, amazing man. I loved him so much, I almost couldn't breathe.

"Aw, Cameron," Inda said, and reached over to rub my shoulder.

An engine rumbled behind us. I was stopped in the middle of the street, no longer on the golf cart path—I needed to get out of the way. But my eyes were swimming with so many tears, my vision blurred.

Sniffing, I swiped my fingers beneath my eyes.

Inda let out a startled yell that was instantly muffled. The world went dark, and it wasn't tears blurring my vision. My breath was hot against the fabric suddenly covering my face. Thick arms grabbed me—thick arms that did not belong to Jude. They were hard and sinewy, pinning my arms down, dragging me out of the golf cart.

I tried to scream through the fabric covering my head, but a hand clamped over my mouth and nose. I couldn't breathe. Someone had my upper body and another set of arms quickly wrapped around my legs, carrying me like a rolled-up carpet. I thrashed and tried to kick, but they had me immobilized.

My heart raced and my lungs screamed for air. The hand still held my face in a tight grip, jamming the fabric into my mouth, covering my nose. I wiggled and writhed, but there were hands everywhere—was I being grabbed by a human octopus?—holding me down. Tying my legs. Binding my wrists.

Finally the hand covering my face eased and I sucked in a lungful of air. I couldn't see, but I was lying on a hard surface. I heard the distinct sound of a van door closing and suddenly I was moving. God, I hoped Inda was okay.

The strangest thing happened in my brain. The words *I've just been kidnapped* flitted through my mind, but instead of inducing panic—which would probably have been the sane response, although not very useful—I felt suddenly detached. Like this was happening to someone else and I was along for the ride. An observer, rather than a participant.

Because this couldn't be happening to me. I couldn't have just been snatched out of my golf cart on the streets of my very safe, gated, secure enclave. I couldn't be riding in the back of a van with a bag over my head, totally immobilized by both ropes and the hands of some very strong men.

But it was happening.

And as if this insane situation needed something else to make it even more terrifying, the hand on my mouth released just as something hard pressed against my forehead. I heard the very recognizable, very distinct sound of a gun being cocked.

My brain did another strange thing. Instead of focusing on the gun pointed at my head, it fixated on the fact that the raspy voices murmuring around me sounded Russian.

32

CAMERON

Fear can do surprising things to a person. Some people crack in the face of terrifying danger. They pass out, or scream, or shake and cower. Others fight back, adrenaline making them stronger, and sometimes reckless.

It made me calm.

The van stopped and the rolling metal sound told me they'd slid open the door. The pressure of the gun barrel against my forehead disappeared and hands and arms once again manhandled me. They hoisted me out—roughly—and carried me... somewhere.

One of my shoes fell off. It was utterly ridiculous how angry that made me, considering Inda and I had been kidnapped by men with guns. She hadn't made a sound, and I firmly told myself she was just being cooperative, like I was. It wasn't because they'd knocked her unconscious. Or worse.

Maybe that was why I was focusing on my now bare foot and the image of my beautiful red suede and crystal Jimmy Choo lost on the ground somewhere behind us. A defense mechanism to keep the eerie detached calmness I felt from breaking.

I had a feeling the other alternative was incoherent screaming, and there was a good chance that would get me killed. So I kept that shoe in my head, letting my mind come up with a loose plan for retracing my steps—or rather, the steps of the men carrying me—to get it back.

Logical? Not really. But it kept me from shaking with mortal terror, so I went with it.

The men spoke in low voices to each other and they were definitely speaking Russian. I heard a ding that sounded like an elevator, followed by a swish. We moved again, then the distinct sensation of rising in a straight line. Definitely an elevator.

I'd been picturing some kind of abandoned dockside warehouse. Maybe with empty crates or pools of dingy water on the floor. Probably a stench, like rotting fish. Or maybe just the reek of gunmetal and bad intentions.

An elevator made me wonder if I was going to be tied to a chair, and when they whipped off the bag that was currently blinding me, I'd find myself in a luxurious office. A man with a cigar and a glass of whiskey would tell me what this was all about while his henchmen stood in the background holding military-grade rifles.

My movie-esque fantasies were as ridiculous as my preoccupation with my missing shoe.

The elevator dinged, the doors opened, and once again I was moving. The man carrying my lower half adjusted his grip. At this point, I just hoped they didn't drop me.

At least one part of my elevator ride conjecture was correct. They tipped me, lowering my legs, and shoved me into a chair. Strong hands pressed against my shoulders, keeping me down, and there was that gun barrel again, hard against the side of my skull.

I didn't struggle while they retied me to the chair. I couldn't see, had no idea where I was or how many men surrounded me, and I had a probably-loaded gun pointed at my brain. I just wanted to survive the next few minutes and hoped someone would take the fucking bag off my head.

It was hard to breathe in here. And the panic that I was successfully avoiding with unrealistic theatrical imaginings was getting harder to ignore—pressing at the edges of my consciousness and making my heart race uncomfortably fast.

Finally, the bag was unceremoniously yanked off my head. I blinked a few times, the light glaringly bright. Was I in some kind of interrogation room with a light shining in my face to confuse me?

No, it was weirder than that. It was a chandelier.

I was in a large hotel suite—or a room that had once been a large hotel suite. The windows were covered with thick sheets of dusty canvas, the wallpaper peeling, and the carpet looked like an entire music festival of rock stars had done unspeakable things that no amount of industrial shampooing could ever clean. The furniture was gone, save the chairs Inda and I were tied to—thank god she was awake and looking around—and a folding table that sat in front of us.

Two men with guns stood nearby and I caught sight of at least two more disappearing through an open door. Maybe they were going to stand guard in the hallway outside.

I looked at Inda. She didn't appear to have any injuries, just messy hair and the misfortune of being tied to a chair. "Are you okay?"

"I think so." She shook her head a little. "I almost passed

out a couple of times. They wouldn't let me breathe. But I'm okay."

"Good."

I strained against the ropes, but they rubbed painfully over my skin. My ankles were tied to the chair, as were my arms. Another rope wound around my chest, over my upper arms. There was no way I was going to wiggle myself out of them. I was bound tight.

Another man walked in and it took my poor, on-the-verge-of-losing-it brain several seconds to process what I was seeing. Because out of all the unbelievable things that had just happened to me, this was the most outrageous.

There was no fucking way.

"Hey, Cami."

I stared at Bobby Spencer, dressed in a beige linen jacket over a shirt with a giant Gucci logo. He swiped off his sunglasses and tucked them into his jacket pocket.

"What the fuck?"

"They didn't hurt you, did they, babe? I told them to be gentle."

My gaze shifted to Inda, wondering if she was seeing what I was seeing—her wide eyes told me she was—then back to Bobby. "No, really. What the fuck?"

"I know, tying you to a chair is a little much, but it's kinda hot seeing you like that. And I had to make sure you wouldn't get away, so..." He shrugged and glanced at Inda. "Your friend is hot, too."

"What... where... what's going on? Where are we?"

Bobby looked around at the dilapidated room and took a few steps closer. "One of my little ventures. I bought this place, I don't know, eight years ago? It was a hot property back in the day, but it's a shithole now. I was going to turn it into the sickest nightclub in Miami with a luxury hotel upstairs. Brilliant, right? A place where the rich and famous can party their asses off and then take the party to their private suites. But the project kind of got halted because, I don't know, I got bored. Shit like this is a lot of work."

I gaped at him for a second, because why did he think I gave a crap about his business plan for what was apparently an abandoned hotel property? But then again, this was Bobby.

"Why did you kidnap me?"

"Technically, I didn't kidnap you. I hired them to do it." He gestured over his shoulder at the men standing guard.

"Why?"

"Why do you think?" he asked, like he couldn't fathom why I didn't automatically understand. "Because you had to make everything complicated by hiring the goddamn Hulk."

It was taking too long for my brain to catch up, but the implications were so unreal, it was no wonder I was staring at him like I'd been hit in the head and couldn't think straight.

Bobby Spencer. It had been him?

"Wait. You're the one who's been fucking with me?"

"I wasn't fucking with you, I—"

"The guy who attacked me in the parking garage," I said, cutting him off. "Was that you?"

He shook his head, once again pulling a *don't be an idiot, Cameron* face. "No. But you broke three bones in my buddy's foot with your shoe."

"Good," I said. "I wish I'd had the chance to puncture his balls, too."

"Cami," he said, his voice irritatingly soothing. "Come on, now. There's no need for that."

"Did you try to run me over on a sidewalk?"

"No, babe, I wasn't even there."

"So you didn't have anything to do with it?"

"Well, I arranged it, but I wasn't actually in the vehicle. That was another buddy of mine."

"What the fuck, Bobby. He could have killed someone."

He shrugged, like it didn't matter. "He smokes a lot of pot, his reflexes aren't great."

I turned to Inda. "Are you hearing this?"

She looked as baffled as I felt. "Yeah."

"Okay, since apparently this is really happening, did you send me those emails?"

"Yeah, I hired a guy. The going rate for a good hacker is high as fuck right now. You'd be surprised."

I ground my teeth together, trying to stay calm. "Who broke into my house and left a fish on my bed?"

He grinned. "That one was me. I'm pretty proud of that."

I was going to kill him. "Was that supposed to scare me, or just gross me out?"

His mouth turned up in a smirk. "You don't get it? Sleeping with the fishes. It's from *The Godfather*."

"Nobody puts a fish in anyone's bed in that movie. It's a horse head."

"Is it? Maybe I haven't seen it."

"Oh my god," I groaned. "How the fuck did you get in my house?"

"I paid one of your cleaners to give me the code. That cost me a shit ton too, but hey, you gotta do what you gotta do, right? Plus, I got a little souvenir."

"You what?

With a disgusting leer on his face, he pulled a black scrap of fabric partially out of his inside jacket pocket. "They were in the hamper, so they smell like you."

Calm, Cameron. Stay calm. You're tied to a chair and there are men with guns. I closed my eyes for a second and took a deep breath.

"Fine, Bobby. You got me. I'm tied to a chair in one of your bad investments and it kind of smells like pee in here."

He scrunched his nose.

"So tell me why," I continued. "Why did you do this?"

He pointed to a manila envelope on the table. A ballpoint pen sat on top. "To get you to sign that."

"I'm not signing a marriage license, no matter how many guns you point at me."

He grinned. "That'll come later, babe, don't worry. No, that's the paperwork to transfer your ownership of Spencer Aeronautics to me."

"What?"

"You keep asking questions, so maybe I'm not speaking clearly, or they stuffed something in your ears when they dragged your fine ass over here. You're going to sign the company over to me."

"Since when do you want Spencer?"

He rolled his eyes. "Since always. It has my fucking name on it. That company was always supposed to be mine."

"You don't know anything about it. You've never worked there. Why do you want to run Spencer?"

"I never said I wanted to run it. I want to own it. You can keep your job, I'm not trying to get rid of you."

"The more you talk, the less sense this makes."

"My father started that company, Cami. And I'm his one and only heir. So I'm sure you can imagine how hurt I was when I found out he's been selling his shares to you." He started to wander slowly in front of us, gesturing with a finger. "Not only is he selling his shares, the old man is about to give you a majority interest. And yes, I know what that means. It means you'll be in control. And I just can't let that happen."

"So you're throwing a tantrum because Daddy isn't giving you the company he spent his life building and to which you've contributed absolutely nothing."

"It was supposed to be part of my inheritance. It's bad enough that my old man is like a goddamn vampire who doesn't age. I don't know if the fucker will ever kick the bucket. But then I find out that by the time he does, the Spencers won't even own Spencer Aeronautics anymore. What kind of fucked up shit is that?"

It hadn't escaped my attention that he wasn't using the armed henchmen to further intimidate me. I was a little surprised he hadn't ordered them to put their guns in my face after my tantrum comment.

"Is your ego really that enormous? Because I'm surprised you can fit in any indoor space and still take it with you."

"This isn't about ego," he said. "It's about what's mine."

"You realize those two statements essentially negate each other."

His brow furrowed. "What?"

"Never mind. Bobby, you're the only child of a billionaire. You already have a trust fund that must be enormous and you're going to inherit your father's wealth someday. You don't need to own Spencer to live exactly the kind of life you've been living until you die of an untreated STD. Or from falling off your yacht when you're too drunk to swim and everyone partying with you is too high to notice."

He snorted. "Yeah, if only that were true."

I exchanged a confused glance with Inda. "Which part?"

"I'm not inheriting shit from my father. He's leaving all his money to some fucking charitable foundation. And my trust fund isn't going to last. The old man's being a dick and says he won't give me more money."

"You're thirty-six. How did you blow through your entire trust fund already?"

He shrugged. "Being an entrepreneur isn't cheap. Most businesses fail, that's just how it goes. I took some hard losses."

"Like when you bought a dilapidated hotel to refurbish and then abandoned the project because you got bored?"

"Yeah, exactly."

I decided not to mention that the failure rate for new businesses was one hundred percent if you didn't put in any actual work.

"Since we're apparently doing the thing where you spill your guts and tell me all your diabolical plans, will you explain something to me?" I asked.

"Yeah, but we need to hurry this up. The boss man is going to be here any minute to sign his part of the agreement."

"We're coming back to the part about a *boss man* in a second, but why did you have me attacked? Why try to hit me with a car? Why break in to my house? I don't understand how any of that was supposed to get me to sign the company over to you."

"It's not complicated, Cami," he said. "Me and some buddies came up with the plan. We figured if we scared you enough, it would be easy to convince you to back down and give me what I want."

Turning my head, I exchanged another look with Inda.

"That plan is terrible."

"No, it would have worked. But you had to fuck it up by hiring that goddamn bodyguard."

There wasn't any point in arguing with him over the

idiocy of his plan, although it didn't make any sense. I shifted in the chair, trying to find a way to ease the growing ache in my legs from the way I was sitting and the fact that I couldn't move.

"So you had me kidnapped. I suppose it was those guys who were following me this morning?" I nodded toward the armed henchman, who stood silently by a wall. "And they trashed my office and planted a bug?"

"A bug?" he asked. "I didn't have them plant a bug. But holy shit, Cami, these guys are so legit. They broke into Spencer headquarters, can you believe it? I told them how I got into your house and I thought they would have been more impressed, but whatever. These guys are fucking professionals. It's costing me a fortune, but it won't matter because I'm about to own a multi-billion-dollar corporation."

"No, you're not."

He chuckled. "Uh, yeah, I am."

"Even if I do sign that, which I won't, it'll be under duress. That won't be a valid contract."

"Whatever, I have amazing lawyers. That's part of what I bought by partnering with the Russians."

Boss man. Sign his part of the agreement. Partnering with the Russians. I felt the color drain from my face. This wasn't just Bobby the douchebag doing something crazy and stupid. He hadn't just hired a group of professional criminals to help him with his half-cocked plot to steal ownership of the company.

He was selling his soul to the Russian mob. And he had no idea what he'd gotten us into.

My brain chose that moment to remind me that Jude didn't know I was gone. And I'd left my phone in my bedroom.

He had no way of knowing where I was. If he even realized I was gone in time.

Panic was starting to win.

"Oh god, Bobby, what have you done?"

"Well, I have shit to do, and I really want to get out to Fort Lauderdale tonight," he said, ignoring me. "There's supposed to be this badass party. Everyone's going to be there." He walked to the table and pulled a stack of paperwork out of the envelope, then pushed it toward me. He picked up the pen and held it out.

"What am I supposed to do with that?" I asked. "I'm tied to a chair."

"Shit, I hadn't thought about how we were going to do this part." He glanced over his shoulder. "Hey, can you guys untie one of her arms or something?"

The henchmen shared a look—I briefly imagined them doing some sort of mental rock paper scissors—then one of them headed our direction.

My mind raced. What could I do with one arm free and the rest of me tied to a chair? Not much. Even if I did get in a good shot against the henchman while he untied me, the other one was armed, and there were more close by.

As if to remind me of that fact, four more armed men filed into the room. Bobby turned and plastered a douchey smile on his face while a man in an exquisitely tailored suit walked in.

The boss man.

I'd never seen him before, but I didn't need to know his name to know he was in charge. People in power often had a look about them. They moved a certain way, as if they had utter confidence that their every word would be heeded without question.

If this guy was the head of the Russian mafia in Miami, he was probably right.

He stopped, his eyes moving from the contract, to me, to his henchman, then to Bobby. "What's going on here?" His Russian accent was obvious, although he spoke English well. "Why the delay?"

"Sorry," Bobby said. "I've just been having a little chat with my Cami. She's ready to sign."

"No, I'm not."

"Cameron," Inda hissed.

"I'm not signing that."

The boss man—he hadn't offered his name, so I didn't know what to call him—stared at me, his face expressionless. He had slicked-back salt-and-pepper hair that was long enough to curl at the back of his neck. Thick beard, mostly gray. And blue, blue eyes, as icy as a glacier.

He was terrifying.

"Of course you're going to sign it," he said.

"How much is he paying you?" I asked. "Maybe we can come to an arrangement."

Was I really going to pay off the Russian mafia to get me out of this situation? Yes, I probably was. Depending on his terms.

The corner of his mouth twitched. "You're very beautiful, aren't you? Had things been different, I would have loved to do business with you directly."

"Why can't we? Nothing is final until the signatures are dry."

"Cami, just sign it," Bobby said, lowering his voice. "Then we can let you go."

The boss man didn't take his eyes off me. "We're not letting her go."

"What?" Bobby asked. "Yes, we are."

"No. That's not possible. She and her little friend are loose ends. I'm afraid the lovely Ms. Whitbury is going to suffer an unfortunate accident."

"You're going to kill her?" Bobby asked, his voice rising. "Hold on a second. You never said anything about killing her."

"It's not your concern," he said.

"Yes it is. I need her. She saved the company from going under. I need her to run it."

"We'll find a suitable replacement," the boss man said.

"That's why you're doing this, isn't it?" I asked, ignoring Bobby's reddening face. "It's not about what he's paying you. If he owns Spencer, and you own him, suddenly the Russian mafia has an aerospace empire."

"No, that wasn't the deal," Bobby said, taking a step toward the boss man. The henchmen all closed in and Bobby held up his hands. "Okay, okay, I get it. But you did not tell me you were going to kill Cameron."

The boss man's phone rang, and he pulled it out of his pocket. "Yes? Understood." He pocketed his phone and turned to Bobby. "I have to take care of something. I'll be back."

Bobby watched, open-mouthed, as the boss man and two of his men walked out of the broken-down hotel suite. Four stayed behind, with three of them taking up positions near the door.

"What are we going to do?" Inda whispered.

"I don't know."

The fourth henchman pulled a knife out of his pocket and came toward me.

"Wait," Bobby said, holding out a hand. "Just give me a second to talk to her before you do that, okay? I want to make sure she's going to cooperate. Trust me, I've got this. We've been friends since second grade."

The henchman hesitated for a second, then put his knife away. He went back to stand with the others.

Bobby glanced around then leaned across the table and lowered his voice. "Cami, I swear to god, he never said anything about killing you. You were supposed to sign and then they'd do the bag on your head thing and dump you somewhere so you could get home."

"Well, you hired the fucking Russian mafia, so I don't know what else you expected."

"This wasn't supposed to happen." He looked around frantically, then turned to me again. "I'll go for help."

"What?" I whispered.

"Just stay here. I'll get you out of this. We can talk about the company later."

I watched with disbelief as Bobby tugged on the lapels of his jacket and sauntered toward the door.

"Bathroom," he said, gesturing out to the hallway. "I don't think the one in here is even hooked up. But I have to take a shit the size of a Coke right now, and trust me, you do not want me to hold it or I'm going to burn the nose hairs off everyone on this floor. The can in the lobby still works. I'll be right back."

The henchmen exchanged irritated glances, then one nodded for him to go.

I looked at Inda and I wasn't sure whether to laugh or cry. Held captive by the Russian mafia in a dilapidated hotel and Bobby Spencer—the dumbass who'd orchestrated the whole thing—was our best hope of rescue?

Yeah, we were fucked.

33

JUDE

Cameron's phone seemed to stare back at me, the glossy rectangle sending a spike of alarm through my entire body.

She wasn't here.

With a deep breath, I banished the panic. I was good in a crisis. Calm. Cold when it was necessary. I drew on my training and years of experience to push aside the fear that something bad had happened to her.

Besides, just because she'd left her phone behind didn't mean she was in danger.

A voice in the back of my head screamed at me that she was. She was in danger, right fucking now, and I needed to get to her.

My instincts had gone haywire, and I knew exactly why. I'd been compromised. I loved her and it was making me irrational.

Logic. No emotion. Focus on the mission.

I grabbed her phone and stuffed it in my pocket, then jogged downstairs.

"Nicholas," I called.

He was still in the kitchen. Meat sizzled in a pan on the stove and if I'd been in a normal state of mind, my stomach would have growled at the mouthwatering aroma.

"Yeah?"

My voice was completely calm. "Cameron left her phone. Would you mind calling Inda? I really need to talk to Cameron."

"I'm sure they won't be gone too long," he said, stirring the meat.

"Just call her."

He stopped stirring, his eyes lifting. "Okay, man. Sorry."

I took slow breaths while he pulled out his phone and called his wife.

The seconds ticked by and I could tell she wasn't answering. He turned off the burner and moved the pan.

"That's weird," he said. "Her voicemail picked up. Should I leave a message?"

"No. I'm going to look for them." I headed straight for the front door.

Nicholas followed. "Dude, you're freaking me out right now. They just went down to the village. They haven't even been gone very long."

"I know." I locked the front door behind us and bounded down the porch steps.

"Then why are you acting like this is an emergency?"

"Because it might be." I got on my bike. "And if it is, we're losing time. Are you coming?"

"Crap," he muttered, and got on behind me.

The two of us barely fit on my bike, but we didn't have far to go. We followed Cameron's driveway out to the street, then crossed the bridge over the canal. The road wound around and the village came into sight up ahead.

Cameron's golf cart was in the middle of the street. Empty.

I stopped the bike and we both jumped off. Nicholas was babbling something, but I ignored him. I took in the scene, looking at every detail. No sign that they'd been hit. No tire marks or tracks. The foliage on either side of the road was undisturbed.

"Inda's phone," Nicholas said, holding it up. "She must have dropped it. Should we go look down at the Tiki Hut?"

I checked the golf cart again and realized the almost silent electric motor was still running. They hadn't broken down and left it here. They might not have stopped intentionally at all.

"No. Someone took them."

"Shit, are you serious?"

"Dead serious." I pulled my phone out of my pocket.

"What are we going to do?" he asked. "Call the police?"

"Cops are too slow."

"How are we going to figure out where they are?" he asked. "Is there another way to track them?"

I glanced up from my phone. Nicholas was a chef, not an intelligence operative. He wasn't even former IDF, like his wife. But his face was determined, his voice calm. He could help.

"If my instincts were correct, there might be." I opened the tracking app Cameron didn't know I had. A little red dot appeared on the map. It wasn't far—in Coconut Grove—but it wasn't here in Bluewater. "Thank fuck."

"What? Is that them?"

"Should be."

"Did you implant a bug in her or something?" he asked.

"No, in her shoes."

"Her shoes? She has like a hundred pairs. You bugged them all?"

"Nope. Just a few." I pocketed my phone and got back on my bike. "She picks her shoes based on her mood. I figured if I ever needed this, it'd be because she was either trying to ditch me or she was pissed at me. Either way, I bugged a few of her boldest pairs of shoes as a precaution."

He got on behind me.

"You bugged the shoes you'd thought she'd wear if she was mad or trying to ditch you?"

"Exactly," I said over the roar of the engine. "And I was right."

THIS WAS a rescue operation with two women as the target. Once the extraction was complete, I wouldn't be able to fit them on my bike—Nicholas and I barely fit—so I had to go back to get Cameron's car.

Nicholas insisted on coming with me and I didn't argue. His wife was missing. A man needed to be able to protect— and rescue—his woman when necessary. I wasn't going to deny him that.

As long as he stayed calm, and stayed out of my way.

The little dot on my tracking app hadn't moved. That was neutral information. It was good if it meant they weren't being moved. A moving target would be more difficult to apprehend than a stationary one. But it could also mean her shoe—the left one, specifically—was no longer on her foot, and I was tracking a piece of clothing, not Cameron.

No way to tell until we got there.

We drove toward the location on the map. The sun was setting, the sky gradually transitioning to darkness. I didn't speed or cut through traffic. I drove her car as if nothing was wrong. It's what I'd been trained to do. Never call attention to yourself. Appear normal.

Nicholas cleared his throat. "Are you armed?"

"No."

"Should you be?

"I no longer own a firearm," I said. "And despite what you've seen in action movies, a lone man with a gun isn't very effective against multiple enemies."

"Then what are you going to do?"

"I'll know when we get there."

He was quiet for a long moment. "Shouldn't we have a plan or something?"

"I have a plan. Find them. Get them out. I'll make up the details as we go." I glanced at him. "Don't worry. I've done this before."

"You're kind of scary when you're like this."

"This is a mission now. And they fucked with the wrong guy."

The tracker in Cameron's shoe led us to a rundown hotel. Metal scaffolding crawled up the side of the building and a makeshift awning protected the sidewalk. It looked like it was under construction—or had been. I didn't see any sign that a crew had been here recently. No trucks or equipment. I circled around to a street that led behind the building, looking for a loading dock or place for deliveries.

Several cars were parked in the loading zone. None of them were construction vehicles.

One was a bright yellow Lamborghini Huracan with a giant spoiler on the back. Good for speed enthusiasts. Perfect for show-offs. That had to be Bobby Spencer's car.

I wanted to pop that fucker's head like a tick, but he was a secondary concern.

The other cars were black SUVs. Tinted windows. Probably bulletproof.

I parked a short distance back. I couldn't tell by the make of the SUVs who we were dealing with. The building looked abandoned, so it could be a regular meeting spot. Or Bobby had hired more than just a crew to pull off a kidnapping.

"Stay here," I said. "Watch the clock. Follow me inside in exactly three minutes."

"What are you going to do?"

"They'll have someone standing guard. I'm going to neutralize them."

"You can do that in three minutes?"

I met his eyes. "I only need two. But I'll wait for you."

I got out and put my hands in my pockets, keeping my head down. A lot of my job had required going unnoticed. Not calling attention to myself. I was a big guy, but most people would be surprised at how easy it was to move in and out of a location if you simply looked like you belonged—even for me. And I was good at it.

So I didn't slink along the outer wall or attempt to stay hidden. I strolled right up to the service entrance where a guy with a buzz cut armed with an AK-47 stood guard inside.

"Hey, man," I said, keeping my hands in my pockets.

His brow furrowed. God, he was young. Couldn't be more than twenty-five, tops.

"Who are you?" he asked, his Russian accent strong.

Before he had a chance to blink again, my hands darted out and I grabbed his gun. He instinctively pulled back, expecting me to try to take it from him. Instead, I moved with his momentum, and jerked the gun upward just enough to hit him in the forehead with it.

The single sharp strike did its job. He crumpled to the ground.

I kicked the weapon away and did a quick visual. Lone guard. That was a good sign. It meant they didn't expect trouble.

They were really fucking wrong.

Stepping to the side, I checked my phone. Cameron's signal was here. I put it away, then stuck my hands back in my pockets and waited for Nicholas.

Sixty-five seconds later, he crept up to the service entrance. His eyes widened at the unconscious guard. "Holy shit. Is he...?"

"No, but he'll have a wicked headache. Let's go."

The service entrance opened to a series of storerooms, a freight elevator—looked broken with doors stuck half-open —and a doorway to a large commercial kitchen. Everything was covered in a thick layer of dust. There were holes in the plaster and random bits of debris strewn about. A single cloth napkin that might have once been white sat unceremoniously in the middle of the hall.

Footsteps sounded from up ahead. I motioned for Nicholas to duck into the kitchen and get down. I stepped through the open doorway and took cover where I could still see who was coming.

The sound of his breathing came first. Whoever he was, he was in a hurry. Shoes pounded against the floor.

As soon as he came around the corner, I darted into action. Sprang out of the kitchen and had him laid out on the ground, pinned down, my hand around his throat, before he had any idea what had hit him.

Bobby fucking Spencer.

"Fuck," he said, his voice a strangled croak with the grip I had on his neck. He grabbed my wrist, but he didn't thrash or try to get me off him. "You gotta help her. She's upstairs. They're going to kill her."

I loosened my grip by a fraction. "Talk."

He took a gasping breath. "I was going for help. Can't call the cops. How did you find us?"

"Where is she?" I growled.

"Upstairs. Penthouse. Dude, I didn't know they were going to kill her. I swear to god, that wasn't part of the plan."

"The Russians?"

"Yeah."

"Is *he* here?" I asked, emphasizing the word *he*. If Bobby had met him, he'd know who I meant.

Fear flashed across his face. "Yeah. I don't know where. He had to go take a call or something."

I glanced up at Nicholas. He stared down at me, resolve in his eyes.

"Is Inda with her?" he asked.

Bobby nodded—as much as he could with me pinning him to the ground. "Yeah, but that was a mistake. They were only supposed to grab Cameron."

I got up, hauling Bobby to his feet by the front of his shirt. He grabbed his throat and coughed.

"Help me keep an eye on him," I said to Nicholas.

"What?" Bobby asked. "Why? No, it's cool man, I'll just go."

"Nope." I grabbed the back of his neck and steered him into the kitchen.

"What are we going to do with him?" Nicholas asked.

"Don't know yet. But I want him where I can see him." I pushed Bobby forward. "And don't test me, you little prick, or I start breaking things, starting with the parts of your body you care about the most."

Bobby nodded. "Okay, fine. Just don't hurt me. I swear, I didn't want to kill anyone. I didn't think she'd get hurt."

Nicholas paused by one of the stainless steel work surfaces and grabbed a large cast iron skillet. Picking it up, he tested the weight in his hand, then raised his eyebrows at me.

I nodded and pushed Bobby again. "Where is she?"

"This way."

We went back the way Bobby had come running. Just past the kitchen entrance, something on the ground caught a glint of light.

Something red.

Cameron's shoe.

I jogged forward and picked it up. I could just see the spot where I'd inserted the tiny tracking device. She'd never known it was there.

Those sexy red heels of hers were about to save her life.

Everyone else in this building? They were in big fucking trouble.

34

CAMERON

*T*he more I struggled against the ropes, the more it hurt. But I couldn't just sit here doing nothing. I twisted my wrists, wincing as the ropes rubbed against my raw skin.

"Don't you know some secret Israeli escape technique?" I whispered.

"No," she whispered back. "I don't think that's a thing."

"Damn. Inda, I have a confession."

She raised her eyebrows. "You want to confess something to me?"

I nodded.

"Okay, what?"

"Sometimes I talk Nicholas into secretly making me food that's not in your meal plan," I said. "Especially key lime tarts. And then I lie to you about it when you ask me if I'm sneaking sugar."

She looked at me like I was crazy and laughed softly. "You know how weird it is for you to say that right now, don't you?"

"Yeah, I do."

"Are we going to get out of here?" she asked, her voice suddenly subdued.

"Yes. We're definitely getting out of here."

Jude was going to find us. I had no idea how. But I knew he would. I knew it in the deepest part of my soul.

And I was too stubborn to give up.

The lights went out, making me gasp, and the door to the suite slammed shut, surrounding us with sudden darkness. I looked around, straining to see. The henchmen spoke to each other—directions, commands, I didn't know; I couldn't understand them. Shuffling footsteps moved through the room.

Someone grunted, like they'd been hit in the gut. They grunted again, followed by a thud. Then a second of silence.

My eyes were starting to adjust to the dark, but it was still hard to make anything out. Just shadowy shapes moving through the room. Men with guns drawn.

Another grunt, this time on the other side of the room. A thud. Silence.

More commands in Russian. One of them seemed to be trying the light switch, but it wasn't working. He went down with a strangled cry and another thud.

A whisper of sound reached my ears. I could just make out the outline of the last henchman, taking slow steps in the dark. Suddenly, he went down, like someone had swept his legs out from under him. He hit the floor with a loud thud. Another grunt, and all was quiet.

The outline of a large man rose in the center of the room. My heart pounded and my eyes brimmed with tears. Oh my god. Please let it be—

"Clear," Jude called.

The door opened, letting in light from the hallway.

Someone else was there, but I had no idea who it was. All I could see was Jude.

He rushed over and crouched next to me, his eyes doing a quick sweep. "Are you hurt?"

I shook my head. Tears broke free from the corners of my eyes, leaving hot trails down my cheeks. "No. How did you find me?"

He reached up to swipe the tears with his thumb. "I bugged your shoe."

"What?"

"I'll explain later." He produced a Swiss army knife from his pants pocket and went to work freeing me from the ropes. "We need to move."

Relief crashed through me, so potent I was almost euphoric. "I knew you'd come."

He cut through the rope binding my left ankle and looked up, meeting my eyes. "I'll always come for you."

That was the second time he'd quoted *The Princess Bride* perfectly in conversation—this time in the middle of a crisis —and a voice in my head screamed, *Marry him and have all his babies!*

Oh hell yes. I was going to.

He cut the rope on my other leg, then freed my arms and pulled the last of it off. I winced at the burns, raw and stinging.

Reaching around, he grabbed something from behind his back—pulled it from a belt loop—and handed it to me.

My shoe.

"Thought you might want that back."

My lower lip quivered, and I had so many emotions swirling through me, I didn't know what to feel first.

"My parents died when I was three and I feel guilty because I don't remember them," I blurted out.

"Cameron, honey, this isn't exactly the time."

Jude moved to Inda and started cutting her ropes while I put on my shoe and stood, noting the unconscious forms of the Russian henchmen.

"I know, I know. I just have so much to say. And for a second I thought I might never have the chance."

It was about then that I realized Nicholas was here, standing next to... was that Bobby?

I glared at him and at least he looked guilty—and terrified. I didn't know why he was here—or if he had anything to do with Jude finding us—but I was going to bury that little shit when this was over.

Inda got free and ran to Nicholas, landing in his arms, while Jude took my hand and hauled me against him. A second later, Bobby flinched, jumping sideways a full foot further into the room. Nicholas moved fast, swinging something large in a tight arc. Was that a skillet? It hit with a low metallic bang and another body crumpled to the ground just inside the doorway.

"Nice," Jude said. "My parents live in Minnesota, but we've never been close, and I only see them once every couple years. I think I kind of scare them. Let's go."

Nicholas and Inda had barely had a chance to hug, but Jude led the way, clasping my hand tightly in his. We stepped over the unconscious man slumped on the floor—he was going to have one hell of a headache—and crept into the hall.

We only made it a few steps before two more men came around a corner.

Deftly maneuvering me behind him, Jude darted forward, shockingly fast. He delivered two swift jabs to the first guy's face, knocking him out cold. Before the second could react, Jude kicked, knocking him off balance. Then he swung around, grabbed the man's gun, and hit him in the nose with it. One more strike from Jude's fist and the guy fell.

"Holy fuck," Bobby said.

"Keep moving," Jude ordered.

He took my hand and led me forward, with the others at my heels.

"Does your fist hurt?" I asked.

"It will later. I really did learn Russian from YouTube. Or at least, that's how I got good at it. I started studying it when I was in the Marines. I wanted to learn it because I thought it sounded tough."

"Milton Spencer paid for me to go to private school starting in second grade," I said as we rushed down the hall. "I went to school with Bobby and he bullied me for being tall and for having red hair."

Jude glanced over his shoulder at Bobby and growled.

"I was messing with you because I liked you," Bobby said.

"You were a dick," I said over my shoulder. "He stopped in eighth grade when I grabbed his nuts in front of his friends and squeezed until he apologized."

"God, you're amazing," Jude said, opening the door to a stairwell.

"There's an elevator," Bobby said.

Jude's eyes were hard as solid amber. "Stairs."

Everyone filed in and we started going down.

"I took the elevator up to save time, but I don't want to risk us getting stuck if they know we're in there," Jude said. "This building is a death trap. And I moved to Miami because I grew up in the Midwest, and once I spent a winter stuck in the Ural Mountains and I never want to shovel snow again."

I laughed, turning at the next landing to keep going down.

"You really are good in heels," he said.

"It's unnatural," Inda said behind me.

"I wear heels all the time because kids used to make fun of me for being tall. So fuck them."

"That's a good reason," Jude said. "Plus they're sexy as hell on you."

He stopped us on a landing and held a finger to his lips. Nicholas and Inda waited on the stairs, Bobby right behind them. Nicholas still carried the skillet, and I had a feeling Bobby knew he'd get whacked in the head if he tried to run. Or maybe he was afraid he'd get shot by one of the Russians.

Jude put his ear to the door, then lowered his voice to a whisper. "We need to wait here for a minute."

I didn't ask why. He knew what he was doing.

"My grandparents raised me and they were wonderful," I whispered, close to his ear. "It was really hard on them, though, because they didn't expect to be parenting a young child again. But there wasn't anyone else. I didn't have any other family. They did their best, but I was alone a lot."

"What happened to them?"

"They both died the same year. Grandma first. Ovarian cancer. Grandad didn't last long after she passed."

He gently touched my face. "Oh, Cameron."

"That was when I quit my job. I wanted to do something my grandma would have been proud of."

Eyes locked with mine, he stroked my cheek.

"I'm sorry I didn't tell you about the video," I whispered. "I was embarrassed, and I didn't want you to find out."

He nodded. "I'm sorry I lashed out at you. And you're not just a job."

Tears stung my eyes again—damn it, that kept happening—and one slid down my cheek.

He glanced down for a second and when our eyes met again, his were filled with emotion. "I left the CIA because a fellow operative was killed."

"Oh god, please don't tell me you lost the love of your life in a tragic mission gone wrong, because there's no way I'll ever compete with that."

"No, I didn't lose the love of my life. I'm looking at her."

I bit my lip and nodded.

"His name was Micah Strickland. I'd worked with him for years. It shook me up when he died. I decided I needed a different life."

I touched his face, feeling his rough stubble against my palm. "It's hard to lose people."

"Yeah."

"We shouldn't be having this conversation now, should we?"

His lips hooked in a small smile. "Probably not."

"I'm in love with you."

He leaned in and planted a hard kiss on my lips. "I'm so fucking in love with you. We're going to talk about this later."

"Yeah."

"First, I'm going to get you out of here," he said, clasping my hand again.

We continued downward. Several of the floors were blocked off, the doors boarded up. Another had no door at all, but a pile of debris spilling onto the landing made it impassable. Jude took us down to what I assumed was the ground floor, although most of the floor signs were missing.

"What do we do now?" Nicholas whispered.

Jude leaned close to the door, like he was listening. "We're going to walk out."

"You guys obviously have this covered," Bobby said. "I can take my own car and head home."

Jude leveled him with a glare.

He swallowed hard and nodded. "Right. I go with you."

"Now," Jude said.

He opened the door and led me through, gently grasping my hand. I walked tall beside him, my hair a mess, my wrists and ankles ringed with rope burns. The fear that had threatened to overtake me was gone. Not just the fear of being killed by the mob. I wasn't afraid of that either, not with Jude at my side.

More importantly, I was no longer afraid to love him.

Jude pulled us up short as a group of armed men ran in from both sides, forming a line in front of us, blocking our way out.

"Oh god," Bobby whimpered.

"Don't piss yourself," Nicholas said.

Inda was behind me. "Stay with me, Nick."

"I'm with you," Nicholas said. "Love you always."

The boss man strode out in front of his men, flanked by two more. He stopped, his dark brow furrowing, his eyes on Jude.

"Ellis," he said, a slight lift in his intonation. Was he surprised?

"Novakoff."

"I did not expect to see you here," Novakoff said. "You have an interest in this situation?"

Jude subtly moved in front of me. "She's *mine.*"

Novakoff gave a slight nod, his eyes still on Jude. He angled his face toward one of the men next to him and spoke softly. "Why wasn't I told of this?"

The man closest to him said something quietly in Russian. Jude didn't move. He stood straight and tall, facing forward, my hand clasped in his.

Finally, Novakoff turned his attention back to Jude. "It appears there has been a misunderstanding. We were unaware of your connection to Ms. Whitbury. I can assure you, it will not happen again."

"Good," Jude said.

"However, he and I have unfinished business." Novakoff pointed to Bobby. "He has caused me a fair bit of trouble."

"We have that in common," Jude said.

"Nah, dog, we're good," Bobby said. "I'll just pay you the rest of what I owe you and we can all move on."

"I'm afraid not, Mr. Spencer," Novakoff said, his voice smooth. "We had an arrangement and you're no longer able to uphold your end of the deal."

"Do you want my car?" he asked, fumbling through his pockets. "Take it. It's a Lambo. It's worth a quarter of a million, easy. That plus the money I owe you. It's wiping out my trust fund, but seriously dude, don't kill me."

"That covers a portion of your debt, but not all of it." Novakoff paused for a moment, as if considering. Then his eyes shifted to me. "Ms. Whitbury, a proposal."

My heart was in my throat, but I kept my expression still. "I'm listening."

"As recompense for the trouble my men caused on his behalf, we will take care of Mr. Spencer for you."

I glanced at Jude. His eyebrows twitched. This was my call.

"May I speak frankly?" I asked.

"Of course," Novakoff said.

"That's very generous, and he deserves everything that's

coming to him." I looked back and shot Bobby a cool glare. "But I don't want to have anyone killed. Even him."

Novakoff tipped his head to me. "Very well. An alternative. I'll give him a position cleaning toilets in one of my clubs. Hard work. Very... messy. He can work off his debt. It will take a long time, but for you, I am willing to be generous. After this, we let him go."

Bobby made a strangled noise in his throat.

It was hard not to laugh at the thought of Bobby cleaning toilets. No inheritance. His trust fund drained. Broke and forced to work for a living? That was a fate worse than death to a guy like Bobby.

"I accept," I said.

Novakoff gestured toward Bobby. "Take him and put him to work."

"They aren't going to kill him anyway, are they?" I whispered to Jude as Bobby tried to negotiate—his voice increasingly whiney—with the two men leading him away.

"No. He's a man of his word."

"All right, Ellis, I trust there is no need for more unpleasantness between us?" Novakoff asked.

Jude shook his head. "We're good."

"*Bol'shoe spasibo*," Novakoff said, angling his head down.

Jude answered with a nod.

Novakoff barked a command in Russian and his men moved aside, giving us a way out.

"Ellis," Novakoff said with another nod. "Until we meet again."

"With respect, Novakoff, let's hope we don't," Jude said.

"Indeed."

Jude tightened his grip on my hand and led us to the exit.

35

CAMERON

*T*he early morning air was warm and the water sparkled in the sun. The lemon trees Bert had planted around the property filled the air with the light scent of fresh citrus. I stretched out my legs on the deck chair and adjusted my sunglasses. I still wore my silk nightie —peach with subtle gold accents—and I just might not bother getting dressed today.

After all, I'd survived being kidnapped by the mob. That called for a day in pajamas.

Jude came out onto the balcony with two mugs of coffee. He hadn't dressed, either. His dark blue boxer briefs displayed his tempting bulge and hugged his thighs. His muscular upper body was on full display. Wide shoulders. Broad chest. Solid abs. Thick, tattooed arms.

"Enjoying the view?" he asked, his mouth turning up in a grin.

"How could I not? Look at you. You're like a tattooed Greek god."

Chuckling softly, he put our coffees down and stretched

out in the other chair. "You're really taking the day off, aren't you?"

"I think it's warranted."

"Of course it is. I thought I was going to have to make you stay home. I was prepared to use force if necessary."

My lips turned up in a smile and I peeked at him over the top of my sunglasses. "Maybe I should resist."

"Maybe you should come here."

He scooted over on his chair. I got up, set my sunglasses aside, and tucked myself against him. With my head on his chest, I draped my leg over his. Snuggled in as he wrapped his arm around me.

"That's better." He gently picked up my arm to inspect the rope burns on my wrist. My skin was raw and slightly bruised on both my wrists and above my ankles. "How does this feel today?"

"It looks worse than it feels. It'll heal."

He planted soft kisses on the inside of my wrist. "I'm sorry I let this happen."

"It's not your fault."

"No, it's Bobby Spencer's fault."

"I'm still wrapping my head around the fact that it was him. Is Novakoff really going to make him clean toilets?"

"That's exactly what he's going to do. Novakoff doesn't fuck around."

I slid my fingers through his chest hair. "Can you tell me what that was about?"

"Which part?"

"The part where the head of the Russian mafia let us go. Was it just me, or was he afraid of you?"

"Maybe a little afraid. He respects me at least." He paused for a moment, tracing slow circles on my arm. "Not long after I moved to Miami, I helped a client with a situation that... let's just say it put me at odds with Novakoff. I did a lot of damage to his organization. But in the process, I also saved his daughter's life. In the end, we came to an agreement. A peace accord, you might say. He stays out of my business and I stay out of his."

"So when his men kidnapped me..."

"It violated our agreement." He took a deep breath. "The last thing I want is to be at odds with the Russians. Or anyone. Believe it or not, I'm a man of peace. But if I have to, I will go to war."

"Thank you again." I snuggled closer to him and his arm tightened around me.

He kissed my head. "I would have torn that entire fucking building to the ground if that's what it took."

"You know," I said, picking myself up to look him in the eyes, "now that it's over, you can finally retire."

The corner of his mouth hooked. "I was thinking I might give up on that whole retirement idea."

"Oh, really?"

"Yeah. I actually hate golf."

"Does that mean you want to keep the job?"

He brushed my hair back from my face. "Cameron, I want this job for the rest of my life."

I smiled. "I don't want you to go back to your loft. I don't want you here because I need a bodyguard. I want you here because I love you. I love you so much and I want you to stay."

"Wow, save a girl from a few guys with guns and I get a mansion out of the deal? I should have tried this years ago."

I lightly smacked his chest.

He placed his fingers beneath my chin and titled my face toward his. Pressed a soft kiss on my lips. "I love you too. So much. I don't ever want to be without you."

Nestling against him, I traced his leg with my toe. Felt the warmth of his skin against mine. I was safe, protected in his embrace.

My heart was safe with him too.

"Did you see Nicholas downstairs?" I asked. "How's Inda?"

"Yeah, he complained about me walking around in my underwear until I reminded him about the sex in the kitchen incident. And she's fine. I think she already went for a run this morning."

"Of course she did, she's crazy. Nicholas was pretty badass yesterday, wasn't he?"

"He was. I'm glad he was there."

Nicholas and Inda worked for me, but really, they were so much more. They were my friends. Family, even. I was surrounded by a lot more love than I'd realized. I'd just needed to open my eyes and see it.

"You know, they might want more room if they decide to have kids," I said. "I bet we could build an extension on their cottage. Add a playroom and a couple more bedrooms. Or maybe combine two of them. The other two never get used. What do you think?"

"I think that's a great idea. You're not going to move Bert into the other one, are you?"

"No, why?"

"He's a magician with plants, but I think I'd feel like a high school kid sneaking around with his girlfriend all the time. He still tells me to have you back by curfew."

I laughed.

He kept rubbing my arm, his soft touch soothing. "What about you?"

"What about me?"

"Do you want kids?"

I bit my bottom lip. "Yes. Do you?"

"Definitely."

A giddy sense of joy swept through me. We were really having this conversation. "I actually want more than one. I grew up alone and it wasn't all bad, but... I want at least two."

"Good," he said. "Because we're going to make fucking adorable little redhead babies. It would be a shame to stop at one."

I laughed and he squeezed me tight against him.

We spent a leisurely morning on the balcony, lying in each other's arms. We kissed, and touched, and played. Got each other so hot, we started right there in the open, in front of the dolphins and sea turtles in the bay. Moved to the bedroom where our bodies tangled in the sheets. We were insatiable. And so in love.

Eventually hunger of a different sort won out. We peeled ourselves out of bed, dressed, and went downstairs. I took a quick call from Derek, just to get an update on the PR efforts.

"What's the latest?" Jude asked after I hung up with Derek.

We sat at the kitchen island, the remnants of our midday grazing strewn across the counter. Leftover chicken and Spanish rice, fresh bread with butter and jam, and a perfectly delectable key lime tart Nicholas must have made this morning.

"Things are looking up. Sydney Phillips posted what she's calling a *clarification* that's essentially a retraction without admitting it's a retraction. And several of the news outlets picked up the story about my charitable foundation."

"That's a better angle than Cameron Whitbury the sociopathic backstabber," he said.

"I didn't start the foundation for the media attention, but right now I'll take the good press. Derek said someone interviewed Everly this morning and she charmed their faces off."

"Sounds like the worst is behind you."

I swiped my finger through the last of the key lime tart and licked it off. "As long as that video Aldrich has doesn't get out. That could do more damage than everything else combined."

"Don't worry," he said with a subtle turn of his lips. "That won't be a problem much longer."

36

CAMERON

I checked Jude's text. He'd said to meet him outside Beach Burgers at ten. It was an odd place to meet, but he'd said he had some business to take care of this morning. The burger place wasn't open for another hour, but there was a tiki-hut style coffee bar that sold breakfast burritos, and a food truck parked nearby with a sign that said bubble waffles. Maybe he thought I'd never had street food before.

Of course I had. I wasn't that fancy.

The sun blazed overhead, and the air felt still, almost no breeze coming off the water. It was going to be a scorcher. I was meeting my friends for DQB after this, so I'd chosen a black and white minidress with thin spaghetti straps. It was adorable, and short, and very much not a business suit. It felt good to tone down the CEO image once in a while.

I'd paired it with my favorite red suede and crystal Jimmy Choos. Because if there was anywhere a girl could wear a pair of red suede and crystal Jimmy Choos, it was Mordecai's Bistro on a Sunday for Drag Queen Brunch.

Plus, they'd always be my favorite shoes. I'd even left the

tiny tracking device Jude had installed. I liked knowing it was there. It gave me a warm fuzzy feeling, like even when we were apart, we were still connected.

And it gave me some fun ideas for a little roleplay. Just because he'd been a real spy didn't mean we couldn't have a little fun pretending. He'd be the sexy, sophisticated intelligence operative and I'd be the seductive femme fatale, my sultry temptations threatening his mission—

"Um, Cameron?"

I turned at the male voice, startled out of my brief fantasy—a male voice who was definitely not Jude. Aldrich stood near the Beach Burger deck stairs, dressed in a pale pink button-down and linen slacks. His hands were in his pockets and his shoulders slumped a little. He wasn't quite looking me in the eye.

"Aldrich? What are you doing here?"

"I came to apologize," he said. His facial hair had started to grow out—he usually shaved—and it wasn't a good look on him. Too patchy. "For everything."

I crossed my arms. "Oh?"

He cleared his throat. "I'm sorry about the video. I shouldn't have shared that with anyone."

"You're damn right you shouldn't have shared it. You should have deleted it like you said you did, not secretly kept it, then passed it around for bragging rights. That was a dick move. And it wasn't even very flattering to your dick."

A handful of people glanced at us, but I didn't really care.

"Jesus, Cameron, keep your voice down."

I took a few steps closer. "I trusted you to keep it between us. And when you told me you'd deleted it, I trusted you again. What you did was a terrible betrayal. It was a shitty thing to do to a person you claimed to have cared about."

"Yeah, I know. I also came to tell you that the video's gone. Every copy. I swear to you, it's true. I checked with everyone and made sure. It's like it never existed."

"Other than the fact that half a dozen of your friends probably jacked off to it like it was porn."

He winced.

"They did? God, Aldrich, that's disgusting."

His eyes darted to something behind me, then back. "Yeah, that is kinda fucked up."

"And what's with buying shares of Reese Howard? Don't try to tell me you just thought it was a good investment."

"I did think it was a good investment."

"Bullshit."

"Fine, I thought I'd get some skin in the aerospace game because I knew it would piss you off. You fucking left me, Cameron. No woman has ever left me. I do the leaving."

"I'm sorry to have ruined your perfect track record. Better luck with the next one."

He shook his head and looked away.

"Aldrich, I left you because we weren't good together. I wasn't happy, and neither were you. I'm not the kind of woman you want. I'm too independent for you. I'm not arm candy. I have a very busy, fulfilling life of my own, and you weren't interested in that."

His brow furrowed. "Is that like saying *it's not you, it's me?*"

"No, I'm saying the problem was you."

He let out an annoyed breath and his eyes darted past me again.

"Jude's behind me, isn't he?"

"Yes."

"Did he put you up to this?"

He hesitated. "He... made a strong suggestion. But I'm serious about the video. It's gone."

I pressed my lips together to keep from laughing. I could imagine how strong of a suggestion that must have been.

"Thank you for the apology. I still think you're an asshole and my biggest regret is that it took me too long to realize it." I took a step closer and lowered my voice. "I hope every time you sleep with another woman, you think of me, and wonder if right at that very moment, Jude is fucking me senseless with his enormous cock. And I can assure you, I will never, ever be thinking of you."

I stepped back, feeling suddenly free, then turned around, dismissing Aldrich from my life forever.

And walked into the arms of the man who'd done more to love me in the short time he'd known me than anyone before him.

He slipped his hands around my waist and kissed me. "Sorry to spring that on you, but I thought you'd appreciate the chance to tie up loose ends."

I looked up at him. At that square jaw and deep hazel eyes. I loved him so much. "How much did you have to threaten him before he agreed to come?"

"Only a little."

I playfully batted his chest.

He gently touched my face. I loved when he did that. "Are you good?"

"Yes. I feel great. Closure."

"Good. That's what I was hoping for."

He offered me his arm and I tucked mine in his. We strolled along the walk, filled with the scent of sugar and deep-fried dough.

"I just wish I didn't have that little doubt about the video," I said.

"What doubt?"

"That someone still has a copy and it'll come back to bite me someday."

"That won't happen."

He said it with so much assurance, I stopped and looked up at him. "How do you know?"

"I made sure."

"Jude, what did you do?"

I could see him trying not to smile, but there was smug satisfaction in his eyes. "A guy I know took care of it. He wrote a program that detects the exact file type and size, down to the byte, and corrupts it. It's essentially a highly targeted computer virus."

"I didn't know that kind of thing existed."

"It's not exactly legal. In most countries, at least. The law is more open to interpretation in some places."

"But how does this not-exactly-legal program know what devices to attack?"

He looked me in the eye. "I made Aldrich tell me."

"Do I want to know how you did that?"

"Probably not."

"Jude."

He casually gestured back to where Aldrich had been standing. "He's fine. You saw him."

I raised an eyebrow.

"I held him by the shirt and leaned him over the edge of a ten-story building," he deadpanned.

I blinked at him. I had no idea if he was serious, or just messing with me. And I decided that maybe it was better if I didn't know.

"We found them all," Jude said. There was an edge to his

voice. "Everyone he sent it to. Everyone they sent it to. I saw to it personally. And even if we missed one, I promise you don't need to worry."

"You're a little scary when you want to be."

"Only when necessary."

I lifted onto my toes and pressed my lips against his. "Thank you."

"Ready for brunch?" He smoothed down his crisp new shirt—dark blue with white hibiscus flowers. "I can't wait to see what Lady Raquel thinks of my outfit."

JUDE HELD the door for me at Mordecai's Bistro. My hair was loose around my shoulders, my outfit was fabulous, my shoes sparkled, and I had good news to share with my friends. And not just the look on Aldrich's face when I'd bragged about Jude's enormous cock.

Although that had felt good.

They were at our usual table, a horseshoe-shaped booth near the back. Emily, her blond hair cut in a slightly new style, her turquoise halter top making her blue eyes pop. Derek, looking smooth as satin in his button-down shirt with the collar open. Luna, wearing an adorable crown of fresh flowers circling her lush dark hair. And Daisy, gorgeous and carefree with violet-streaked blond hair—I had no idea what her natural hair color was—and a shimmery purple top that made her boobs look fantastic.

Jude and I squeezed in with them. Usually it was just us girls at DQB, but none of us minded if our men joined once in a while. We all loved Derek, and my friends loved Jude. And the way the queens gushed over our men was satisfying in an *oh hell yes he's mine* kind of way.

Lady Raquel—dressed in an exquisitely gaudy red sequined gown and long blond wig—took our orders. Then we got down to business.

"All right, bitches, what's new?" I asked and took a sip of my mimosa.

"We're seeing incredible results with the scar treatment," Emily said. "Things are progressing better than I hoped for."

"That's amazing," Luna said. "Wild Hearts just got a new distribution deal, which is huge for the company."

We all gushed at Luna's awesome news.

Daisy took a sip of her bloody Mary. "I spent a glorious weekend on the Mediterranean with a Greek hottie. It was my reward for closing my latest deal."

We raised our glasses to Daisy's accomplishment—and her Greek indulgence.

Finally, it was my turn. "I'm in the market for a new Chief Operations Officer. Noelle Olson turned in her resignation."

"That's such good news," Emily said.

"I still wish you would have fired the dumb bitch," Daisy said.

"This is perfect because I don't have to look like the bad guy," I said. Noelle might not have been behind the efforts to ruin my life, but she'd been a thorn in my side for a long time. I'd been ecstatic when she'd made her announcement a few days ago.

"Where's she going?" Emily asked.

"An electronics manufacturer. She claims she wants to get out of aerospace and take her career in a new direction. Personally, I think her little stunt with that blogger backfired. It made her look like a traitor, and no one in our industry wants to touch her."

"Karma," Luna said, raising her glass. We all raised ours and drank to that.

"Oh, and thanks to a certain someone," I said, winking at Jude and squeezing his thick bicep, "I no longer have to worry about that stupid sex tape, *and* I got to tell Aldrich that he's an asshole to his face."

"Yes, girl," Daisy said, reaching across the table to give me a high five.

"His life has certainly taken a turn for the worse," Derek said.

The others nodded and I felt like I was missing something.

"What do you mean?"

Emily's eyes widened. "You haven't heard?"

I glanced at Jude and he gave me a subtle shrug. "I wanted to let them tell you."

"Apparently he has a thing for recording his sexual activities," Emily said. "A video of him with a foreign model who's barely legal got out. And from what I hear, it's not flattering."

"It's not," Daisy said. "It's really, really not."

"Not only that," Emily continued, "When Reese Howard found out, they immediately fired him from their board of directors. He's on so-called personal leave from his own company, and word on the street is they're forcing him to resign."

I gaped at her. "You're kidding. No wonder he looked like shit this morning."

"Indeed," Derek said, idly stirring his drink with a straw. "He contacted my firm to help him sort out the crisis, but I'm afraid I had to tell him we're far too busy to take on any new clients right now."

"Oh, speaking of," Daisy said, "I have an acquaintance

who's in a bit of trouble and she could really use Alpha Group's help."

"Of course. Have her give my office a call, I'm sure we can fit her in."

I zeroed in on Daisy. "D. Why did you say the video isn't flattering?"

Her mouth curled in a wicked grin. "I have a copy."

Everyone leaned forward.

"Obviously you have to show us," Luna said.

Daisy brought out her phone, housed in a gem-encrusted case. "You're going to love this."

She queued up the video and we all squeezed together so we could see. It opened in an expensive hotel suite. Aldrich lying on his back. He was undressed, but thankfully we couldn't see too much. A young woman with a deep tan and porn-star-sized fake boobs started to climb on top of him.

She glanced down and her eyebrows drew together. "Is something wrong?"

Aldrich lifted his head. "No. Fuck, I don't know what's going on. That never happens to me."

We watched with morbid curiosity and a healthy dose of horror as the woman tried to help Aldrich achieve an erection. She tried. He tried. But no matter what they did, he couldn't get it up.

Finally, she got frustrated and told him off in a language that might have been Portuguese. She grabbed her clothes, and the phone doing the recording, and the screen went dark.

"Can you even?" Daisy asked, laughing so hard she had to swipe a few tears from beneath her eyes.

"I almost feel bad for him," Luna said. "Almost."

"Karma indeed," I said. "That was an absolute train wreck."

Jude sat back and stretched his arm behind me. He had that smug look in his eyes again.

Not that I blamed him.

We spent the rest of brunch chatting. Our wins and losses. Plans, ideas, and the exciting things we had coming. The food was wonderful, the drinks were great, and the company was the best part.

I was feeling a bit tipsy when we finally got up to leave. Jude led me toward the front with his large hand on the small of my back. Maybe it was the drinks, or maybe I was just that happy, but I couldn't seem to stop smiling.

"Um, excuse me," a woman said behind us.

Jude and I turned, and my breath caught. It was one of the romance novelists. I'd seen them sitting in the booth next to us, but they'd been quiet today, all four of them wearing headphones and typing furiously. She had long brown hair and her teal blue shirt said *I turn coffee into love stories.*

"Hi," she said. "Sorry, I know this is so weird, but let's be honest, I have kind of a weird job, so why not, right?"

Jude and I shared a glance. I was too giddy to reply. I'd never spoken to one of the romance novelists before.

She had to look up at Jude, who was well over a foot taller than her. "I was just wondering if you've ever done any modeling, or thought about doing any modeling, or would maybe consider doing some modeling. Specifically for a book cover. A romance novel. You're absolutely exquisite and you look exactly like a romance hero and I can already picture the cover and it would be stunning. And I mean no disrespect." She glanced at me and held up her left hand, flashing her wedding ring. "I'm not hitting on him. I'm super married. High school sweethearts. I know, we're so cheesy."

I tucked my arm in Jude's. "Actually, he's my bodyguard."

Her eyelashes fluttered, her lips parted, and she made a little noise that sounded like a cross between a soft laugh and a moan. "Bodyguard. Oh my god. I just had the most amazing idea. Holy inspiration." She dug in the pocket of her cropped jeans and shoved a business card at Jude. "That's my card. If you're interested, email me. I have to go. All the ideas. Must type before I forget."

Jude looked at her card while I watched her go back to their booth, feeling a little awed.

"Book cover model," Jude said. "I don't know, might be fun."

"Oh my god, Jude, is she going to write a bodyguard romance?" I breathed. "I love that idea."

He held her card out to me. "Maybe you should email her. Tell her what happened to you. It might give her more inspiration."

I took the card and glanced back at her table. Maybe I'd do just that.

37

JUDE

I stood in the doorway of the spacious master bathroom while Cameron slipped off her heels. Casually crossing my arms, I leaned against the frame, admiring her. Long legs. Narrow waist. The curve of her ass. She unpinned her coppery red hair and shook it out.

"Sense a security threat?" she asked, glancing at me over her shoulder.

"There's definitely a threat. A persistent one."

"Sounds serious. If only I had a big, strong bodyguard to protect me."

I wasn't exactly Cameron's bodyguard anymore. Not always, at least. I'd put a security team in place so she had protection when it was required. She no longer needed someone shadowing her every move, especially at Spencer headquarters. But she'd agreed that she needed a more robust personal security strategy now.

Often, it was still me.

I coordinated with both the Spencer Aeronautics security team and the guys in Bluewater. Hired a couple of guys I trusted to be on hand for when we needed a little extra muscle. I was confident she was in good hands, whether she was kicking ass in the boardroom, catching up with her R&D team at Spencer's airfield and test facilities, or attending a black-tie gala at a hotel downtown.

As for Jude Ellis, one-man security operation and professional problem solver, he was finally retired. But I'd reached out to an old contact from my days in the CIA. Turned out, he was having a bit of trouble adjusting to life as a civilian. I knew what that was like. He decided a move to Miami and all the referral business he could handle was the perfect solution.

What could I say? I was a problem solver.

"I should probably take a closer look," I said, taking slow steps into the bathroom. "Just to be sure."

Approaching her from behind, I swept her hair aside and leaned in to kiss her neck. She sighed at my touch and I rubbed her upper arms, moving in closer. Her back arched against me as I nibbled and kissed her skin.

"Uh oh," she said, pressing her ass against my erection. "He's packing heat."

"Do exactly as I say, and nobody gets hurt," I growled into her ear.

Sliding my hand through her hair, I gripped it in a tight fist and tilted her head to bare more of her neck to me. Sucked on her soft skin.

"All right, beautiful," I said, my voice low. "Take your fucking clothes off."

She hesitated. Our eyes met in the mirror, hers flashing with challenge, her lips turning in a hint of a smile.

I reached down and started slowly drawing the hem of her skirt up her thigh. "What did I say? Take your clothes off."

"Make me."

A low growl rumbled in my throat. I let go of her hair, grabbed her skirt, and hiked it up her legs to her waist. Planting my hand on her upper back, I pushed her forward over the counter to bend her over.

"You still want to be a bad girl, Cameron?"

Our eyes met in the mirror again. She bit her lip and nodded.

God, that fucking thong. I tucked my fingers beneath the slim strip of fabric and slowly slid it over the curve of her ass.

I pulled it down her legs and kissed my way up the backs of her thighs. Then licked her slit a few times, quick darts of my tongue, enjoying her breathy gasps.

My dick was hard and aching for her. I stood and she watched me in the mirror while I slowly unbuttoned my shirt. She arched her back, shifting toward me, her arms braced on the counter.

I pulled my shirt off, one arm at a time. "What do you need, beautiful?"

"You know what I need."

"I'll give you what you need when you do what I say. Can you do that?"

She bit her lip again. "Maybe."

Holy shit, I loved her. That wicked gleam in her green eyes made me crazy.

"Do you want to know what I'm going to do?"

"Yes."

I let my shirt drop and cupped her ass cheeks. "I'm going to rip the rest of your clothes off." I smacked one side with a sharp crack. She gasped. "Then I'm going to pick you up, toss you over my shoulder, haul you to the bed, and lick your pussy until you beg me to stop."

"You don't want to fuck me right here?" she asked,

arching her back, putting her beautiful pussy temptingly on display.

I smacked her other ass cheek and she let out a little whimper. "Stand up."

She slowly straightened. I pulled her skirt back over her ass and unzipped it. She shimmied out of it, letting it fall.

"Buttons," I ordered.

She took her time unbuttoning her blouse while I watched in the mirror. I pulled it over her shoulders and down her arms.

I was done taking my time. I unclasped her bra and tore it off, then tossed her over my shoulder, smacking her ass cheek again.

She giggled as I dropped her on the bed. I climbed on, pushed her legs open, and went to work on her delicious pussy.

"Oh my god," she moaned as I mercilessly attacked her clit with my tongue.

I licked her, swirling my tongue around her clit. Made her writhe against the sheets. She tasted so fucking good. I slid a finger inside and her slick walls trembled. Two fingers and she cried out.

I was relentless. Flicking her clit with my tongue while I fingered her. I could feel her heat build, the pressure growing.

"Touch your nipples," I ordered.

With a groan, she slid her hands over her round tits and pinched her nipples. I almost had her. She dropped her legs open wider, her body moving against the sheets.

I loved making her let go. Making her lose control. In this moment, I owned her body.

But she owned my fucking soul.

She started to come, and I growled against her. She

clenched tight around my fingers, coming in my mouth, her rhythmic cries making me insane with lust.

"Stop. Stop," she panted, finally. "Oh god, stop. I can't."

I planted a soft kiss on her clit and slid my fingers out. She leaned her head back, breathing hard, her arms stretched out on the sheets.

Stripping off the rest of my clothes, I let her catch her breath. Then I climbed on top of her, settling between her legs.

She ran her hands up my chest and around the back of my neck. Kissing her deeply, I slid my cock inside, groaning into her mouth. She felt so good. Every single fucking time. I'd never get enough of this woman.

I pumped my hips, driving into her. Kissed her soft lips. Delved into her mouth with my tongue. Pressure built fast and I lost myself in the feel of her. So good. So perfect.

I'd never felt this way about anyone before. Never shared such a deep and powerful connection. Loving her—being open enough to love anyone—was a risk. But she was worth it. I'd risk anything to be with her.

I growled with every thrust, my muscles flexing, my cock sliding in and out of her wet pussy. Rolling to the side, I flipped us over. She braced herself with her hands on my chest and rode my cock hard—hips tilting, her hair falling around her shoulders.

She leaned down, still rolling her hips, and brushed her nipples across my chest while she rode up and down. I loved it when she did that. It was sexy as hell.

My cock was rock solid inside her, aching for release. She moved faster and I held her hips, driving in and out, grunting in a steady rhythm.

Her pussy clenched and she started to come again. That was all it took to make me come undone. I groaned as my cock pulsed, finding sweet release inside her. Riding the waves of pleasure as they crashed through us both.

When she finished, she collapsed on top of me, her pussy still twitching with the aftereffects of her second orgasm. I caressed her soft skin, breathing her in. Enjoying everything about this moment.

God, I wanted to love her forever.

"I'm going to marry you," I said. "You know that, right?"

She picked herself up and brushed her hair out of her face. "Is that a threat or a promise?"

"Promise." I cupped her cheek and brought her mouth to mine for a deep kiss. "I guess this isn't exactly a grand display, but Cameron, I know what I want. And I don't have any reason to wait. I want to spend the rest of my life with you."

The playfulness left her expression and her mouth softened. "Are you really proposing?"

"If you want me to wait until I have a ring and—"

"No," she said, cutting me off. "Don't wait."

"All right." I tucked her hair behind her ear. "Cameron Whitbury, will you marry me?"

"Yes," she said, her eyes filling with tears. "Yes, I'll marry you, Jude Ellis."

I rolled her onto her back and propped myself up over her. Looked into her beautiful green eyes, then leaned in for a kiss. Tasted her soft lips.

"I was hoping we wouldn't have to wait." She sniffed a little and swiped beneath her eyes.

"Me too."

"We should celebrate," she said, rolling toward the edge of the bed.

Reluctantly, I let her get up. She slipped on a satiny robe and tied it at the waist. Something on the bedside table caught her attention. Tilting her head, she picked up an envelope.

"What's that?" I asked.

"Inda left me a note. She said this was delivered today and it looked important, so she brought it up here to make sure I'd see it."

She set the note down, opened the envelope, and pulled out what looked like a letter.

"Oh my god," she said, her eyes tracking the text. "It's from Milton Spencer's legal team. Confirmation of our buyout agreement, and he's giving me the option of accelerating the timeline."

"That's great news."

"It's amazing news. It means I can buy him out now. But..." She trailed off as she kept reading.

I waited for a moment while she read.

She sucked in a breath and her eyelids fluttered.

"Is everything okay?"

"Yes," she said, almost breathless. She touched her lips, her eyes still on the letter. "I can't believe this."

"What?"

"Milton amended his will. He's leaving all his assets to the Thomas and Dorothia Whitbury Charitable Foundation."

I sat up in bed, leaning on my forearm. "Cameron. Holy shit."

"I know. This is... I don't even know what to say. There's a provision to begin distributions now, once a year until he passes. After that, the balance will be donated." She looked up at me with tearful eyes. "Jude, this is unbelievable. It's so much money."

"That's incredible. Did you have any idea he'd do this?"

"Not a clue. He never said anything that even hinted he might donate his wealth to charity."

"Maybe he's trying to make up for Bobby."

She laughed. "Think of all the things we can do. Scholarship funds and desalinization plants to provide fresh water. Food distribution programs and domestic violence shelters. Education initiatives. Have you heard of that guy who invented a vessel that cleans plastic out of the ocean?"

"I don't know, maybe?"

"The technology is genius. I'll get him to build a hundred of them. Oh my god, Jude, I'm going to have to hire so many people to help me give all this money away."

"Come here."

She dropped the letter and dove at me. I wrapped my arms around her, hauling her on top of me. Holding her tight.

"I love you," she whispered.

"I love you too, beautiful," I said.

This woman. I was so proud of her. So in love with her. She was smart and sarcastic and stubborn and driven and so fucking incredible. I'd never really know how I got to be the lucky man who got to share his life with her. But I was. And I was going to spend the rest of my life by her side. Protecting her. Keeping her safe. Supporting her. And loving her with everything I had.

EPILOGUE
CAMERON

*T*he Ritz-Carlton ballroom was gorgeous—and packed with people. I'd briefly considered a beach wedding and small reception, but it had quickly become clear that Jude and I were either going to run off somewhere and elope—also something I'd briefly considered—or we were going to have a zillion people at our wedding.

Now that we were several hours into the reception, I was glad we'd opted for the zillion people. And for the Ritz-Carlton.

The entire population of Bluewater had turned out to watch me and Jude exchange wedding vows. The WWs, the tech geniuses, the bohemian artists, the retired and semi-retired business moguls—everyone.

A number of people I worked with were also in attendance, as were Jude's parents, who'd flown in from Minnesota. They were nice and seemed happy for their son —if a little bewildered by the two of us. I got the feeling they knew enough about their son to be the tiniest bit afraid of him, even though I could see they were proud of him, too.

My best friends had stood with me as bridesmaids and their significant others had been Jude's groomsmen. A fabulous wedding party for my dream wedding.

Everything about this day had been perfect. The weather had been lovely, the flowers beautiful, the food fantastic. My custom gown, designed by an up-and-coming designer who'd been a student in the Kid-Ovation program its first year, was more beautiful than I could have imagined. Jude looked unbelievable in his custom-tailored tux.

Although he looked amazing no matter what he wore. Or when he wore nothing, which was my favorite look on him.

And the eighties cover band we'd hired for the reception? Killing it.

I sat at a table with a half-eaten slice of the ten-tier wedding cake Nicholas had designed and baked for us. He'd surprised us with key lime filling on the bottom layer and I was considering doubling his salary just for that. He sat with Inda at a table nearby, her bare feet in his lap. He gave her a foot massage while she rested her hands on her pregnant belly. I could tell why people said pregnant women glowed. Inda looked amazing. I couldn't wait to meet their little girl in a few months.

Jude came back to our table and handed me a glass of champagne. He'd taken off his jacket and his tie was loose around his neck, the top buttons of his shirt undone. He was so sexy and delicious, and I was starting to feel like it might be time for us to make our exit so we could get on to the next part of the wedding experience.

Or maybe we'd just duck into a closet somewhere.

He took my left hand and traced his thumb over my ring finger. We'd had a jeweler make a replica of the ring my grandma had worn. It was rose gold with a pale opal in the center, surrounded by a halo of diamonds.

"I like seeing this on you," he said.

I knew the feeling. Ever since I'd slid Jude's wedding band on his finger, I couldn't stop looking at it.

"I'm just glad we have a way to get women to stop throwing themselves at you. Now everyone will know you're taken."

He grinned. "Getting territorial already?"

"Always. You're mine."

He reached over and grabbed me, scooping me into his lap. "That works out pretty well, because you're fucking mine."

Giggling, I draped my arm around his broad shoulders. The band started a new song, "Lady in Red," and I glanced at the packed dance floor.

"You want to dance to this, don't you?" he asked.

"So much. I love this song."

"It's a good thing you have so many other amazing qualities, because your taste in music is highly questionable."

"Are you kidding me? This is a classic."

He chuckled and we got up. He took my hand and led me to the dance floor.

I rested my head against his chest, and he put his arms around me. The lights twinkled, my best friends all slow-danced with the loves of their lives next to me, and the man I loved held me in a protective embrace. And I knew I was going to remember this moment for the rest of my life.

The song wound down and Jude kissed my forehead.

"What do you think? Time to make our escape?"

"Think we can sneak out?"

"I could get us out." He winked. "But maybe we should do the goodbye thing."

Jude signaled the wedding coordinator and she put the bride and groom exit plan into action. The band announced our impending departure, and everyone gathered to offer us a final goodbye.

Our friends, family, and loved ones all cheered as we waved goodbye. Daisy had smuggled in bubbles—her maternal side was so adorable—and they filled the air. We rushed out front, hand in hand, to our waiting limo.

The drive to Bluewater's private airfield wasn't far, but we made good use of the time, making out in the back like a couple of teenagers. The driver opened the door, but we were too busy pawing at each other to notice.

He cleared his throat. "Would you like me to circle around the runway for a while?"

Jude climbed off me and swiped the corner of his mouth. "That's okay."

I straightened my dress and he helped me up. Then we both climbed out of the car onto the airstrip where my private plane was waiting.

"Lovely wife," Jude said, gesturing for me to walk up the steps ahead of him.

I picked up the bottom of my dress and made my way up the stairs and onto the plane. Our luggage was already packed and stowed on board. A post-wedding snack, complete with more champagne, awaited us.

The only thing missing was the pilot.

"Jude, we have a little problem."

"No we don't." He closed and latched the outer door, then started cuffing his sleeves.

"What do you mean? We don't have a pilot."

One corner of his mouth hooked in a grin.

"What are you up to?" I asked.

Without a word—but with a mischievous look in his

hazel eyes—he went up to the empty cockpit and sat in the captain's seat. He motioned for me to sit next to him.

I sat down and followed his lead, buckling the seat belt. Then watched in awe as he slipped on the headset and started the pre-flight check.

"You know how to fly this?" I asked, putting the second headset on.

"Yep."

"You just happened to know how to fly a plane."

He didn't answer, just winked.

"Where did you learn how to fly?"

"I'd tell you, but then I'd have to kill you. And considering I just married you, I'd like to keep you around."

I shook my head, laughing softly. "You're something else, Jude Ellis."

"Are you ready for our next adventure?" he asked.

"Ready."

I was more than ready. I was excited to start this new phase of our life together. To be his, body and soul, for the rest of my life.

The day I met Jude, I hadn't thought I needed him. It turned out I couldn't have been more wrong. I needed him more than anything. My partner. My friend. My husband. My love.

Would you like a peek into Cameron and Jude's happily ever after? Turn the page to see where they are in ten years in a special bonus epilogue.

Want more Bluewater Billionaires?

. . .

EMILY HAS a billion-dollar deal that's falling apart and a naked stranger in her bathtub who says he can make all her problems disappear in **Lucy Score's The Price of Scandal.**

LUNA LOSES the public's adoration after a corporate scandal and there's only one man—a big, bearded dog-rescuing biker—who can help her save it all in **Kathryn Nolan's Wild Open Hearts.**

NIGHTLIFE-LOVING **Daisy** is forced into the mom life when she inherits a baby... and the baby's other broody, serious, sexy guardian in **Pippa Grant's Crazy for Loving You.**

～

BONUS EPILOGUE: CAMERON

Ten years later

I rested my elbow on the bar and traced my fingertip over the rim of my martini glass. The bartender—a smartly dressed woman with a platinum blond pixie cut—mixed a drink behind the bar. A man in a suit jacket, no tie, sat at the other end, contemplating his whiskey on the rocks, and small groups of people held quiet conversations—mostly in Czech—in the seating area behind me.

The Black Angel's Bar was in the renovated cellar of the Hotel U Prince and was one of the best bars in Prague. A crystal chandelier hung from the arched exposed-brick ceiling, the dim light adding to the mysterious ambiance. The dark wood bar was carved with intricate details and the light gleamed off bottles stacked on glass shelves. The nineteen-thirties décor somehow complemented the Gothic opulence of the centuries-old building.

But neither the lavish surroundings nor the excellent gin

martini could soothe the jumpy feeling in my stomach while I waited for Jude to arrive.

My shimmery black Versace gown did glorious things for my boobs. A difficult twin pregnancy eight years ago had widened my hips, and my boobs had never returned to their original size. Not that my husband was complaining, and this dress maximized all my hard-earned curves. With my red hair in loose waves around my shoulders and a pair of sparkly gold Louboutins on my feet, I felt confident and sexy.

I slipped my phone partway out of my black clutch. I wasn't supposed to be Cameron Whitbury-Ellis tonight, but once my thoughts strayed to my twins, I couldn't help but check to be sure I didn't have any messages. Jude had brought me to Prague, one of his favorite cities, for our tenth anniversary and our first vacation without Fiona and Carter since we'd become parents.

They were staying with their Auntie Daisy and Uncle West, so there was no doubt they were having fun. The biggest challenge would be getting them out of the trampoline room for meals and bedtime. Especially without their favorite person—Daddy—to lure them out.

Once upon a time, weekend Jude had surprised me with his leather jacket and vintage motorcycle. But that guy had nothing on daddy Jude. He was the sweetest, gentlest, most loving and patient father. He loved those little ginger babies with his entire enormous heart, and it was every bit as precious and ovary-melting as I could have imagined.

A text from Daisy with a photo of our two little redheads happily eating breakfast on her balcony eased my mommy heart. They were fine. I tucked my phone away and went back to sipping my martini.

I felt Jude's entrance before I saw him—although, like

me, he wasn't Jude Ellis tonight.

The hairs on the back of my neck stood on end and my heart gave a tiny flutter of excitement. I pointedly ignored him, lifting my martini to my lips, my eyes downcast, and left a blot of red lipstick on the glass.

The air felt charged with electricity. I risked a quick glance from the corner of my eye as he took a stool two down from mine. His suit jacket fit his wide shoulders perfectly. A sprinkling of gray had made its way into his hair, especially at the temples, and the silver in his stubble made him more handsome than ever.

He was still an intriguing mix of rugged and sophisticated, with his square jaw, capable hands, and the way he wore a suit like it wouldn't slow him down no matter what dangers he faced. The sight of him made my heart beat harder, and a familiar tingling trickled through my body, settling between my legs.

It reminded me of the first time I'd seen him, standing in my office, a giant wall of man. More than a decade had passed since that day. A day I'd had no idea would change everything.

Who would have thought I'd have Bobby Spencer to thank for meeting the love of my life?

It had been ages since Bobby Spencer's name had crossed my mind. I hadn't seen him since the day he'd had me kidnapped by the Russian mafia. About five years later, Jude had received an anonymous text indicating he was alive and unharmed, but appropriately miserable, his life of luxury long behind him.

The bartender slid a glass of whiskey to Jude. He wasn't looking in my direction—I didn't catch so much as a flick of his eyes—but I could feel his attention centered on me.

I re-crossed my legs, the high slit in my gown revealing

an almost obscene amount of thigh. Jude's jaw ticked and he took a sip of his whiskey.

We'd roleplayed at home a thousand times. Sometimes he was a by-the-book intelligence operative and I was the temptress intent on thwarting his mission. Other times I was the spy and he was my devastatingly handsome foreign contact with a tendency to distract me from my mission.

Our games never lasted long. A little improvised banter and we'd be hastily making our way upstairs to the privacy of our bedroom.

But here in Prague, five thousand miles from home, Jude had suddenly dropped into character in the hotel lobby upstairs. He'd touched my elbow, leaned in close, and told me he knew the truth about me, and I wasn't going to compromise his mission. Without another word, he'd walked out.

A short time later, I'd received a text from a number I didn't recognize. A tip from "my handler" that Agent Brick Holt—one of the teasing spy names I'd given Jude since he wouldn't tell me any of his former aliases—would be at the Black Angel's Bar tonight. It was my last chance to gain the agent's trust and complete my mission, otherwise my life was forfeit.

That meant tonight I was Sienna Rose, Brick Holt's nemesis—and only weakness.

I'd replied simply with, *I'll do what's necessary.*

I'd also decided that tonight, Sienna Rose was going rogue.

Clutching my drink in my manicured hand, I smoothly moved to the stool next to Jude. He took another sip of his whiskey, pretending to ignore me.

"You shouldn't be here," he said, his voice quiet.

"I know you don't trust me," I said, keeping my voice soft

and eyes forward, as if hiding the fact that we were speaking.

"I don't trust anyone."

"Professional hazard. Neither do I."

He was quiet for a moment and took a casual sip of his drink. "I thought I made things clear. I know who you are. I know who you work for. You might as well take that dress home. It won't work."

I trailed a finger across the low-dipping neckline. "No? Such a shame."

"Don't insult me, Sienna."

"I know you aren't so easily tempted. But there was a time when you couldn't resist."

"Things change."

I took a sip of my martini. "Things do change, Brick. Perhaps more than you realize."

His posture stiffened, ever so slightly. "How so?"

"I want out," I whispered, giving my voice a slight edge of fear.

"Come on, Sienna. We're not amateurs. Do you really think I'll fall for that line?"

My hand trembled as I set my glass down. I felt the tingle of fear in my chest as if this were real. As if I was about to put my life on the line for the man who was supposed to be my enemy.

"You're right about me. I'm a liar and a thief. They sent me to steal your secrets by any means necessary."

He turned his face a few centimeters in my direction. "But?"

"But I can't. I can't betray the man I..."

A growl rumbled deep in his chest and when he spoke again, his voice was dangerously low. "The man you what? Say it, Sienna."

I turned toward him, letting him see my face. As if I was suddenly allowing myself to be vulnerable and real for the first time. "The man I love."

His jaw hitched and he leaned in close. "Don't fuck with me. That night in London, I thought we had something. Then I come to find out you betrayed me—"

"No," I said, cutting him off, laying my hand on his arm. "No, Brick, I've never betrayed you. I've never given them anything. I lied to you, but I lied to them, too. I didn't tell them about London. I didn't tell them about us. They think I failed, and tonight's my last chance."

He slid his hand around to the back of my neck and held me in an iron grip. "If you're lying..."

"I swear on my mother's grave I didn't betray you. And I never will. If you walk away from me tonight, I'll accept your choice and face my death willingly. They'll kill me if I fail, but my life won't be worth anything without you."

He fisted my hair and his brow furrowed. "They can't have you."

I exhaled with relief. "Then I have to run."

"They'll never stop hunting you."

"I know." I lowered my eyes, his hand still in my hair, keeping me in his control. "I can't ask you to risk everything for me. I don't deserve it."

"We all have a past, Sienna. I just want your future."

I met his gaze, a little thrill running through me. His hazel eyes were filled with love and compassion. I didn't know how long we were going to play—how far we'd take our game—but it felt like I was falling in love with him all over again.

He let go of my hair and traced his fingertips down my neck. Something seemed to catch his attention and he glanced over his shoulder.

"Damn it," he whispered. "Either you're every bit the lying vixen I feared you were, or they're onto you."

I shifted so I could see past him. A man I didn't recognize wandered into the bar. He was dressed in a black shirt and dark jeans, his hair buzzed short.

"Don't pretend you don't know who he is," Jude said. "Jax Draven, your boss's right-hand man."

"They know," I hissed, wondering who the guy really was—and what he'd think if he knew we were pretending he was a bad guy. "They must have sent him to kill us both."

He leaned in so close his lips brushed my ear. "If you come with me, I'll save you. But then you'll be mine."

"I'm already yours. What's the plan?"

"Don't make eye contact. Follow my lead."

I nodded and picked up my clutch, keeping my eyes down. Jude slid off his stool, adjusted his jacket, and positioned himself between me and the stranger. He offered me his arm and as soon as I tucked my hand in the crook of his elbow, we were ducking out of the bar.

Stifling a giggle, I held onto Jude's thick arm. That had been fun. We went up to the hotel lobby, but he didn't turn us toward the elevator to return to our room. Instead, he picked up the pace, walking us quickly outside.

Streetlights illuminated the ancient buildings of Prague's Old Town Square. My heels clicked against the intricately paved sidewalk as I hurried to keep up.

"Where—"

"Shh," he said, cutting me off. "Don't look back."

I resisted that temptation for all of two seconds before tossing a glance over my shoulder. The man from the bar was behind us.

"Jude—"

"For fuck's sake, Sienna, don't use that name here."

Oh my god, we were still playing. But who was following us? Did I need to be concerned?

Not that I would be with Jude around. I always felt safe with him, no matter what was happening.

That tickle of pretend fear grew, snaking through my belly and making my fingers and toes tingle. I walked alongside him, my hand still tucked against his solid bicep. The night air was cool on my bare shoulders and arms, but the heat of arousal—enhanced by the excitement of our game—warmed me from the inside.

It was early enough that the square was still teeming with people. Tourists and locals out for a bit of nightlife in one of Prague's most historic—and beautiful—neighborhoods. I noticed a man peel away from his spot next to a building across the street. He kept his hands in his pockets and his eyes in front of him, but there was no doubt in my mind he was following us.

My eyes flicked to the other side and sure enough, another man did the same.

"There are three," I whispered.

"Five. You certainly pissed them off."

"Should we stay in the square? Will they attack us in public?"

"Probably not, but we need to lose them before more show up."

The buildings in Old Town Square were built right next to each other with very few alleys or walkways in between. We made our way quickly across the widest part of the square to where the roadways narrowed. People packed in tightly in the smaller space and the scent of flowers and baked goods filled the air.

Jude dropped my arm but took my hand in his, leading me forward through the crowd. We darted around small knots of wandering people in the increasingly narrow space between the old buildings. Risking a quick glance behind us, I caught sight of all five men, none of them far behind.

My stomach tingled with excitement and anticipation and my heart raced. The street widened, coming to a three-way intersection. A car whizzed by, the pedestrians simply stepping out of the way to let it pass.

Jude didn't hesitate in choosing a direction. He led me across the street, but instead of continuing around the corner, he took me through a restaurant's open door.

It was pub-style, with dark wood paneling, a bar with at least a dozen beer taps, and large wooden tables surrounded by benches. A chalkboard above the bar had the menu written in Czech and English, and a folk band played on a small stage.

We rushed past the tables, earning a few surprised looks from patrons. Jude didn't seem to notice. And despite the server calling to us first in Czech, then in English, Jude took us behind the bar and straight into the kitchen.

The cooks looked up, blinking at us in shock as we swept through without stopping. I had no idea how Jude knew where he was going, but I didn't question it. We must have been quite a sight. Jude in a suit and tie, me in a designer evening gown and gold heels, bursting through a Czech pub's kitchen while the staff gaped at our audacity.

There was a door at the back and I half expected it to lead to a pantry or storeroom, or maybe an alley outside. Instead, I found myself at the bottom of a narrow, rickety staircase. Jude turned around and fiddled with the door-knob, locking it.

"Do you think they followed us in?" I whispered.

"Maybe, but the staff will delay them."

"They didn't delay us."

One corner of Jude's mouth turned up. "I know. Come on."

He took my hand and gently nudged me in front of him. There wasn't room on the stairs for us to walk side-by-side, so I went first.

"All the way up," he said.

Not for the first time, I was grateful for every leg day Inda had put me through as we hurried up four flights of stairs.

The sound of someone banging on the door below echoed in the tiny stairwell and my heart jumped into my throat. I raced up the last section of stairs, but the door at the top was locked.

"Are we trapped?" I asked, pulling on the useless doorknob.

Jude put his big hand on the small of my back and stepped up next to me. "If you'll allow me."

He reached into his pocket and pulled out a large old key. It was thick with a circle on the end of the handle, like something you'd see on the belt of an old-fashioned police officer guarding a bank of jail cells. He slipped the key into the lock, jiggled the handle a few times, and opened the door.

A rush of cool air greeted us. He took my hand and led me through, ducking because the door was so small.

We emerged on a flat rooftop. A single table with two chairs sat off to the side, decorated with a white tablecloth, two place settings, champagne glasses, and an ice bucket with a bottle of champagne.

"I thought we could celebrate your defection to the good guys," he said. "Sienna Rose."

"Does Agent Brick Holt always keep a table for two at the ready or am I special?"

He slipped his hands around my waist and leaned in to rub his nose against mine. "Special? That's an understatement. You're the greatest thing that's ever happened to me."

"Are we still being chased by bad guys?"

"I think we gave them the slip."

I laughed softly and twined my arms around his neck. "Who were they? How did you do all this?"

His lips turned up in the slightest grin. "I'd tell you, but then I'd have to kill you. And you don't want to know how hard it was to get a key lime tart in Prague. It'd be a shame to waste it."

"Oh my god, you really are the greatest man in the world."

He placed his fingers beneath my chin and tipped my face up to meet his lips. "I love you, Cameron. Happy anniversary."

"I love you too, Jude. Happy anniversary."

We stood on a rooftop in Prague, kissing beneath the stars. No matter where we were, or what we were doing—board meetings, birthday parties, conferences, manufacturing facility site visits, back-to-school nights, Bluewater HOA meetings, or running through the ancient cobblestone streets of a foreign city while pretending to be spies—Jude always had my back. He was my partner, my lover, my husband, and my best friend. We'd spent more than a decade together—created a family together—and our love had only grown stronger.

We truly had found happily ever after in each other.

∼

I HOPE you enjoyed this peek into Cameron and Jude's happily ever after!

AFTERWORD

Dear reader,

I hope you enjoyed this little romp through Miami with Cameron and Jude. This book was a ton of fun to write. I love writing banter and these two had some great back-and-forth exchanges.

The concept for the Bluewater Billionaires came from a conversation between myself, Lucy Score, Kathryn Nolan, and Pippa Grant. We wondered whether readers would be into a twist on the billionaire trope. What if it's not the hero who has all the zeroes in his bank account, but the heroine? And what kind of badass man would it take to be the perfect hero for her?

That was something all four of us REALLY wanted to write. So the Bluewater Billionaires were born.

One of the things I loved about writing this book alongside three other authors was how we each took a broad concept (a lady billionaire romance) and made it our own. The four books touch on some similar themes, but they're also distinct and different. We had plenty of space to make the books our own, with our own interpretations, characters, and voices.

When it came to The Mogul and the Muscle, I kicked around a few ideas before I landed on a bodyguard romance. It's a theme I hadn't written before and it fit perfectly with our Bluewater concept.

Cameron is accustomed to handling things for herself and doesn't particularly like to rely on others. That would require letting them get close. She shies away from allowing anyone "in," largely because she knows the pain of losing people close to her. She's used to going it alone, so she doesn't think a bodyguard is necessary.

Jude wants to live an ordinary life, whatever that means (he isn't really sure, to be honest). He's a former intelligence operative trying to retire in sunny Miami, but he keeps getting roped into security jobs. He doesn't want to take on another client, but he's a softie at heart, and can't say no to a favor for his friend.

These two begin their relationship with some skepticism toward each other. They circle around the feelings that develop for quite a while in the name of "keeping it professional." If you read between the lines, it's clear they're both doing it for deeper reasons. They both have a hard time trusting others, particularly when it comes to being intensely vulnerable.

As much as I loved writing their banter, it was watching them open up to each other that was especially gratifying. The rescue scene at the end, where they both word-vomit details of their lives despite the fact that it's really not the time, had been in my head for a long time before I wrote it. I loved the idea that in the midst of this slightly wacky external conflict, they both decide to lay it all out there and make themselves vulnerable to each other.

I hope you loved Cameron and Jude's story as much as I did. And if you haven't, check out the other Bluewater Billionaires romantic comedies. Cameron's BFFs Emily, Luna, and Daisy have fantastic stories and fabulous HEAs.

And if you enjoyed The Mogul and the Muscle, it would be awesome if you'd leave a review on Amazon and Goodreads.

xoxo,

CK

P.S. Curious about that scene with Cameron's new hire, Everly Dalton, and her slightly rumpled billionaire boss, Shepherd Calloway? You can read Shepherd and Everly's story in **Faking Ms. Right: A Hot Romantic Comedy.**

ACKNOWLEDGMENTS

Thank you so much to all my readers for coming on this journey with me. I love your beautiful faces!

Thanks to everyone on my team who was a part of making this book a reality. Kari for the beautiful design work and graphics. Nikki for suggestions, encouragement, critiques, and for helping me keep my head above water. Elayne for your editing work so my books are always polished and professional.

Thank you to David for your never-wavering belief in me, and to my family for supporting me in this crazy job.

And thank you to Lucy, Kathryn, and Pippa. Not only for sharing this quirky Bluewater world with me, but for being my people. I love your guts.

ALSO BY CLAIRE KINGSLEY

For a full and up-to-date listing of Claire Kingsley books visit www.clairekingsleybooks.com/books/

For comprehensive reading order, visit www.clairekingsleybooks.com/reading-order/

The Haven Brothers

Small-town romantic suspense with CK's signature endearing characters and heartwarming happily ever afters. Can be read as stand-alones.

Obsession Falls (Josiah and Audrey)

Storms and Secrets (Zachary and Marigold)

The rest of the Haven brothers will be getting their own happily ever afters!

How the Grump Saved Christmas (Elias and Isabelle)

A stand-alone, small-town Christmas romance.

The Bailey Brothers

Steamy, small-town family series with a dash of suspense. Five unruly brothers. Epic pranks. A quirky, feuding town. Big HEAs. Best read in order.

Protecting You (Asher and Grace part 1)

Fighting for Us (Asher and Grace part 2)

Unraveling Him (Evan and Fiona)

Rushing In (Gavin and Skylar)

Chasing Her Fire (Logan and Cara)

Rewriting the Stars (Levi and Annika)

The Miles Family

Sexy, sweet, funny, and heartfelt family series with a dash of suspense. Messy family. Epic bromance. Super romantic. Best read in order.

Broken Miles (Roland and Zoe)

Forbidden Miles (Brynn and Chase)

Reckless Miles (Cooper and Amelia)

Hidden Miles (Leo and Hannah)

Gaining Miles: A Miles Family Novella (Ben and Shannon)

Dirty Martini Running Club

Sexy, fun, feel-good romantic comedies with huge... hearts. Can be read as stand-alones.

Everly Dalton's Dating Disasters (Prequel with Everly, Hazel, and Nora)

Faking Ms. Right (Everly and Shepherd)

Falling for My Enemy (Hazel and Corban)

Marrying Mr. Wrong (Sophie and Cox)

Flirting with Forever (Nora and Dex)

~

Bluewater Billionaires

Hot romantic comedies. Lady billionaire BFFs and the badass heroes who love them. Can be read as stand-alones.

The Mogul and the Muscle (Cameron and Jude)

The Price of Scandal, Wild Open Hearts, and Crazy for Loving You

More Bluewater Billionaire shared-world romantic comedies by Lucy Score, Kathryn Nolan, and Pippa Grant

~

Bootleg Springs

by Claire Kingsley and Lucy Score

Hot and hilarious small-town romcom series with a dash of mystery and suspense. Best read in order.

Whiskey Chaser (Scarlett and Devlin)

Sidecar Crush (Jameson and Leah Mae)

Moonshine Kiss (Bowie and Cassidy)

Bourbon Bliss (June and George)

Gin Fling (Jonah and Shelby)

Highball Rush (Gibson and I can't tell you)

~

Book Boyfriends

Hot romcoms that will make you laugh and make you swoon. Can be read as stand-alones.

Book Boyfriend (Alex and Mia)

Cocky Roommate (Weston and Kendra)

Hot Single Dad (Caleb and Linnea)

~

Finding Ivy (William and Ivy)

A unique contemporary romance with a hint of mystery. Stand-alone.

~

His Heart (Sebastian and Brooke)

A poignant and emotionally intense story about grief, loss, and the transcendent power of love. Stand-alone.

~

The Always Series

Smoking hot, dirty talking bad boys with some angsty intensity. Can be read as stand-alones.

Always Have (Braxton and Kylie)

Always Will (Selene and Ronan)

Always Ever After (Braxton and Kylie)

~

The Jetty Beach Series

Sexy small-town romance series with swoony heroes, romantic HEAs, and lots of big feels. Can be read as stand-alones.

Behind His Eyes (Ryan and Nicole)

One Crazy Week (Melissa and Jackson)

Messy Perfect Love (Cody and Clover)

ABOUT THE AUTHOR

Claire Kingsley is a #1 Amazon bestselling author of sexy, heartfelt contemporary romance and romantic comedies. She writes sassy, quirky heroines, swoony heroes who love their women hard, panty-melting sexytimes, romantic happily ever afters, and all the big feels.

She can't imagine life without coffee, her Kindle, and the sexy heroes who inhabit her imagination. She lives in the inland Pacific Northwest with her three kids.

www.clairekingsleybooks.com

Made in the USA
Middletown, DE
29 May 2024